THE GAMES WE Play

For my love of the game.

CHAPTER ONE

"OH MY GOD!" The gorgeous woman that had spotted me was quickly approaching as I had attempted—and failed—to lay low. "Oh my God! Kace? Kace Jackson? Can I have your autograph and a pic? I cannot believe this! My sister is going to literally die when I send her this pic."

I loved my fans, scouts honor. But Cam was going to be here soon, and the gorgeous fangirl with the bright green eyes had to be gone. Especially before she drew more attention my way. Quickly, I tried to quiet her down by signing her napkin and grabbing her phone to take the pic myself. Then I glanced back toward the entrance of the bar looking for Cam.

Not here. Good.

Unfortunately, she wasn't leaving. She started talking, and I began drumming my fingers on the table, torn between being rude and playing nice.

Shit.

"You played so amazingly last night; I watched the whole game. That double play you turned to end the 9th inning was spectacular."

I was getting annoyed, not only at the fact that she was still there, but also because she was giving me *the code*. The one where the person said dumb shit like "spectacular" when referring to a routine double play, that translated into, *"You can fuck me if you want."*

She wasn't even aware she was doing it, but I had played that game so long that I knew with a few sweet words, she would have been following me to the bathroom for a quick fuck.

I could use one.

But more than that, I wanted to spend some much needed time with Cam. I had to get the woman away from my table, and I was going to need help.

Mary, my regular server at The 678 Club, always made sure we had a private area. People tended to approach us less when we were behind the metaphorical rope. Not to mention, Mary liked to shoo people away like a mother hen, making 678 our favorite place to hang out.

Mary had no kids of her own, but she took to me and Cam instantly, nurturing us in a way. Well, as nurturing as a 54-year-old, hardened cocktail waitress got. She called me sweetheart, patted my back when I coughed, and kept the 'sluts' away.

Her words.

But Mary also served us drinks, offered us cigarettes—we didn't even smoke—and cussed like a sailor. She was special and reliable, so as the fangirl continued to chat, I looked for her to come save me. One wide-eyed look from me, and Mary would know exactly what to do. She would get fangirl away, secure our table, and get me a drink.

All before Cam showed up.

Where the hell was Mary?

Wednesdays at 678 were out of routine for me. As a professional baseball player. I had very little time during the season to go out on a Wednesday night. We were right in the middle of our season, we traveled out of town a lot, and I was my team's captain and star player. Bottom line was, it was a bad night to be out. But it was a special occasion.

A vow that Cam and I were trying to keep.

Our buddy, Josh, was a former member of a kids camp that Cam and I sponsored. He was nineteen years old and no longer went to Camp 2020, but we had stayed in touch as he worked hard to do well for himself, by himself. He accepted nothing from us except our friendship, and Cam and I had promised to see him play when we could.

Cam supported Josh—one hundred percent—so he knew it was important, but he had been hesitant about going out. Cam cared about me, and wanted to do what was best for me. A midweek party—midseason—wasn't good for me.

The place was dead, maybe a hundred people total, but compared to Saturdays, when I usually went to 678, I considered it almost empty.

So, where was Mary?

The fangirl was still talking, although I couldn't tell you what she was saying. I had checked out the minute she'd started, driven by the fear of Cam coming in at any minute.

"Ya know, darlin," I cut her off, tacking on words like *darlin'*, hoping it would make me come across a little nicer than I was feeling. "I am here to see my friend play a gig, and I would appreciate it if you left."

Fangirl just stared at me confused.

No words.

I sat down in my booth, hoping she got the hint.

She didn't.

Instead, she sat down next to me.

What the fuck?

"Kace," she purred, "I know you don't want to be lonely tonight. I can keep ya company while you watch the show." She was batting her fake eyelashes, squeezing her tits together, and scooting closer.

Code.

She was right, I didn't want to be alone. I wanted to be with Cam. It had been two weeks since I had last seen Cam, and call me a pussy, but I needed time with him. We didn't often go that long without hanging out, and I missed the fucker.

"Oh my God!" She started squealing again. "Cam Nichols? I cannot believe this! Both of you in one room!" I didn't have to look behind me to assume Cam was there.

"Fuck," I mumbled under my breath.

Cam didn't mind the attention, but didn't enjoy the game the same way I did. Our deal for the night had been no fangirls, no drama, no autographs, no pictures, and no quick fucks. I wanted to keep up my end of the bargain, hence trying to get fangirl away from me the moment she started squealing. But the wide-eyed look Cam gave me as he approached the table indicated he thought I had already reneged on our deal.

Cam was a true professional, though. He gave the fan a fake smile, signed the napkin for her, took a pic, and then sat down across from me.

She still didn't leave.

Where. The. Fuck. Was. Mary?

"So, I was what, five minutes late? You get bored that fast, Kace?" Cam's smirk was half teasing, half annoyed.

"Nope, fangi…um… *she* found me right before you walked in, she was just leaving." I shooed her like a bird, channeling my inner Mary. Probably not my finest moment, but I was far from being Mr. Polite.

It worked. She left, stomping and huffing like I had sent her to time out.

Geez.

Cam just sat quietly across from me, eyeing me.

"Where the hell is Mary?" he finally asked.

"That is the million-dollar question. I was looking for her

when that girl found me and wouldn't leave. I haven't seen her yet."

Cam looked around, but he couldn't find her either. It was becoming obvious that Mary wasn't there, making me assume that Wednesday was her night off.

If Cam and I stood a chance at a decent evening, we had to get some boundaries in place. Maybe I should have called ahead, but that had never been necessary before. That was *our* place. Our regular hangout. Not just the two of us, but our entire teams as well.

Before we could flag a waitress down—to ask for Mary, of course—another woman started to approach me from behind. I couldn't see her, but I *felt* her. Every muscle in my body tensed, and all I could see were Cam's bright blue eyes looking over my shoulder, wide in anticipation of an approaching fan. I couldn't tell if he was annoyed, or enamored. Either way, I didn't need him getting skittish and bolting on me.

Don't get me wrong, Cam didn't shy away from the attention *all* the time. He was the number one quarterback for the best football team in the league—attention came with that job. But he didn't love it with the same enthusiasm I did.

Without a second thought, I stood up to cut the new fangirl off before she could reach Cam. What I didn't anticipate was fangirl's lack of joy to see me. She was missing the big eyes and the jaw drop. She didn't squeal, or jump. She didn't even smirk or squeeze her tits together.

She was, however, the most gorgeous woman I had ever seen. Long blonde hair, lush pink lips, and a body that made me want to cry. Her complexion indicated she spent time poolside, or at the beach—'sun-kissed' being her makeup of choice.

She wore a small heel, that added to her height, and cut off jean shorts that showed her long, lean legs. The dark lights in the bar made her white tank top stand out and she looked like a goddamn angel.

As I admired her continued approach, I forgot about Cam for a minute. I forgot that I promised him no games. I forgot that he was even there.

Or that he even existed.

That was, until he stood up beside me, shoulder to shoulder, building a wall for her to run into. "Holy shit."

Okay, I got my answer—*enamored.*

He spoke so lightly, I barely heard him, but he was definitely seeing the same thing I was seeing. The kinda girl that could literally knock the breath out of a man with just a look.

I was currently that man.

From the looks of it, Cam was also that man.

If I took my eyes off of her, I would be willing to bet every man in there would be *that man.* Moving my eyes wasn't an option, though.

Cam was like a brother to me. I would kill for him. I would even "shoo" willing women away and give up a chance at pussy. I would give him anything, and everything.

But not her.

If she was going to fangirl, start fawning, and try to get a piece of one of us, then it was going to be me, and I wasn't going to say no. I'd stay with my original plan, to keep the fangirls off Cam, and I couldn't wait. I was going to let her eat me alive.

Before she could reach us, I took two steps forward and grazed her shoulder with the tips of my fingers.

Soft. My touch, and her skin. But before I could say any words, she jumped. Not in excitement, but like she had seen a snake.

Huh?

"Please don't touch me," she said, firmly, and with a little irritation in her voice. Her eyes roamed over my entire body, and I stood stock still waiting for her to say something else. The tension was palpable, but despite her reaction to my touch, I wasn't entirely sure the tension was all bad.

After a few quiet seconds, I broke the spell.

"Um, I thought…" No, not a good idea to say what I thought.

She was still silent, her gaze moving to Cam. She was taking him in the way she had just done with me, roaming her eyes over his arms, his hands, and his face.

She didn't have to say a word for me to know she was talking to herself inside that gorgeous head of hers. I wondered if her internal dialogue sounded like mine.

Isn't this the part where she screams and fawns?

"You thought…?"

Stay the course, Kace.

"You wanted a pic, a hug, an autograph?" I rambled all the normal things fangirls wanted, but the confusion on her face mimicked my own. Neither one of us could believe I had said that out loud.

Saving me from making a bigger ass out of myself, Cam finally spoke, "Did you need something?"

There weren't a lot of people on our side of the bar, and she had been coming directly for us. His question came off a bit crass, but Cam wasn't a rude guy. He was always the good guy. So, without even looking his way, I knew he was having that same internal conversation we were all having.

He was just as baffled as the rest of us.

"To take your order," she said quickly, crossing her arms over her chest.

Apparently, she was a server. A very offended server.

Shit.

I felt like I would have seen that woman before, maybe even sensed her like I had a moment ago. There was no way she had worked there very long, because I would never forget her.

"Where's Mary?" Cam asked first, wondering the same thing I was.

Her eyes softened a little, and she bit the inside of her cheek, debating her answer before she spoke. "Mary is sick. She's going to be out for a little while, a month or two, I'm filling in for her until she's well."

"Sick? How sick? The flu, strep throat, pink eye?" Sure, we never swapped numbers with Mary or even saw her outside of the bar, but we cared, and we were both rattling off questions.

"That's as much as I feel comfortable sharing. What can I get you to drink?"

She didn't have a pad and pencil; she didn't have the standard black on black club uniform. For a minute, my mind thought she was, indeed, a fangirl. Just a super psycho variety, with lying issues and Julia Roberts' level acting skills.

It's happened before. Some women played all kinds of games. But non-fangirl—as I was now thinking of her—didn't give me the psycho vibe.

"Well, Mary usually takes care of this, but we need a private booth, two IPAs, and someone to tell Josh we are here, dude isn't answering his phone..." Cam trailed off as he looked around like Josh would hear his name and pop out of nowhere.

"Excuse me?"

If looks could kill, we would be dead and buried. No one would find our bodies. She was back in her annoyed stance, and I was extremely thankful I wasn't the cause of it that time.

"Two beers, that's it, we're good." I said quickly, saving him the way he had me earlier.

There wasn't a doubt in my mind that she thought we were egotistical pricks. Probably big heads to make up for small dicks. But what I did know was that she had no idea who we were. And I kind of wanted to keep it that way.

ali

I HATED BEING A SERVER. It was not my dream job.

It wasn't even my *actual* job.

But when Mary asked me to fill in for her, I couldn't say no. She was my neighbor, an old friend of my mom's before she died, and the kind of person who would tear her skin off for someone else, just to keep them warm. I would do anything for her.

She knew I had been a server in the past and had the experience. It had been two years since I last worked in a bar, but it was like riding a bike. It still made me anxious, though. I hated feeling vulnerable and scared. Bars did that to me. They scared me and I had to keep reminding myself it was all temporary.

Mary asked me to fill in for her knowing I would happily leave once she was ready to return. Management allowed me to replace Mary by her vouching for me but if I got fired, Mary got fired. Pretty harsh for a sick woman, but I was willing to bet Mary didn't fully explain the extent of her illness.

She had been diagnosed with stage two breast cancer. Mary wasn't one for regular doctor's visits, so she was lucky it hadn't spread by the time they found it. She had a double mastectomy and was given a chemo and radiation plan—and a warning that she may be too sick to work for a while.

That was where I came in. Ali Hansen, cocktail server extraordinaire—sarcasm—and Mary's replacement for the foreseeable future.

The 678 Bar, named after the area code of the original owner, was the best in the entire city of Atlanta. People lined up to work there because the atmosphere was amazing and the tips in one night were enough to pay most people's entire month of rent.

Mary was an original at 678. She had worked there long before it was such a big place. She thrived in that environment and never had any desire to leave or do anything else. It was perfect for her and I wanted to be perfect *for* her. I wanted to make her proud and give her a reason to fight and return to work.

Unfortunately, it was a nightly battle to ensure I didn't fly off at the mouth, roll my eyes, or punch any of the customers. *Did I mention I hate this?*

I was a loner and preferred quiet.

In my real job, I was a freelance writer for a publishing company that required my written words, not my spoken ones. I spent my days at home, at my desk, writing in a notebook, old-school style, about various topics as needed by the publishers. Only on occasion would I have dinner with Mary downstairs at her apartment.

A few deep breaths, Ali. A shot of tequila, and you're good to go.

And I was, until those two guys showed up—Mr. Sexy and his friend, Mr. Gorgeous. They stood up and knocked me off my game. I had been headed to their table, but I hadn't focused in on them until they were standing in my way. Even before Mr. Sexy reached out for my shoulder, I was aloof and running through the motions of work without paying attention to who I was approaching.

I still didn't know who they were, or who they thought they

were. What I did know, was that his touch had made me jump so far backward that I could have won some Olympic sport that involved backward jumping. I had been taken by surprise; by his touch or by my reaction, I wasn't sure. There was just a wave of electricity that coursed through my body.

But I compensated for my initial jumpiness by freezing in place for an awkward amount of time. *Good job, Ali!* I was trying to piece together their actions, their requests, their concern for Mary, their incredible eyes, their assumptions. Despite their obvious egos, a knot of intrigue formed in my head. I wanted to know more. Not just about them, but about me.

Why was my spine tingling? Why was I suddenly so overcome with the inability to talk? How long had I been standing there?

And wait….

Did they seriously just insinuate I went over there to hit on them?

I needed to clear my head, and they weren't the kind of guys you could do that around.

"Two beers, right." I walked off before they asked for anything else. I didn't even know what kind of beers they asked for but I planned to ask Tony, our bartender, if he knew them.

Like Mary, Tony had been there since the beginning of time, and he seemed to know everyone who walked through those doors. But as I approached the bar, Tony was distracted by a red head half his age and I knew any words other than, "Hey, I need two beers," wouldn't register.

By the time I returned, both guys were sitting down so I set their beers on the table in front of them and attempted to get away again.

"Hey whoa…" I wasn't sure who said it, but I paused and looked up, my eyes bouncing between the two of them.

"I think we got off on the wrong foot just a minute ago. Mary just usually handles everything, so we were shocked to learn she was sick." Mr. Gorgeous was doing the talking.

"Right. Well, Okay." What else was I supposed to say?

I turned to walk away from the table, but Mr. Sexy spoke again. "Hey, what's your name?"

I turned back quickly, *who me?*

Of course, you, Ali. You're the only person trying to flee their table at warp speed.

"Ali," I said softly. My name was a reasonable request.

"Ali, I'm Nick, this is my partner JJ." Mr. Gorgeous was doing the introductions.

Wait, partner? As in….

"Ohhhh I see! Wow. Okay." My obvious relief was laced with complete disappointment. Not that I was interested in them, but it was unfair that so much male hotness was put into men that would never be interested in me. Yet, knowing they weren't interested in me also made me breathe easier.

"Wait no, noooooo, no… fuck no. Dude." Mr. Sexy, who I now knew was JJ, was upset. "Why did you say partner? Why not friend, pal, compadre? I would have even accepted being your bestie for the restie. But please don't let this woman think we are bangin'… fuck man."

I giggled, then covered my mouth to hide it from not only them, but myself. I didn't giggle. Arrogant JJ was squirming in discomfort, and even though I had just met him, I felt like that wasn't something that happened very often. Nick was smiling at me, enjoying the fact that I found JJ's discomfort so hilarious.

The tension had been broken, and the laugh had calmed my nerves and settled my soul.

I took a deep breath.

Instead of retreating, I bounced my eyes back and forth again getting a better look at them without the uncertainty that was coursing through my body earlier.

They were friends, good friends. They knew Mary, and Josh—tonight's musician. They both had light, dirty blond hair, and blue eyes. But despite those similarities, they didn't look related.

Nick had a lighter complexion, no facial hair, and a natural smile. He seemed to be more of the quiet type, the kind that preferred keeping to himself. He wore loose-fitting jeans and a light blue button-down shirt with the sleeves rolled up to his elbows, showing off his perfect forearms. He looked like the all-American boy. *Man.*

JJ, on the other hand, had a natural tan, as if he worked outside every day, with day-old scruff on his face, and a smile that could more likely be described as an arrogant smirk. He wore a tight black t-shirt, with 6+4+3=2 written across in white, and dark, tight jeans. His hair looked like his hands had run through it a million times. He had tattoos with intricate designs woven through bigger ones covering both his arms. Nick didn't have any tattoos—at least none I could see.

They were both equally good looking, but in completely different ways.

Clearing his throat, JJ gathered himself and drew my attention. "Nick and I had decided we would be competing for your attention tonight, so he's playing dirty."

I shook my head, again, this time trying to rid myself of the crazy ideas I had. Ideas that involved them fighting, with no shirts.

Dirty.

"I'm not looking for attention, or games, so I'll pass, thanks." I didn't even believe myself when I said that, no way were they buying it. The music was about to start, and I had a few more tables to tend to beforehand, so with one last smile, I turned away.

I didn't make it far, they were determined to keep me spinning in circles.

"Oh, hey, Ali?"

Looking over my shoulder, I raised one eyebrow and smiled at Nick as if to ask, "*Yes?*"

"JJ was right." His eyes flicked to his friend, and then back to me, my smile faltering at the uncertainty that was sinking in. "I definitely play dirty."

I staggered as the butterflies in my stomach took flight. There was no doubt that my face was turning a bright shade of red. I glanced at JJ, gauging if he noticed how affected I was by Nick's words, because I felt like I had a sign on my forehead that blinked, *"I like it dirty."*

But he was barely looking at me. With his eyes on his beer, he began nodding an affirmation. "Same."

On some level, I knew they were just trying to get a reaction out of me. I knew their words were meaningless, and were meant to be funny. But I couldn't laugh. I couldn't play along. And come to think of it, they weren't laughing either. They were just staring at each other. Almost as if they were having a conversation without saying a word.

I had to shake away the daze that had come over me, so I finally walked away and snuck into the bathroom, feeling unnerved and out of sorts. My only goal was to get my shit together and to fall back into my defensive mindset that had somehow faltered so quickly around Nick and JJ.

If I were anywhere else, I wouldn't have overanalyzed everything. Their charm and good looks probably sent most women into a tailspin.

I was no different.

But I had waited tables before, in a bar. It taught me a few hard lessons that I carried with me every day.

Most men were egotistical assholes.

Most men took, took, took for their own entertainment and pleasure.

Most men didn't care who they hurt in the process of self-gratification.

You could say I was a bit circumspect. Like I said, I hated that job. I was scared of that job. I was only there for Mary. I would get my shit together, for Mary.

Mary didn't know about my past.

No one did.

The invisible tether I felt around Nick and JJ was most likely the result of two years' worth of my "solitary anxiety" crumbling under the pressure.

That was all it was.

I could deal with that and power through.

There was just one problem—my gut was telling me Nick and JJ weren't *most* men.

cam

I COULDN'T REMEMBER the last time someone *didn't* know who we were. Our faces were plastered all over the city— benches, the sides of buildings, billboards, newspapers, magazines, you name it.

It came with the territory when you had a story like ours.

Kace and I grew up together—our parents had been best friends for as long as we could remember. We went to school together, we played sports together, we vacationed together, and we spent our weekends together. I was the only boy of four kids, Kace was an only child. We lived next door to each other, and were never separated until college.

Kace was a top-rated baseball prospect in high school. The guy could do it all—hit for power, steal bases, play every position on the field. He was getting scouted by pros when he was sixteen. There wasn't any doubt that he would skip college and get drafted straight to the big leagues.

I was the quarterback for our high school football team, and led them to district and state championships. Division one colleges were recruiting me just as long as Kace had been scouted by the pros.

Like Kace, my future was predetermined by my talent. Kace was drafted by the Atlanta Kings in the first round of the MLB draft. Our home team. Our dream team. I went to college out of state, but after three years, I was drafted to the NFL with the Atlanta Jets. Again—our home team. A dream come true.

Kace started in the minor leagues, but was brought up to the major league level the same year I was drafted, making us both rookies in our respective sports in the same year, in the same town. Our town.

To a certain extent, it had been a fairytale.

We were both named Rookie of the Year, five years ago. We have both stayed with our teams, and have become the highest-paid players in our sports. We have maintained our friendship. We have created a charity called Camp 2020—we both wear number twenty on our jerseys—and we own several businesses across the city.

There were some downfalls, though.

We didn't see each other enough. Kace played all summer, I played all fall, and we overlapped a little in-between. When football ended, we would spend a month together before baseball started again.

We didn't have any real friends outside of ourselves. We had people in our lives—acquaintances—but we were primarily a duo. There were not very many people we trusted. Sounded cynical and ridiculous, but besides each other, and maybe Josh, everyone we met wanted something from us.

Money.

Fame.

Perks.

Tickets.

It was hard to tell who wanted to be around for the right reasons. It got exhausting and heartbreaking, and eventually, we learned that it was just us.

Women came and went, and we let them use us because we

were basically using them. They wanted to say they'd slept with a ballplayer, maybe get a fancy dinner out of it, or a few of the finer things that surround us. We just wanted to have sex—guys are simple like that.

Despite saying we would fight over Ali's attention, we would never let a woman come between us. But without even discussing it verbally, we agreed she was different, special.

Plus, she had no clue who we were. Our faces weren't limited to Atlanta networks, we were all over the damn country, so I wondered what rock she had been under.

I had introduced us by our nicknames—names we only occasionally called each other—just to keep up our anonymity for a little while. Kace was JJ because his full name is Kace Jackson Jr, and he called me Nick because my full name was Cam Nichols.

No one said we were super creative.

We learned that to do normal things, we occasionally had to use normal names. Cam and Kace couldn't do things that JJ and Nick could. Every time someone mentioned our two names in the same sentence, there was no doubt about whom they meant.

So, giving Ali our nicknames wasn't lying.

Right?

After my parting *dirty* comment, she ran off with a fiery blush running up her neck and to her cheeks. I could almost feel that blush in my bones, and I wanted to make her do it again.

"If I believed in love at first sight, this is what I imagined it would feel like." Kace was eyeing Ali as she walked around our area of 678, serving drinks, and making small talk with customers.

"Well, that is going to make what I have to say kinda awkward… cause she's mine."

Of the two of us, I was more likely to hold a relationship. Sometimes, I actually tried to see the same girl more than once. Kace thought that "repeats were reckless" and was more jaded than me.

In his defense, no woman had ever seen past his fame and money. They all wanted something from him, and he'd kept them at arm's length to avoid being exploited.

I'd had a steady relationship in college, and always wanted that again.

"No, I mean it," he mumbled, barely taking his eyes off Ali. She was smiling and having polite conversations with the people around her.

"Right," I finally said, my sarcastic tone letting Kace know I knew he didn't mean it.

"Not kidding, man. Something just happened to me. I don't even know what the fuck it was."

No smirk, no smile, no wink. No signs he was bullshitting me. *Was he serious?*

"Same." I mimicked his earlier remark to Ali. No smile, no bullshit.

He glanced back at me and studied my face for a quiet minute, and I stared back. We were mirroring each other's facial expressions, both relaying how serious we were.

Maybe I was wrong, maybe we would fight over a girl. Because I had known Ali a total of seven minutes, and I already knew she was more than a game.

As much as I thought Kace needed to be home, he talked me into going out, and admittedly, Wednesdays at 678 weren't that bad. There weren't nearly as many people as on a weekend, and even though we'd hoped for a private area, we seemed to be keeping low key.

Aside from Kace's original fangirl, we had been left alone.

Kace was right, we needed to be there for Josh when we could. He grew up jumping from one foster family to the next, sometimes even ending up on the streets. No one wanted to adopt a sixteen-year-old with a penchant for throwing punches and staying in trouble. Then one of his foster families brought him to Camp 2020, hoping it would help him connect with people, and the rest was history.

Despite his circumstances, he was a good kid. He had passion, talent, and a beautiful outlook on life. Now that he was too old for the Camp, we still kept in touch with him, always promising we still had his back, no matter what.

"Did you get ahold of Josh? Tell him we were coming? I tried texting him but he hasn't responded."

Kace, taking his eyes off Ali, joined me back at our table. "I texted him when I left the house, but I haven't heard back from him either. Not sure if he saw it or not."

"What time does he…." The lights lowered before I could even finish my question, as an emcee jumped onto the stage and introduced Josh. I was so pumped to hear him play that I started to stand and holler, but Kace pulled my arm down, reminding me to keep a low profile.

Josh walked onto the stage with his guitar and began an acoustic set of covers he had put together. He was amazing, and belonged on a bigger stage than 678.

When Josh started his rendition of *Tennessee Whiskey*, Ali came to drop off two more beers. With the lights dimmed, the lyrics in the air, and a shy smile on her face, I felt something.

The three of us looked between each other, constantly changing the face we were looking at. All trying to figure out what that *something* was.

Then she was gone, turning on her heels to tend to other

tables. But she never came back, and I couldn't spot her anywhere.

After almost thirty minutes, *Molly* brought us another round.

Molly. A twenty-something-year-old redhead that I could imagine Kace taking to the bathroom later. But when she came on to him, thrusting her cleavage in his face and offering herself up as an appetizer, Kace backed away and asked what I was about to ask myself. "Where's Ali?"

Molly jerked up and straightened her spine, a snarl on her face at Kace's dismissal. I thought she was going to stomp away, but despite her sour mood, she answered with a shrug.

"Home."

CHAPTER FOUR

FAKING BEING SICK WAS EASY. With my sweaty face, shaking hands, and missing brain cells, Tony didn't even question me.

I didn't feel too much better the next morning, either.

After I ran out of work, I walked the few blocks to my apartment building. I had thought about checking in on Mary before I headed up to my apartment, but decided not to bother her so late. I knew I would ask her about Nick and JJ, and I was telling myself that I didn't want to know anything about them.

The next morning, I was sitting on the fire escape of my sixth-floor apartment, overlooking Centennial Park, trying to find my brain among the joggers and "morning people". I figured it must've been out there somewhere. I must have dropped it on the way home because I sure the hell didn't have it in my possession.

If I had, I would have been back to my old self, and clearly, I was not.

At least I got to stay home. Tony called early in the morning and told me he'd covered my shift for the night. *Be ready and rested for the Friday scrum.*

Friday was going to be my first official weekend in the three weeks I had been at 678. My anxiety was happy for the day off, and I planned to spend it in my happy place—home.

Thanks to my late Grandma, I had an amazing, rent-controlled apartment. It was a studio, but bigger than a lot of places in the city that went for double the rent. Everything had been updated to look modern and sleek.

My favorite part of the apartment was my bed. My king-size barely fit into an alcove, leaving no room to walk on either side of the bed. There were big built-in shelves on both sides of the bed that were filled with all my favorite books.

Instead of a headboard, I had a big window that took up the entire wall. It was also the only window in the apartment, and the one I climbed out of every morning to get onto the fire escape.

When my grandmother had lived here—alone—she'd kept a twin-size bed in the alcove which allowed room for a nightstand, and a bench. She'd hung a curtain to separate the spaces, so guests couldn't see her "bedroom."

I preferred my huge, cozy bed to walking space, but I had a curtain up at the foot of the bed, to block out the living area that consisted of just a couch and a TV. Most of the time, I kept it pulled back to let the light in from the window, but the curtain made me feel safe on the nights I needed the veil of security.

I had never intended on moving to the city, especially into my grandma's apartment, and being there without her was hard at first. But I couldn't ever bring myself to let the place go, either.

For a year after she'd passed away, I'd paid the rent, checked in on occasion, but I'd never stayed very long.

Then Alan happened.

Two years ago

I had been a normal college student, living in an on-campus apartment, and having the time of my life. The American dream in every aspect—good friends, a great education, a fun job, and a boyfriend that doted on me.

While waitressing at a bar on campus, I met Alan—a good looking, nerdy type of guy. He had a gangly build, but charisma and confidence that rivaled a thirty-something-year-old George Clooney. He wore black-rimmed glasses, was extremely smart, very well- versed on most topics, and was a senior majoring in Criminal Justice.

At the time, I thought he was perfect. Alan treated me like a queen, and often reminded me how amazing he thought I was. When he said the L-word six months into our relationship, I never hesitated to say it back. I felt Alan was *it* for me.

The day after we'd declared our love for each other, I was set to work a Friday night shift at the campus bar. Fridays were always busy as people—students and out-of-towners—started *pre-gaming* for Saturday's football games. Getting Fridays off during football season was impossible.

Alan tried to tempt me anyway, giving me a million reasons why I shouldn't go to work. He tried to reason that we were in love, and he didn't feel comfortable with me working at the bar.

That became our first major fight.

I had worked at that bar for three years, ever since I had started at the University. It wasn't glamorous work, but it consistently paid my bills, and I enjoyed the atmosphere. I wasn't leaving my job.

Alan seemingly shrugged it off, and I was thankful for that, but it was soon after when work became miserable for me. Men started touching me inappropriately, calling me vulgar names to get my attention, spilling their beer on me, and not tipping me. I had complained to management, but there were no cameras in the bar—therefore no "proof"—and every time it happened, the ones involved denied it.

"It's their word against yours, Ali, my hands are tied."

Telling Alan was pointless. He just encouraged me to quit even more, telling me he would cover my bills for a few months while I looked for different work. Confiding in my friends seemed to scare them away, proving they weren't my friends at all.

At that point, I wanted to take Alan's offer and quit, but Grandma's apartment held me back. Alan didn't know about that apartment—that I was still paying that bill—and for some reason, I'd never wanted to tell him.

I coveted Grandma's apartment. It was a sacred place where she taught me to play the piano, bake, and where we relaxed together. It was where I went to escape when I needed to get away, and even loving Alan didn't make me want to share that part of my life with him.

So I turned down his offer, and kept grinding. But things didn't get better.

They got worse.

Whatever made a man think it was okay to grab a woman by the shoulder, spin her around, and grab her breasts was beyond my understanding. And for what? A laugh among friends? Was it *that* funny? A sick *game*?

I couldn't figure out why that was happening to me, and at work, in public, of all places.

One month after the harassment started, I began noticing a trend. The same men started showing back up, attempting to impinge upon me again. Up until that point, no two people were the same—which had made it hard to arrange an accusation on my part.

By the time I recognized the repeat offenders, the games had escalated. Although nothing had ever happened to me outside the bar, I started to fear for my safety, always looking over my shoulder.

I called the police, told management, reported it to campus security, but there was never any follow up. I lost faith in the system, in the people that surrounded me, and ultimately, I quit.

But I couldn't shake the feeling that something more was going on. The harassment felt so deliberate and targeted. I was still scared all the time.

Three weeks later, everything finally started clicking into place. The cards began to fold one by one, and it started the day Alan came over to pay my rent for the first time.

He had gone to the leasing office himself, but had later joined me for a night in—dinner and a movie on my couch. Despite my continued fear, the grief over quitting my job, and the added guilt of letting him pay my rent, Alan was happier than he'd ever been.

"You should move in with me!" he suggested as we sat on my couch, preparing the movie.

"What? Don't you think it's a bit early on for that kind of decision?" I loved Alan, but we were still getting to know each other.

"Ali, I plan on marrying you, no reason to keep this shithole when we can get on with our lives together." He looked genuinely serious.

"Married? I haven't even met your family, Alan. We have a lot of steps to take before we consider marriage."

He stood up from the couch, hands on his hip, looking down at me, and snapped. "So, you plan on letting me pay your way, but you won't consider marrying me?"

"Whoa, I plan on letting you loan me money, but I will pay you back when I get a new job. I never planned on using you, Alan. But marriage is a big step in the far future."

"That is exactly what you do, every day. You use me and take me for granted, and I clean up all the pieces without complaining, don't I? I only want one thing, and that is to start discussing marriage with you. I want to propose soon. I have a fucking ring, Ali. And I don't want to pay your goddamn rent when I have a nicer apartment off-campus that's big enough for both of us. It is a waste when the end game is the same."

At that point, Alan had started yelling. I could rationalize that I had hurt his feelings, and for that, I was sorry. But I was not going to be yelled at and talked down to. He was upset, I got it. He wanted to be together, I loved that. But he needed to cool down before we continued the conversation.

"Alan, please leave. I have had the worst month of my life. I have been treated poorly every day in that bar by men who think it's okay to dehumanize me while I work. I will not sit here in my home and be berated and cursed at by someone who is supposed to love me." At some point, I had also stood up, hoping it drove my point across, but I never raised my voice.

"My home."

"Excuse me?"

"This is my home. I paid for it today, this place is mine, just like you are. You have no job, no money, and you walk around this campus like a scared, fucking animal. Do you think you can tell me to leave? You can't, Ali. You need me. To be honest, in two weeks, you will need a new place to live. I just put my name on the leasing info—and you have two weeks to be out. The landlord didn't even bat an eyelash when I told her we were getting married, that you were moving in with me. That I was going to surprise you—because that's the way this night was supposed to fucking go. You should be thanking me." He paused, long enough to snort at my shocked expression. "She already has someone else lined up for this place, and has told them they can move in. So, you know what? I am going to leave, long enough for you to get your shit together and realize what I have done for you. When you get over being a bitch, you know where *we* live."

With that, he stomped out of my apartment, slamming the

door before my brain could wrap around what the hell had just happened.

The whole time he spoke, I had no words in rebuttal. That was the first time Alan had shown me that side of himself, and he left me speechless.

But much to his chagrin, I didn't run to him.

Instead, I went back to the bar, telling management I wanted to try again, lying that I wasn't scared anymore, that I had just needed a few weeks to clear my head.

They gave me the job back because I was too good at it for them to turn me down, and I started the night after Alan and I had our huge fight.

I had planned on calling him, eventually. But I was still so angry, and I was pretty sure I didn't want to continue our relationship at all. I loved him, but I knew I would never see past the way he spoke to me. I needed to find a way to tell him it was over, and a part of me wanted to earn the money I owed him first, so I could pay him back as part of the breakup. I would even find a new place to live.

Stepping foot back in the bar didn't feel as weird as I thought it would. It had only been three weeks, but that was the longest I had gone without being there since I took the job the first time.

Most of the faces were familiar and the night started without a hitch.

Until I recognized a face.

I didn't know his name, but I knew he was one of the guys that had harassed me before. I couldn't run or complain, though. I needed that job more than ever.

So, I approached him with caution, and while I expected unsavory behavior, all I got was huge "deer in the headlights" eyes, and a quick beer order. The two unfamiliar friends with him ordered beers as well.

I was confused because I expected a repeat performance, more games, but they didn't come.

He was surprised to see me, that much was clear.

While I waited on their beers at the bar, I snuck a glance back to their table, but he was gone. I scanned the room. *No way he left that quickly.*

After a minute, I spotted him down the hallway that led to the bathrooms, on the phone, hunched over and not wanting his conversation to be heard. I motioned to the bartender that I would be back for the beers in one minute, and crept down the hallway. With his back turned toward the bar, and the noise of the other patrons, he didn't know I was walking up behind him.

"Dude, I thought you said she finally quit? She's here…Yes, I'm sure it's her…. Fuck no, I'm not doing that shit again, besides I'm with Kendall and Jason, they are not Pi Kappa Phi, and your shit needs to stay in house… well, figure it out, this is your only heads up." He hung up quickly, not waiting for a response.

I started to turn away, thinking I would get back to the bar before he noticed me, but I didn't. He spun around, and by the look that was on my face, he knew I'd heard him. He didn't say a word to me, though, just shouldered past me and went back to his table.

I hustled back to the bar and had Jenny, another server, deliver their beers by telling her I needed to use the restroom. Instead, I walked back to the hallway and tried to piece together everything I had heard.

Pi Kappa Phi? That was Alan's frat. He didn't live there anymore, but he was still in that circle, and a part of that house.

Then, just like a vision, it all clicked.

Alan was behind the harassment. I started placing every face of every man that dared to lay a hand on me, and every single one of them was Pi Kappa Phi. *How the hell did I not see that earlier?*

Alan always wanted me to leave that job. Then he wanted me to leave my apartment. He wanted me under his thumb. When I refused to quit my job the first time he suggested it, he took it as a slap in the face, refusing to lose, and put those guys up to the harassment to get his way.

And it worked. I quit.

I also lost my friends.

He was my knight—telling me he'd help, that he'd protect me, that I could count on him.

Making me *need* him.

What he didn't expect, was that when it came down to it, I wasn't the type of girl to roll over and let him treat me so blatantly ugly. He didn't expect me to choose the crummy job over his temper tantrum.

But I did.

I still shuddered when I thought back on what happened next.

Alan ended up confronting me as I left the bar that night, and I stupidly confessed that I knew his game. That I had figured out what he had done to me. But I shouldn't have poked the bear alone, in the dark. All I could do was ask him *how?*

How could he do that to me? How was he able to convince everyone in the frat to do something so heinous? How did he think I would react when I found out? How long had he been planning on sequestering me from everything, and everyone, I knew? How could he think I would allow myself to be treated like that?

So. Many. "Hows".

Alan didn't answer any of them. Instead, he backed me into an alley and held me against a wall, his hands tight around my neck. It was the first time I realized he would physically hurt me, if not worse.

His eyes were soulless, pure rage behind his black frames.

When he had finally let go of me, I had to gasp for breath while bent at the waist. He took a deep, pompous breath of his own—the action somehow making him look bored.

"When you wake up, go home. I'll be waiting for you to fix this." Before I could even consider what he meant, he backhanded me so hard that I fell, temporarily blacking out.

Two years later, I could still feel the pain of him squeezing me around my neck, and the sting of that hit.

Alan underestimated me, though.

He left me.

He thought I would follow.

But I didn't. Just like I hadn't the night before. I may have been too scared to call the cops, since they weren't much help the first time around, but I didn't stay either.

I ran.

Fifty miles away from campus, I found safety in my secret hiding place, Grandma's apartment. Until I figured out what to do next, I sold my car, and used that money to live. Since I didn't dare go near the college, I never finished my degree. I tried waiting tables again, but someone simply brushing my arm would send me into a tailspin of fear.

My major had been in creative writing, and although I didn't graduate, eventually I started writing columns under a pen name and selling them to local websites and news outlets. They were meaningless columns, but they helped me pay rent without having to leave home too often. Though my dad insisted I visit him every once in a while. He lived a few hours away, so without a car, that wasn't easy, but I was able to borrow Mary's car on certain days.

After a few months of doing all that, I applied to the publishing company where I currently work. The pay was better, and I worked on my own time, from my own home, taking assignments that spoke to me, and made me *want* to write. But I never felt the need to get a new car.

The squawk of a bird shook me from the daydream about my past, and I realized I had lost a lot of time that I should have spent working. Not to mention my coffee was cold. With the unexpected day off, I needed to get ahead, because I knew working the bar over the weekend was going to take everything I had.

kace

THURSDAY'S GAME had been a grind… and Friday's… fuck, they were all grinds, especially with the playoffs so close, and our team closing in on the division lead. By the end of the week, the whole team was exhausted and needed some time to relax. My big mouth mentioned Cam and I were going to 678, so every fucker in the clubhouse thought that'd be a fan-fucking-tastic idea.

Don't get me wrong, I loved my teammates. They were my friends—my family—they meant everything to me. But I was hoping Ali would be there, and since she still didn't know who we were, having my team there would be a dead giveaway. All I wanted was one more conversation with her before she figured it out.

If she hadn't already.

There was a chance she had talked to Mary since we last saw her, or had seen one of our billboards in town. Hell, Cam's face was painted on the side of the bridge near exit sixty-two, if she happened to venture that way. There was also a chance she had an epiphany and remembered where she had seen us.

Regardless, we were all piled in Uber XLs, headed to the bar

Friday night. The noise in our car was loud, the guys were hyped up and ready for a night out after winning a big game earlier in the day. I was unusually quiet, looking out the window, lost in thought.

"Yo Cap?" Chase, our catcher, always called me Cap—short for Captain. Leader of our team. Didn't matter that he was a few years older than I was, in his eyes, I had earned the respect, and distinction, that came with leading our team.

"Yeah, man?" I mumbled, without turning away from the window.

"Why the long face? Mom shorten your curfew again?" Okay so he gave me a few jabs about being younger, but I loved him for it.

"Ha, yeah, gotta be home by 9." My heart wasn't into a rebuttal.

I wasn't sad or mad, though. I was anxious. Which wasn't like me at all, and Chase was picking up on it. "You feeling okay? For real."

"I'm good, man." I finally turned to look at him, hoping to convince him I was fine. It wasn't like I could tell him a woman I had met for fifteen minutes had me squirming. "A little tired. Crazy game we had, huh?"

"No doubt, Cap. That win had my blood pumping and ready to go."

"Hell yeah!" I faked an excited fist bump. "Cam is already there."

"Oh good. I haven't seen him in a while. He hasn't been to any games lately." Chase, and everyone else, knew how close Cam and I were. He was a staple at my games when his schedule allowed him to be there, just like I was for his.

"He's gearing up for preseason training camp, working his ass off all day. I bet he's ready to let loose, too."

"Well, we can arrange that. How about I give you two first dibs, because you look like you could use a good fuck, Cap."

He nudged me playfully but he wasn't wrong. It would certainly help with the uninvited anxiety I suddenly had. The problem was, there was only one girl I wanted to see—Ali—and something told me she wouldn't be up for a quickie in the bathroom.

Cam was standing by the bouncer in front of 678 with his head down in his phone as we pulled up to the curb and got out.

"Nick!" I yelled, using his nickname so no one on the streets knew to look around for *Cam Nichols*. "You not going in?"

"Yeah, I just walked up. I wanted to talk to you first." He paused to look around at the guys before adding, "Alone, out here, for a minute."

My teammates shrugged and made their way past us, approaching the bouncer to get access to the bar. When they were all out of ear's reach, I nodded at Cam. "What's up?"

"You think she's here tonight?"

He didn't have to ask who *she* was. We hadn't spoken since Wednesday, but we both knew something was up when it came to the gorgeous new server.

"I hope so."

"Do you? Cause with your entire team here tonight, it's gonna be hard to be normal guys who get to talk to girls in bars, like normal humans."

"Yeah I know, but I don't get to tell them where they can and can't go. Doesn't change the fact that I want to see her again."

"Not gonna lie man, I was hoping to be *Nick* just one more time." He let out a big sigh and shoved his hands in his pockets. We rarely met, or got to know, anyone who didn't already know everything about us before we opened our mouths. It was nice being regular guys sometimes, and probably why were both so attracted to the same woman. A first for us.

"So, what's the plan, Cam? We gonna brawl over this girl?" I was only half-joking.

"Maybe," he snorted back.

"Let the games begin." I tapped my hand to his chest and forced a laugh out of him before turning toward the door.

We walked up to the bouncer, who I didn't know at all, but he knew us. He opened the door without even checking our IDs, or asking questions, just a nod. "Good game today."

"Thanks, man."

The bar was crowded, in its usual Friday night glory, so we kept our heads down as we waded through the crowd. I resisted the urge to peek around for Ali, knowing that the guys had probably secured a VIP area, and I needed to get up there first.

As we approached the steps, we raised our eyes to meet those of another bouncer standing outside the private area, who nodded at us as we walked up the two stairs leading to the platform of the VIP section. It was the first time I had sat in that particular section, and it was like being on a stage, on display. I was overthinking it when I finally locked eyes on Ali.

She was standing in front of Chase, hands on her hips with one leg kicked out resting her weight on the other leg. Her back was to us, and she was nodding at something Chase was saying. Her long hair was down in waves and moved across her back as she moved her head.

My eyes snapped toward Chase, and I immediately imagined he was hitting on her—and she was letting him. Jealousy flared up in my chest, making it hard to keep moving forward.

Motioning for Cam to move back a bit, we wait out their conversation. I couldn't afford to punch a teammate in public—especially when I didn't have a legit reason to do so. It was safer where we stood, and Cam seemed to understand without me having to say it out loud.

It felt like four hours, but the whole interaction was probably thirty seconds.

Then, Chase reached out to grab Ali's forearm. The touch was innocent enough, maybe his way of being endearing, but she jumped back.

Just like she did with me.

She shook her head *no*. I imagined she was telling him not to touch her, the same way she did the other night. A part of me felt relieved that it wasn't just me she didn't want to touch her, and the other part of me felt relieved she didn't want Chase touching her.

However, the biggest part of me needed to hit something, and Cam was mirroring my every move. His body was rigid, and his fists were clenched tight at his sides. We stayed tense as we watched Ali recoil, getting a glimpse of her face as she finally turned and walked away.

Something clicked. The terror in her eyes. The way her face paled for a minute. The way she came out of her skin long enough to armor herself.

Something was wrong.

Something happened.

Someone hurt her.

I looked over at Cam, wondering if I could read his mind—his eyes, his face. But he was stoic. Staring. Waiting. Then he finally looked over at me and sighed. "Looks like we better get ready to rumble."

I nodded, agreeing without needing more context. He either meant with each other, with Chase, or with whoever hurt Ali. So whichever it was, he could count me in.

CHAPTER SIX

Cam

UNDER NORMAL CIRCUMSTANCES, I wouldn't think too much of Chase hitting on a woman in the bar. But two things were running through my mind. One, Ali didn't like to be touched, *so don't fucking touch her, Chase.* Two, who should I hit?

Make that three things because I couldn't help wondering why I felt the sudden urge to punch something?

Someone.

Anything.

As much as I wanted to hate Chase, I knew he wouldn't hurt Ali. And in truth, he didn't do anything that Kace hadn't done. Ali got jumpy when other people's hands came toward her. I could make an argument that working in an environment with an overwhelming amount of drunk and uninhibited people would get old. A natural defense would be to recoil every time someone got handsy.

But that didn't feel like what was happening. She didn't come across as being simply annoyed. Her fear was too pronounced.

She recovered quickly; much quicker than she had with Kace. She smiled at Chase and shrugged off the discontent as she stepped back and turned toward the steps that Kace and I had just come up. That was when we finally approached the guys and took the seats at the end of the grouped tables.

"Cam, my man!"

"Chase, long time no see." I sat in the chair next to him, someone I considered a friend, even though we only hung out through Kace.

"Kace drag you out again?"

"Something like that. You already order?"

"Yeah, and I told the hot waitress to bring two extra beers for you two."

"Thanks, man." Clearly he thought Ali was hot. *We probably all did.*

"Hot?" Kace scoffed, not letting Chase's words go away that easily. "The woman that was just standing here? The one I just saw jump ten feet away from you? Hate to break it to ya buddy, but that looked rough."

"Yeah well, I said she was hot, not that I was trying to hit it."

"Looked to me like she was shooting down your game," Kace smirked, digging for information while disguising it as banter.

"Nah, she's hot, but she's not single. I don't mess around with another dude's woman."

"Not single? Is that what you were over here talking about?" Shit, I didn't even consider the fact that she may be seeing someone.

"No," Chase huffed, "but when I reached out to thank her for naming almost every local IPA they had on tap tonight, she flinched like she had a man."

"How does that mean she isn't single?"

"Available women don't walk away from my touch, fucker." Chase laughed and turned his attention to the other guys, unknowingly sending my head into a tailspin of thoughts that I didn't get time to process.

Over Kace's shoulder, I spotted Ali weaving back through the crowd with a tray of several draft IPAs, and I knew she was headed our way. It took her a few minutes to navigate the crowd, but it was made worse by two drunks that had started pushing one another directly in her path. Kace noticed where my attention had gone and looked back over his shoulder. We both watched as Ali made a move to get around the commotion.

Then, everything became a blur of movement and chaos.

Ali had made it past the fight but as she stepped up the steps to our section, one of the drunk fuckers pushed the other one again. Drunk guy number two fell back, his body falling into Ali's back and in turn, pushing her forward. Her tray and all the drinks went flying, crashing into a pile of glass and ale, as she braced herself for the fall.

Kace was slightly closer to the action, and before Ali hit the ground, he jumped up and caught her by the arms, raising her back to her feet. I had rushed forward as well and was standing directly behind them. I thought Kace would see if she was okay, but instead, he spun her around to face me while he faced the fight. His back was against hers, creating a shield, knowing I was there to make sure she wasn't hurt. Holding onto her arms to steady her, I saw that she was visibly shaking, and for a moment, I thought it may have been because I was touching her and making things worse. Yet, I didn't let her go.

"Hey, hey, Ali. I got you. It's okay." She looked up at me, recognition immediately showing in her eyes before leaning into my touch and taking a deep breath.

"I hate this job," she whispered.

I couldn't help but laugh a little. If it were me that had just been pushed while holding twelve glasses of beer, I would hate that job too. "Are you okay, though? Anything hurt?"

"I'm fine, JJ caught me before I face-planted." *She remembered our names.* Our fake names, but still.

Kace was still being a wall for her to hide behind as the scuffle continued, but he heard her. "I got you, sweetheart. And security being right by the stairs is making it quick to clear them out."

"I, um, I need to clean up this mess." She started to pull away, assessing the broken glass at our feet, but I wasn't ready. Kace and I had her sandwiched in between us, and until those guys were kicked out of the bar, I didn't want her to move.

"Wait until it's all clear, there is too much glass." I started to move my hands up and down her arms in a soothing manner and she nodded then took another deep breath.

The other guys had gotten up from our table and were watching the whole scene. Most of them were watching the two guys fighting—not for a show—ready to jump in if they needed to. Chase included.

Several of the patrons in the bar had noticed our crew standing on the stage-like platform surrounded by ropes, recognized us, and were using that chance to take pictures. I kept my head down, my forehead almost touching Ali's. It was intimate, in a way. Being so close to her, listening to her breathe, not speaking, just comforting.

I forced myself to glance up when I heard one of the managers of the bar apologizing to everyone, and assuring them that their night could continue in peace. Kace started to move forward, away from Ali, and she took one final breath before stepping aside and away from my touch.

No longer being blocked by Kace's large frame, the manager spotted Ali and came forward. "Ali, are you okay? We need to clean this mess up stat."

"Yes ma'am, I'm good and will get this cleaned up. Can you ask Tony to remake the entire order for the VIP section, please?"

"This was the VIP order? Shit!" The manager started to lose her concern for Ali, which didn't sit well with me, even though I knew it was normal for businesses to worry over their VIPs. Ali didn't look fazed; she just began throwing big pieces of glass onto her now empty tray as the manager stomped off to replace the order.

The other guys had made their way back to the table,

engrossed into their full conversations once again. Kace and I were inching closer to the mess, both bending down to help Ali with the glass.

"What are you doing?" Her face was covered in concern.

"Helping," Kace shrugged.

"No! You guys are clearly in the VIP section. My boss will kill me if she sees me letting you clean my mess."

"Okay, first of all, this isn't *your* mess, this is those fucking assholes' mess. Second, your boss will have to go through me if she has the nerve to get mad at *you* for *me* making my own decision."

"It doesn't work that way." She turned from Kace to look at me. "Don't you think about it either."

Too late, I was already carefully piling the glass in my hand, trying not to cut myself. I just raised one eyebrow at her and smirked, making her shake her head in defeat.

With all three of us cleaning, it took no time at all to get the major pieces of glass up. By the time a busboy had made his way over with a broom and mop, Ali's part was done, so she left to dispose of the mess while Kace and I sat back down.

"What the hell just happened?" Chase asked.

"I just looked back at the exact right moment and saw the whole thing unfold. I was thinking she was going to get hurt if I didn't keep those guys from falling into her again." Kace was eyeing me as he fibbed a little. We didn't just happen to look back, we were fucking staring.

"Yeah, well, thank God you were there, she would have fallen right into that glass."

"I think she realized how close she came to being shredded up. Took me a minute to calm her down," I added.

Chase nodded, accepting our story before turning back to the conversation he was having with his teammate. It was technically all true, and we would have done that for anyone. Probably even helped them clean up. The difference was, we wouldn't have been watching anyone else as close as we were Ali. She had our attention long before she needed it, and no one else knew that.

For some reason, I didn't feel like drinking anymore. I just needed some air, so I got Kace's attention and pointed up, letting him know I was going to the rooftop.

He raised one brow at me in question asking, *Want me to go with?*

We were such girls sometimes, I swear. But I turned my lips down and shook my head. *Nah, just need air.*

I knew 678 had a rooftop area that was mostly used for the staff to have a smoke break. Taking the steps two at a time, I pushed the heavy door at the top open. As the door shut behind me, the music from the bar immediately disappeared and was replaced by the faint noise of sirens and traffic below.

Walking around the corner to an area I remembered had some old benches, I immediately paused at the sight of a lone figure leaning on the half-wall that surrounded the edges of the roof.

Ali.

Her hair had been pulled into a ponytail and her apron was gone. I could see her long legs, toned and tan, peeking from below her cut off shorts, down to the heels she was wearing. She hadn't noticed anyone had come up to the roof, so I took advantage and had a longer look before I took a step forward to get her attention.

"Everything okay?"

ali

NICK'S VOICE STARTLED ME, and I jumped. These guys were going to think I was a scaredy-cat, but I had been a bit jumpier since I met them. I *felt* something shift in me that night, making my belly clench and my head spin, and I had been like that since.

Before turning to face Nick, I took a minute to school my face into a smile, then turned. "Hey there, I'm good, yeah. Thanks for the help back there, never a dull moment around here."

Nick was tall, with broad shoulders and long legs. He was wearing faded jeans and a Henley shirt with the long sleeves pulled showing his forearms, and the buttons at the top undone just enough to see some of his smooth chest.

He didn't move, stayed ten feet away, and considered my words. "I guess not. That happen all the time?"

"Not *that*, but something is always up. I guess it comes with the job description."

He shrugged, unconvinced. "If you say so. Just not sure any job should come with a 'may fall into a bed of broken glass after getting pushed by drunk grown men' warning label."

"You're probably right," I laughed, then added quietly, "I need to go thank JJ again, too. I don't know how he got there so fast. It was like he had superpowers." *God, I was lame. Next thing you know, I would be asking if he was a damn vampire.*

After a beat of silence, I steered the conversation away from me, and onto him. "What are you doing up here?"

"My drink, it never came, so I came looking for it myself."

"What? Tony told me to take five and he would get the other girl to take the drinks. I swear if Molly flaked out, I'll kill her." I started toward the door, on a mission to make sure my tables were covered, mostly for Mary's sake.

"Wait," Nick was laughing. "Okay, I actually just came up for air. I didn't stick around to wait on my drink. I'm sure it got there just fine."

In my attempt to get to the door, I had moved closer to him, and he smelled so dang good. When he held me up earlier, his smell permeated my brain, and I didn't know what the scent was. But now I was sure someone should bottle it up and label it *Nick*.

Maybe they already had, which made me wonder. "So, the other night, when you and JJ wanted the ropes and red tape, you weren't kidding, huh?"

"No, we weren't." He actually looked a bit embarrassed. "But it ended up being the best night, even without it."

"I'm so sorry. I have only been at this for three weeks and I hate it. I'm still getting the hang of the regulars."

"Like I said, we had a good time. At least, until you disappeared."

I tried to ignore the blood that rushed to my face. I turned and edged back to the wall, hiding my obvious embarrassment. "I, um, started feeling a little off. My head was spinning so I went home in case I was coming down with something."

"Well, I am glad you're feeling better." He was now standing next to me, both of us looking down at the traffic, our elbows touching as we leaned on our arms.

"Yeah, false alarm." I wasn't going to admit that it was him and

JJ that got my head spinning, or that I had left because my 'sickness' was a *fear of making a fool out of myself* disease.

He probably already knew that was the reason. He was there, he wasn't blind.

"What I said that night still stands, though. JJ and I have a five round UFC fight planned for next weekend. The winner gets to ask you out on a date."

He had turned to rest one arm on the wall and was facing me, a teasing smirk on his face. "What are you… just friends? Brothers? Coworkers? I mean, what's the deal there?"

"You really don't know?" He let out a small snort and shook his head in disbelief.

"Know what?"

"Never mind. JJ has been my best friend since we were kids. He's closer than a brother to me."

"So, is this," I twirled my finger around in a circle, "your favorite game?"

"We've never played this game before. It's new." He leaned in a little with a charming smile on his cocky face. I could feel him baiting me.

"Well, I think it's pretty dumb to go five rounds with a lifelong friend like that. Especially when all the winner gets is a rejection from the girl who doesn't want to date either of you."

Unfazed, he pulled his phone from his pocket and sent a text off, then slid it back into his pants before answering me. "Maybe. But you're probably worth an honorable try."

My faced burned in response to his charm. He was really good at being the prince.

Meanwhile, I didn't have a comeback. All I could think of was how broken I was, definitely not worth the trouble. But I quickly decided that wasn't his business, nor was it something I wanted to talk about.

"I…" Before I could settle on telling him I should get back to work, the door to the roof opened and JJ walked out. He quickly shoved both hands into the pockets of his jeans and strolled toward Nick and me with an arrogant smile.

"We doing this right now?" JJ asked Nick.

My eyes bounced between them, but I remained quiet because my mouth had gone a little dry at the sight of JJ. He had a similar build to Nick's, and wore dark jeans and a dark grey t-shirt with a black silhouette of a goat in the center of his chest. Unlike Nick's coiffed hair, JJ's was wild.

"Eh, she said it's a losing game," Nick shrugged.

"You fucked it up, didn't you? You called me up here to fix it?" The smile on his face let me know he was teasing. And before Nick could even respond, JJ turned to me and got serious for a minute. "You okay, sweetheart?"

"Yeah, thanks again. Being a bloody mess would have stifled the tips a little."

JJ just stared, making me nervous all over again. He seemed more imposing than Nick, with a big personality that made me feel inferior. Nick's lack of tattoos and softer demeanor put me more at ease.

Why did I care?

I cleared my throat and remembered that it didn't matter what anyone thought. "I better get back to work."

"But I just got here," JJ spread his arms wide.

"Well, I've been here fifteen minutes. Time's up on my break."

"How long have you been up here?" JJ asked Nick.

Nick looked at his watch and bounced his head like he was doing hardcore math. "Um, ten minutes."

"And you just now texted me?"

"Yeah, well, don't ever say I don't love you."

A laugh escaped my mouth, his comment reminding me of when he called JJ his partner and I thought they were lovers. JJ didn't miss it either, rolling his eyes before saying, "Man, how many times are you going to try convincing her we're an item?"

"You trying to tell me you don't love me?" Nick put his hands on his hips, mocked scorn in his stance.

"Of course, I love you, I'd marry the shit out of you. But you're plan B, baby."

Now I was laughing harder, and I bit, too curious. "What's plan A?"

"You." His response was fast, and he wasn't laughing anymore.

I wanted to roll my eyes at myself, again, for walking right into that one.

"Y'all are ridiculous." It would be embarrassing to actually think that one of them was into me. Not only were they way out of my league, but they were playful and put on a great show.

However, in the five minutes we had all three been standing there, I had loosened up a little. Their friendship and banter was contagious, and we had gone from super awkward introductions, to almost falling on my face, to easy laughter.

"I really do have to get back to work. Thank you, not just for helping me earlier, but for this." I pointed between us, hoping they realized I meant their company and light. "I needed this."

With a small smile, I reached out and touched JJ's bicep, and then with my other hand, I touched Nick's wrist. It was an ironic move on my part but touching them felt okay. When JJ's back was against mine earlier and Nick held my arms, it felt good. I knew I was safe, and although they didn't know my fears, or the extent of my issues, I hoped that deep down they knew how much that small gesture on my part meant.

kace

WE ALL MADE our way down the stairs and back to our stations—Cam and I to our table and Ali to the bar. My arm was tingling where Ali had touched me. It was like she was trying to say she trusted us, but I could've just been overthinking it.

"Hey," I leaned across the table a little, to talk lower to Cam. "Why did you text me to come to the roof? Doesn't make sense you'd invite me to steal the girl and win the game, Cam."

He just smiled an easy smile and shrugged. "I thought it would make her happy. She told me she thought you had superpowers."

My eyes widened and then beaded, not believing him.

"Swear."

I started to flex and tell him I most definitely had super-powers but stopped when Ali came to the end of the table between me and Cam.

"Anybody need another round?" She was asking the entire table and a few of the guys were holding up their empty glasses to indicate they wanted another. But once she got the table count, she focused on me. "How about you? That beer hot, yet?"

"Actually, I haven't touched it…. So probably."

"I will bring you a fresh one. And you?" She looked to Cam.

"I'm in the same boat, hot beer," he replied.

"I'll be right back with fresh ones, guys."

Cam watched her leave over the top of my shoulder with a look of shock on his face. "Why does she make me want to hit shit?"

"I don't know the answer to that, but I feel you. I've been borderline raging since I laid eyes on her. That woman just raises the testosterone in me, I guess."

"And the jealousy, protectiveness, and vulnerability? Is that all testosterone, too?"

"No, that's a fucking crush. We are apparently teenagers again, with hormones, acne, and a crush."

Cam was laughing at me when Ali walked back up and delivered the beers, saving ours for last. When she placed them in front of us, she lowered her tray to her side took a deep breath. "I don't know why I think you need to know this, but I've been cut for the night. Molly is taking over my section."

"Cut? Why would they cut you? That's bullshit."

"No! Seriously! I *want* to go home. Tony knows I do, he's the one that cut me. Any time we have too many servers on the floor and need to send someone home, I volunteer. But um, yeah. I just wanted to tell you. I don't know why. See ya around."

"Let us walk you out," I quickly suggested before she got too far. The word *us* came out naturally for some reason. *Damn I really I would lose at this game, I suck at it.*

"No need. I leave out the back and only live a few blocks away."

"You walk home? This late?" I asked.

"Every night."

"We can walk you home," Cam said, coming up with a new plan to escort her.

"Guys, I appreciate that, but it's not necessary. I just wanted you to know why Molly was taking over for me... again. Besides, walking home in the dark with two strange men sounds scarier than walking alone."

She had a point. She worked there more nights than we were there, so it wasn't like we could start walking her home every night. She had a routine she felt secure with, and I respected that.

"Okay, sweetheart. Just do me a favor..." I trailed off, waiting for her to look at me. "Stay on your feet. No falling up the stairs on the way out. You got me?"

"Yes, sir," she saluted with a smile, making me suppress a very turned on groan.

"And hey," Cam added and winked. "See you soon."

Two weeks.

That's how long it'd been since we'd been at 678 and gotten to know Ali a little more, telling her we'd see her again. But I had to leave that following Monday for a road series in Philadelphia and Miami. By the time I had gotten home, Cam was neck-deep in preseason media days. We had agreed we wouldn't go back to the bar unless we could both go because it would be too easy for one of us to get attached without the other there to knock us back down to reality. And neither of us were letting go of how much I wanted Ali.

I still wasn't sure what we were going to do about our mutual attraction to the same woman. It wasn't like it was a little crush, or the need to fuck her. This was a full-on arrow to my heart. When I told Cam that it was the closest to love at first sight I had ever seen, I wasn't kidding, and I knew he was feeling the same way, because if he knew I was into a girl, and he was just so-so, he would back down.

Ali was going to test our friendship. But until we knew more about her, we couldn't decide what to do about it. Cam informed me that she told him that neither of us stood a chance, but we all knew that was a lie. The first night we all met was so ignited with flames, I was surprised we didn't catch fire. She was definitely feeling it for one of us.

But who?

I was sitting in front of my locker after our big win that afternoon when my phone started ringing, breaking me from my thoughts.

"Hey," I greeted Cam.

"Hey! Watched the game today, good win. You guys needed that."

"Yeah, we did. If only I had contributed."

"That hat trick got you hard," Cam laughed.

Failure was part of the game. There were good days, and bad days. Normally, I could laugh at myself after a game like that, striking out three times. But I didn't have it in me.

I ran a hand down my face and sighed. "I don't know what happened. I couldn't have hit the broad side of a barn."

"You were stepping into the swing too early. You weren't waiting on the pitch."

"Thanks for your insight, Mr. Quarterback." My sarcasm was thick, but he wasn't wrong. Baseball may not have been his sport, but he was an athlete, nonetheless. He had also been watching me play since I was four years old, and he could see exactly what I was doing, even if others couldn't. *Even if I couldn't.*

"Just looking out. Hey, what're you doing tonight?"

"Going home. Wallowing in self-pity. Avoiding the recaps of the game. Watching your interviews from today. What you got going on? Have you eaten?"

"I still have to meet with the media team for our pregame videos. I am ready for media week to be over with." Media days were essential in every sport. It allowed all the news outlets to get their questions in and get insight on the teams before the season.

That way, once the season started, the players weren't hounded over inconsequential information. We also had to use that time to do anything the team needed for promos. It was good to get it all over with but exhausting for everyone involved.

"Want me to bring you some dinner or something? I can pass by the stadium on my way home." I was nice like that.

"No, I have a much bigger request."

"Um, okay… just remember I played nine innings of crap baseball. I'm not in the mood for much."

"Not even if it involved Ali?"

"I'm listening." I sat upright on my stool, wondering what he was going to ask and ready to say yes.

"Maybe you should go to 678 and *check* on Ali?" Cam said, but made it sound like a question. That was a weird request. We agreed not to go separately, so I didn't understand why I needed to *check* in on her.

"What's this about?"

"Well, two things. I don't want her to think we forgot about her because we've been away for two weeks. We should have slipped her our numbers. And the biggie… one of the reporters earlier today showed me a picture from the bar a couple of weeks ago. All the guys on your team standing there, you in front of Ali, and me rubbing her arms. My forehead is leaned in, intimately. Your face looks like you wanna kill someone. And this guy just asked me who the lady was. I—"

"Who's this reporter? What was his angle? Who took the pic?" The amount of questions I had was endless. I knew people in the bar were taking pictures of the scene, so I didn't know why I started panicking. "You didn't tell them who she was, did you? Ali won't appreciate being the center of our media storm."

"Hell no, I didn't tell him. I told him I didn't even know her name, that she fell in front of us, and we were being good Samaritans by making sure she was okay." He took a deep breath and continued, "But then he said he could tell it was at 678, and would find her name for his article. I just think maybe you should pop in and make sure no one has been asking for her. Maybe we should warn her about the picture. I know these reporters like to pursue anything they think is associated with us."

"Fuck." A month ago, I laughed at something a fan said while I was signing autographs before the game, and she had three reporters around her before the first inning was over... wondering what she said to make me laugh. I rolled my eyes at the memory. I was used to the interest the media took in my life, but sometimes they took it too far.

"And Ali isn't a random fan. Hell, she isn't even a fan. She won't know what the fuck is going on."

"Well, I can't say this is a difficult task, Cam."

He groaned and huffed before nicely saying, "Tell her hey from me."

"Will do. I'll call you when I head home." *We really were girls sometimes.*

"Later, man."

I lifted my head and looked around the locker room. Almost everyone had gone home, just a few guys lingering by their lockers. Home was where I should have been going since we had a big game the next day.

Cam was normally the responsible one, keeping me home, telling me to rest. He must've really wanted me checking in if he'd suggest I go out on a game night—with no babysitter.

As if he was reading my thoughts, a text popped up.

CAM

Don't stay out late, fucker. Drink water tonight, and for the love of God, eye on the fucking ball tomorrow.

ali

I DIDN'T REGRET HELPING Mary, but I was going to need a prescription for anxiety meds before too long. It had been a few weeks since I last saw Mary because I was afraid I would ask her about Nick and JJ.

Then I decided I *wanted* to ask her about Nick and JJ, and I also needed just to check on her. But every time I texted her, asking her if I could drop by, it hadn't been "good timing." I was determined to try again on Tuesday.

Monday night at the bar wasn't exactly the busiest night of the week. I had been able to sneak to the roof quite a few times to get some fresh air. The same roof where Nick and I had finally had a conversation that wasn't solely based on awkward silences and stares. A tingle ran down my spine at the thought of them both standing there, gorgeous and perfect. I took a deep breath and let it out slowly as I looked over the edge of the roof.

Giving myself a few more minutes, I turned around and decided it was time to get back to work. Navigating the pipes that ran across that section of the roof, I was careful and kept my head down so I could see where I was stepping.

"Don't fall."

A scream almost escaped, but I put my hands to my chest and let out a relieved breath at the man I knew belonged to that voice.

JJ.

"I will have you know," I said, trying to look composed. "I haven't fallen in two whole weeks, thank you very much."

"Thank God. I would hate it if something happened to that perfect face."

I flushed at his comment, but he and Nick were professional smooth talkers, and I had to get over their charm.

"What're you doing here?" I had already made the connection that he and Nick were regular patrons and VIP, but it had been a couple of weeks since I had seen them.

Not that I was keeping track or anything.

"At the bar, or on the roof?"

"Both."

"Came to see you." He was smiling with a sincere look in his eyes. "That is the answer to both. Didn't look busy down there, so I thought maybe you got cut tonight. Decided to check up here, just in case."

"I was just getting ready to head back in."

"Five more minutes?"

I bit my bottom lip, trying not to smile. "Okay."

My only defense against a man like JJ was distance, but he moved toward me and reached his hand out for me to take. I didn't flinch at the movement, or get jumpy while he stayed still, a few feet away from me. He was making me move forward to take his hand, letting it be my decision. It was a very intentional move, and I knew he had caught on to my aversion to being touched.

Judging by the look in his eye as I approached, I would say he not only knew, but savored the trust I put in him as I took his hand. He led me over to a bench that sat in the center of the roof and motioned for me to join him, never letting go of my hand.

For a few seconds, he just smiled and stared at me. It wasn't as awkward or uncomfortable as it would have been with anyone else.

"Cam says hi," he finally blurted.

"Who?"

His eyes widened and he shook his head. "Sorry, I meant Nick… Nick says hi."

"He's not here?" I didn't need to see him, but I was kind of sad he wasn't there with JJ. My heart and my head were making me crazy.

"Nah, he had to work. I just told him I was going to pop in and say hi."

"To me?" I asked, disbelieving.

"Yes, to you. Why else would I be in a bar, alone, on a Monday night?"

I couldn't pretend I wasn't flattered. Surely there was a woman in his life, though, right? He seemed too perfect to be a liar or a cheater, but I knew all too well how deceiving looks could be. I was wrong once before and I needed to keeping reminding myself that most men *sucked*.

"What is it you do, for work, that is?" I leaned back, wanting to ask a million other questions but didn't want to get too deep.

He started bouncing his knee a little, seeming nervous all of a sudden. "You really don't know?"

Was I supposed to know who he was? He was VIP here in 678. I knew that much. He was cocky as shit about it, too. At least he was the first night I met him. There were a lot of actors in the area, movies were always filming in Atlanta these days. He must be one of them.

Which didn't help much, because unless his name was Brad Pitt or Tom Cruise, I was clueless when it came to pop culture. I watched maybe four movies a year because my nose had always been in a book or doing research for pieces I was writing. My TV was used for the local news as background noise and occasionally a late-night sitcom if I couldn't sleep. So, I had no clue who JJ was. I wasn't sure if I was annoyed that he thought I should know, or intrigued by what he was going to tell me.

For some reason, he seemed more at ease with my confusion.

Before he answered me, or before I answered him, his phone started ringing. Looking to the screen, he smiled. "Nick," he said to me, indicating he was going to answer it.

"Hey! You finish up at the office?" A minute of silence and then, "So you headed home?" Another beat of silence. "Yeah, I am sitting here at 678, rooftop." He smiled at whatever Nick was saying. "Yeah, get some rest man. I am headed out soon." Nick's turn, and JJ rolled his eyes. "Yes Mom, I promise I am only drinking water. And yes, I will text you when I'm home safe." He laughed at himself, or maybe Nick's response to his sarcasm. "Okay hold on a minute."

Suddenly, he held the phone out. "Nick wants to talk to you."

If my eyes could leave my head from surprise, they would have been rolling around on the ground. *What?* I mouthed. *No way.*

JJ just smiled wider and mouthed back. *Just for a second. He's not the chatty type.*

I took JJ's phone, curious about what Nick was going to say, and also, admittedly, anxious to hear his voice. "Hello?"

"Hey, gorgeous." Nick sounded tired but happy. "You doing okay?"

"Um, hey there. I am. How are you?"

"Busy. But since JJ was getting a chance to hang out tonight, I thought I would barge in with a phone call while I drove home."

"Yeah, he mentioned you had to work tonight."

Nick sighed, "Yeah, and one more long day tomorrow, but then a few days off. Hey, I have a quick question though," he said, changing the subject mid-thought.

"Oh sure, what's up?" I was trying too hard not to sound like an idiot.

"What's your favorite color?"

I wrinkled my nose in confusion. "My what?"

"Favorite color," he repeated.

"Um, red, I guess."

"Okay one more. What is your favorite number?"

"Are you doing a survey or something?"

"Nah, just pissing JJ off. Is he red yet?" I looked up to JJ and laughed at the questioning eyebrow he had raised. *Is he done?*

"Almost."

"Then my work here is done," he laughed.

"You two are a mess, you know that?" My southern accent came through strong, and I was feeling more and more relaxed every time they made me laugh.

"Gotta keep him grounded, Gorgeous. Tell him I'll call him tomorrow. And I really hope to see you again, soon."

"I will." The smile in my tone was undeniable, and before he could hang up, I added, "Oh, and Nick, it's 20, my favorite number is 20."

Hanging up, I handed the phone back to JJ who had a glint in his eye as he looked at me. Then he visibly shook off whatever was running through his mind and sighed, "He loves making me crazy."

"You two are cute," I blurted, even though it was true. Their laughs and banter showed how much they cared about one another. It was the kind of friendship I had been missing in my life.

"Yeah, well, there is currently no one in my life that I care about more than Nick. When you grow up the way we did, experience the things we have, and learn that we are the only people we can trust, you kinda cling to one another. We keep each other in line."

"I haven't had a best friend, or even a friend, in so long, I'm jealous of you two." I tried a small laugh to lighten up my statement because I didn't want to come across as pathetic.

"I have a hard time believing that."

"Believe it. I'm not much different than you, I guess. I learned the only person I can trust is myself."

"Well," he raised his hand, and then pointed to the phone, "now you have two friends. Nick and I are good friends to have."

"Thought this was a game?" I teased.

The side of his mouth quirked up, showing off a boyish charm I hadn't noticed before. "I don't think that keeps us from being friends."

For almost a full minute, we sat in silence, staring at one another and sizing each other up with goofy smiles on our faces. *I could use a friend.* Then the door to the roof popped open and one of the busboys poked his head out. "Hey Ali, Tony is looking for ya."

"Shit, I'm coming." But I didn't jump and run. I waited on him to shut the door before turning back to JJ and shrugging. "Thanks for stopping by."

"Hopefully it's not forever before Nick and I get back in here." He looked down at our hands, still intertwined in a friendly and natural way.

Perfect.

"Well, I'll be here as long as Mary needs me."

"How is Mary? What's going on with her?" He pushed at the reminder.

"That is a story for another day," I sighed and stood. "Gotta get back to work." I also needed to make sure Mary didn't mind me telling them about her diagnosis.

Like I said, I wasn't entirely sure how honest she'd been about her absence. No one at 678 had asked me anything, so I just kept quiet.

We made our way to the door and down the stairs, no longer touching. As we approached the bottom step, JJ tugged slightly at my back pocket and leaned into my ear. "Be safe. See you soon."

When I stepped off onto the floor, I looked back at him, but he was already walking towards the exit.

It took me three more days to finally get Mary to agree to a visit. She sounded tired on the phone, but I needed to see her, to check-in. I guilted her by mentioning my only day off because of all the jobs I was working, and I probably should have felt bad, but I didn't. I was too worried about her to care. She didn't have any kids or family that I knew of, and she was going through a very tough time. She needed people in her life more than she realized.

I walked down to her second-floor apartment and knocked at eight in the morning. My arms were full of a picnic basket filled with breakfast pastries, a thermos full of coffee, orange juice, and a picnic blanket. We lived right across from the most serene park in Atlanta, and I was hoping she would agree to a breakfast picnic under one of the shade trees.

"Good fucking gracious, Ali, what do you have?" Mary asked as she opened the door. Her voice was deep and raspy, years of smoking playing a role. Her bright red hair was up in a French twist and she wore leggings and a loose-fitting top. She looked to have lost a little weight in the weeks since I had seen her.

"Mary! I've missed you!" Mary wasn't a hugger, so I tried to express my excitement with my words and happy facial expressions. I lifted my arms to show her all my surprises. "I was hoping you'd walk across to Centennial Park with me for a morning picnic!"

"Is that what all this is? Shit, honey, I thought you were just wanting to check-in, see that I'm still alive." Her words didn't match her expression. She was going to come; I could see it in the twinkle of her eyes at the idea of a picnic.

"Well, I do, but I also want to spend some time with you. I

haven't seen you out and about, so I thought a picnic would be perfect for getting some fresh air."

"Yeah, yeah..." She trailed off, waving her hand in annoyance. But again, her actions didn't match her face. She had a hint of a smile that grew bigger as she turned around to grab her sweater. "Let's go, Hot stuff."

She locked up her apartment and we walked down to the first floor. Despite being sick, Mary was still fit and quick. She preferred using the stairs and didn't mind the walk across the street to the park.

The sun was shining, not a cloud in the sky, and not too hot considering it was mid-August. We were able to find a spot under a tree and I made quick work of laying out the blanket and pouring us each a cup of orange juice.

As Mary settled in, she took a sip of her juice and coughed. "What the hell?" Her face was scrunched in distaste. "This is plain. Where's the vodka?"

Mary was serious and I rolled my eyes with a laugh. "Sorry, Mary, didn't think morning-drinking was part of your medical regimen."

"Fuck that! Besides, a stiff drink helps me rest, and that fucking doctor is always telling me to fucking rest." Mary grunted, then pulled a mini bottle of vodka from her sweater pocket and added it to her juice.

God, I loved that woman. She was hardened by life, not always having the easiest circumstances along the way, but always good for a laugh. Mary would do anything for anyone but the facade she showed the world hid her huge heart.

She and my mom, Margie, had been friends in high school, and kept in and out of touch over the years. Mom had told me stories about Mary, but I had never met her personally until I was sixteen. That was the year Mom died in a car accident and I didn't take it well. Grandma didn't take it well, either, but Dad took it so much worse. Mary reached out to me, letting me know that she—coincidentally—lived in the same building as my grandma, and would be around if I ever needed anything.

She would sometimes visit with me and Grandma, or I would have dinner with her. But like my mom and her, we stayed in and out of touch.

I went off to college. She worked a lot.

I was barely ever in the city unless it was to visit Grandma. But once she died, those visits were even fewer.

Until Alan happened.

Once I moved back, Mary became my only friend, and apart from the people she worked with at 678, I was her only friend as well.

Mary never knew the truth about why I moved into Grandma's. I told her college sucked, and she accepted that answer. No questions. She would have never asked me to take her shifts if she had known the truth—which made me both thankful and pissed that I never told her. She needed me to keep her position steady, and I was happy I could do that for her. But it forced me to deal with demons I didn't want to deal with.

Maybe it was a blessing in disguise.

Working at 678 forced me out of the shell I had built around myself. The people I worked with were great, and the clientele at 678 was, for the most part, pleasant.

Plus, I met JJ and Nick—two of the sexiest, and most charming, men I had ever met. I knew nothing would come of our meeting, but I would be lying if I didn't say they hadn't added a spark to my mostly introverted existence.

I felt high in their presence, and figured should just enjoy it while I could.

I needed friends, I reminded myself.

For the most part, Mara and I had been silent. There really wasn't much to talk about—she wouldn't answer me if I asked about her chemo. I knew she was tired, and it was taking its toll on her. I had already updated her on how work was going, although I did have a few questions I was working up the nerve to ask her…

"Um, so… I have a question." I pursed my lips and eyed Mary, who was busy peeling the skin off the grapes before eating them. "I met a couple of guys a few weeks ago."

That got her attention for sure. "Whoooooa. A couple of guys? As in two? You go, honey!" She nudged me.

"Yes, and no. Not like that. Or maybe like that. But not really." Ugh. *This was confusing.* "They seem to know you. Told me they always have you wait on them, and you always take care of them."

"You will have to be more specific. Do they have names?"

"JJ and Nick."

"Hmmm, that doesn't ring a bell at all. It doesn't mean they don't know me, though. JJ and Nick? Hmmm." She drifted off in thought, searching her brain for who I may be referring to. I guess I shouldn't have been surprised that she didn't know them off-hand. After all, she waited on hundreds of tables a week.

"Yeah, well, they asked how you were, and I just didn't know what to say. Your business is your business, but I feel like they care and want to know," I hedged.

"Well, my business is my business, is right. I don't need no random bar fools knowing my fucking business," she huffed.

"Okay, they just seem to be concerned and I feel bad not telling them the truth. But I will keep it to myself, promise." I tapped her hand and she smiled at me.

"Good. Now tell me something else about JJ and Nick."

I side-eyed her. "Like what?"

"Fuck if I know, just that you got a little twinkle in your eye when you said their names, and I wanna know what the fuck that's all about." Mary and her use of the word *fuck* knew no bounds.

I sighed a deep, exaggerated sigh. "They are two of the sexiest men I have ever seen—of course, my eyes are interested. My head, however, has no space to worry about how my eyes feel. I don't need man drama right now."

"Your eyes and your head aren't the part of you that needs a man, Ali. Your head is an independent and intelligent woman that needs no man. Your *vamama* on the other hand…" I shoved her before she could finish. I did not need Mary telling me what my *vamama* needed. Or her definition of "vamama".

"Mary!" I groaned but she was already laughing at herself —and me.

"Oh, my word!" Mary yelled out of the blue, then stood up quickly and started throwing her grapes.

What the hell?

I looked up and around her small frame to try and determine what was going on. My eyes followed the direction of her rogue grapes to the sidewalk that circled the park. Two men were jogging side by side, and I realized she was throwing the grapes *at* them.

I was starting to think she had finally lost her marbles. *Or grapes?* But when the two joggers got past her body, that had been blocking my view, I gasped. "Oh my God."

"Cam and Kace, get your asses over here," Mary started yelling.

Now I was convinced she was losing it because the two joggers were Nick and JJ, and she was calling them something else while throwing grapes at them. I was both concerned, and embarrassed.

I stood quickly and started to pull Mary's arm down, but once I was standing, my view improved, and I realized Nick and JJ had already seen her and were headed our way.

They both had huge smiles on their faces, and were looking at Mary with tenderness in their eyes. No doubt they knew her, but she must have been confused about who they were.

I stepped out from behind Mary—and the tree she was standing next to—and smiled at their approach. I decided if I couldn't beat the crazy, I'd just join, but when Nick and JJ noticed me standing there, they both stopped abruptly as if they had hit a wall. Their smiles faltered, and they both looked a little worried.

Well, okay then.

I guess there was no need to worry about my eyes and head—or my *vamama*—because they were not exactly happy to see me. I tried to turn around and hide my embarrassment. I thought they'd be happy to see me. They had, after all, seemed to both like me, but they also told me I was their little game.

God. I was most likely overthinking everything.

Mary met them a few steps off our blanket as I turned back around and plastered an uneasy smile on my face. They were both hugging her and asking her how she was, and she freely told them all about her diagnosis and wellbeing.

What the hell happened to her business is her business? We were literally just talking about those two guys not four minutes prior and she called them "random bar fools."

I put both hands on my cheeks and wiped toward my mouth, trying to decide if I was going to say something or wait the crazy out. I intertwined my fingers in front of my mouth and stayed quiet, but the motion was enough to catch the eye of JJ. He was still listening to Mary but also looking toward me every few seconds.

Mary eventually noticed him eyeing me and looked back. "Oh, how rude of me, guys this is Ali, my neighbor, and my friend. Ali, this is..."

"We've met," Nick said, cutting Mary's introductions off. He started to reach out to me, his arms going up like he was going to hug me, but then quickly brought his arms down back to his side. "She's been at 678, Mary. We've been asking her how you've been, but she wouldn't tell us shit." His smile showed his playfulness in the comment.

Mary dramatically slapped her forehead, then she turned to

me. "Why didn't you tell me they were asking how I was? These are my babies! Of course, you can let them know how I am."

I had no words. Just an extremely confused WTF face directed at Mary. I raised my arms and started to ask her where the hell her brain went, but I stopped when I felt a light touch running down the back of my arm. The kind of touch that I would have jumped from had I been at the bar. Or had I not known what it was.

Or *who* it was.

But I knew.

JJ had moved closer and had started moving his fingers from my shoulder to my elbow. Lightly. So lightly. Goosebumps covered my arms and I had to take a deep breath to keep my heart from stuttering. Mary had started to sit back down, inviting the guys to join us. Nick was standing just off the blanket, watching JJ behind me. He nodded slightly to JJ, telling him something without using any words.

I started to look back, but before I could, he leaned in close and whispered in my ear, just like he had at the bar, "Game over."

CHAPTER TEN

Cam

SINCE KACE LIVED close to Centennial, we often found ourselves jogging the path that lined the entire park. Not very many people were out on a weekday before noon, so it was a great place to go without being noticed.

I had finally finished up media week, which was a relief. And after Kace told me he didn't think the reporter—with the picture of me and Ali—had made his way to 678 yet, I was even more relieved. He told me he slid his number into her back pocket just in case, but he didn't tell her about the picture, and that bought us more time. We both wanted more time to get to know her without the acclaim of our fame.

Of course, that morning, as we jogged in Centennial, that plan went to hell.

We had been lost in conversation about Kace's batting stance when the first grape fell at my feet and I looked up.

Apparently, in my head, grapes fell from the sky.

Then the next grape hit Kace in the leg. "What the hell?" he barked. He didn't look up, though. Apparently, he had the good sense that morning to remember grapes didn't fly.

We both stopped and looked around, only to have another

grape hit our backs. We turned quickly, toward the direction of the grape, and saw Mary—a sight for sore fucking eyes.

We had been worried about her, but Ali had kept whatever was going on with her mum.

She was wearing black leggings and a t-shirt. She looked tired and definitely looked sick, but she also looked damn happy to see us.

We started walking toward her, ready to drill her with a million questions. But as we approached, the person sitting on the blanket behind her stood up and stepped to the side.

Ali.

Holy fuck, it was Ali.

Kace registered her presence as well, because we stopped mid-stride, at the exact same time. There was nothing I wanted more than to see her outside of 678, where we could talk and get to know one another, but I also knew, in that instant, the jig was up.

I prayed she wasn't mad.

Or worse—a fangirl.

Most of my fear was surrounded by her reaction. Ali was gorgeous, kind, and complex. Kace and I both talked about getting to know her, seeing if she was maybe into one of us, seeing where it went, and so on. But I knew, without a doubt, that if she freaked out over our status because of who we were, I would be out. The dream would be smashed. Maybe not for Kace, because he fed off fangirl behavior, but I just couldn't subject myself to it anymore.

As I stood there, realizing Ali was about to know who we were, I feared that it would be the last time I looked at her that way. With reverence and awe.

Damn, she was so beautiful. She wasn't wearing any make-up, her hair was thrown up into a bun on her head, and she was wearing tight workout shorts and a tank top. She looked worried, and maybe a little confused.

Mary was quickly cutting the distance between us with her arms up, waiting on hugs. We refocused on her and scooped her into our arms, peppering her with questions about her health.

I was dumbfounded when she said the word cancer. Somewhere deep down, I knew that was a possibility, but hearing it confirmed was gut-wrenching. She spoke so fast, filling us in without letting us get any more questions in, but also answering any questions we may have had.

Ali was silently standing in place on the blanket that she and Mary had been picnicking on. I glanced her way just as Mary decided she needed to introduce us all.

"Oh, how rude of me, guys this is Ali, my neighbor, and my friend. Ali, this is…."

"We've met," I said quickly, not quite ready to see Ali's face when she heard our real names. "She's been at 678, Mary. We've been asking her how you've been, but she wouldn't tell us shit." I smiled at Ali, so she knew I was playing with her.

Kace had made his way to the other side of Ali, his eyes locked on mine, telling me what I already knew—she was about to find out who we were. Right after Mary finished her rant about how Ali should have told us everything. Ironic, right?

I nodded to him, letting him know I understood, and to do what he needed to do. Then he leaned in close to whisper something in her ear.

"Sit, sit, sit," Mary instructed. "Ali packed us a breakfast big enough to feed two whole football teams."

Ali had moved forward, away from Kace, and was taking her seat next to the picnic basket. We all joined her, each claiming a corner of the floral printed blanket.

"Yes," she said. "I have a ton of food here. I didn't really know what Mary would want. You guys should join us."

Whatever Kace had said to her rattled her a bit, but I knew the secret wasn't out yet. Mary had started chatting about the weather, but I barely heard a word she said as worry took root in my stomach.

Time to pull the band aid off.

"Hey Mary, I think there's something we need to tell Ali." Mary immediately took interest in what I was saying, and Ali was staring at me as if I were a two-headed monster. "It's not that bad," I added, hoping it eased her concern.

She looked to Kace, still staying relatively silent as he spoke. "Well, so—"

"Oh God Kace," Mary cut him off. "Did you fuck her? Kace, I swear to God I will kill you. She's not one of those sluts that you can fuck around with." She started swatting at his shoulder as he tried to get her to stop talking.

"No, no, no, no, Mary. No." He looked at me for help. Instead, Ali spoke up.

"Mary, he didn't….do that…. with me. Oh God, this is embarrassing. Guys, I think Mary is confused about who you guys are." Ali was rubbing her forehead, clearly concerned with Mary's outburst.

"Confused?" Mary registered. "I'm not confused. These two boys are the biggest pain in my asses there ever was. Well, not you Cam, but Kace makes me work too hard, and is probably the reason I have cancer."

"MARY!" We all three said at the same time.

"Oh hush, I'm just fucking around. But I'm not confused." She pointed at us in her motherly manner. "Spill it."

Here goes.

"Ali, my real name is Cam. Cam Nichols." And then I pointed to Kace. "He is Kace Jackson." I left it at that, waiting for the truth to register in her features, but it never came.

Kace piped up, hoping to add in something to ease the news. "But we do go by JJ and Nick… sometimes. Well, just to each other. People don't always recognize us by face, but always by name, and we just wanted to get to know you before we came clean."

She didn't look mad, so that was good. She didn't look *anything*, so that may not be good.

What was she thinking?

"Are you meaning to tell me that you two lied to her about your identity like you were damn superheroes, and now that I'm here, you little fuckers are busted?" Mary scoffed and rolled her eyes.

"Basically," I mumbled.

"But she did say I was kinda like a superhero, so, this is actually how the story is supposed to go," Kace reasoned.

Mary started laughing, a full belly laugh with tears rolling down her eyes.

Ali had yet to speak at all.

"Look, Ali. JJ and Nick are monikers we use when we just want to be regular guys. We didn't mean to deceive you."

"Okay. What the hell is going on?" Ali finally asked. "I feel like I stepped into some twilight zone. Apparently, everyone here knows something I don't. You two have seriously large heads. My real name is Allison, no big deal." She shook her head in annoyance.

Mary had stopped laughing, and was now paying attention. "I still don't think she knows who you are, you maniacs."

"I don't," Ali smiled uneasily. "I'm going to be honest here— this is the strangest conversation I've ever had. The dramatics are too high considering we barely know each other. And you owe me nothing, guys. I'm incredibly embarrassed. That's it."

I didn't think she knew who Cam Nichols and Kace Jackson were so we were the ones that should be embarrassed. We spent weeks trying to be JJ and Nick, only to realize it didn't even matter.

"Cam and Kace," Kace said. "Those are our names, and we

should have told you that from the get-go. All this awkwardness could have been avoided."

"Why does it even matter?" she asked.

Mary took pity on us and answered. "Honey, I know you don't follow sports, but these two play for the Kings and Jets. I think when they realized you didn't recognize them, they wanted to keep it that way."

Kace and I were nodding our agreement with Mary.

"Okaaaay. Well, thanks for clearing that up. You two out for a run? Come to the park often?"

She was changing the subject. Maybe even pretending as if the last fifteen minutes never happened. I was a man, so I was definitely okay with that route.

"Yeah." I pointed across the park to the 60-story high rise. "Kace owns the top floor of that building, so Centennial is an easy jog when we get the chance to hang this way."

She followed my finger to the building and nodded, unimpressed.

"What about you? Come down this way a lot?" Kace asked.

"Actually, Mary and I live in that building right there." She pointed to the six-story, historically aged building.

I knew the building well, being I was from Atlanta. It was an old brothel hotel from way back when. Over the years it had been turned into a lot of different things, but ultimately landed on small apartments with the ground level being used for commercial space. Currently, there was a sandwich shop—that Kace and I frequented often for their double meat pastrami deluxe—in that space.

"Only a few blocks from 678," Kace mused, thinking back to when Ali told us she walked to work and back.

"Yeah, I moved back to the city two years ago and reconnected with Mary, who was friends with my mom once-upon-a-time—"

"Two of the sexiest men you ever met!" Mary shouted, interrupting Ali.

We all jumped and looked at Mary, staring at her silently.

"That is what you said." She pointed to Ali. "I just figured it out! You goons told her your names were Nick and JJ. And Ali did ask me if she could give you an update on me, but I told her hell fucking no because I didn't know a Nick and JJ. But she was talking about you little fuckers all that time and when I asked her about this Nick and JJ, she said you were the two sexiest men she'd ever met. Holy shit, Ali!"

Ali was as red as the grapes Mary had thrown at us. Her eyes were wide, and she was silently begging Mary to shut up. Poor Ali was embarrassed, again, but I don't think my smile could have gotten any wider. Kace didn't appear to be too sad, either.

"Aw shit! I don't think I was supposed to say that out loud," Mary shrugged. "Okay, well, I'm tired. Ali, honey, I'm going to go lay down. Kace, Cam… you two make sure you eat the rest of that food and walk Ali home for me."

Before Ali could protest, Mary popped up and walked across the street, entering a door next to the sandwich shop that I assume led to the apartments. She did that on purpose.

The instant Mary had left, though, something changed. The air. The electricity. The tension. Mary had been a barrier that I didn't realize was there until it wasn't. In a way, things were more relaxed. We were more relaxed.

But we were also more charged.

Ali bit her lip and sheepishly smiled. "I'm so sorry about her. She's wild sometimes."

"And honest?" Kace asked, fishing for some truth to what Mary had just blurted out.

"Yeah." Ali's smile changed to a cheeky one. "But she didn't say anything you two obviously don't already know, what with those big egos, and large ass heads y'all carry around."

Kace and I laughed out loud at her wit, loving when she teased back.

I scooted closer to her and brushed some hair out of her face, tucking it behind her ear. "Well, your ego may not be as large as ours, but you're pretty damn sexy yourself."

She flushed again, pink creeping up her neck. Her shade of rosy skin was my new favorite color. We fell into an easy conversation after that, telling her about how we grew up, practically brothers. She told us about being an only child and losing her mom when she was sixteen. She filled us in on her connection to Mary, and we told her stories about how we came to rely on Mary's help at 678.

We all laughed at impressions that Kace and I did of each other. Ali added one in of Mary ordering her first Uber eats delivery: *"What the fuck are you charging me a delivery fee for? It wasn't even a block away."* We spent an hour and a half talking—and finishing Ali's picnic—but not once did she ask us about baseball or football.

Not until Kace brought it up. "Shit, I need to get going. I have a game tonight and I'm supposed to be at the stadium in two hours." Kace ran a hand through his hair, upset he had to leave.

"A game? So, you play baseball? Because I don't know much about sports, but I do know football season hasn't started."

"Yeah, the Kings."

"So, you play football? The Jets?" She turned to me next.

"Yeah, we both came up the same year and have played for the last five years."

"Sorry, Mary said Kings and Jets, and I knew they were the pro teams here in Atlanta, but she didn't specify who played for which."

Kace popped up in a squat, his forearms resting on his knees, and smiled at Ali. "You have no idea how fun it is to tell someone who I am, from my very own mouth."

No truer words. It felt good. Which gave me an idea.

"Have you ever been to a King's game?" I asked Ali.

"No. And before you ask, no I don't hate sports. I just honestly have never had the chance, so don't hate on me."

"How about you come to Kace's game with me tonight?" I suggested.

They both turned their heads my way. I had already planned on going to the game, I was going to sit in his private box with his family, but like we always did, Kace read my mind. "I could get you tickets next to the field."

"I don't know, I mean, maybe." She bit her lip as her eyes looked from me to Kace, conflicted over what to do.

I wanted it to be an easy yes for her, so I added, "Kace is swinging at the air right now, trust me, you don't want to miss the fun we could have watching him strike out five times at the plate."

"That does sound like fun," she laughed, as Kace groaned. "Okay. Count me in."

"As glad as I am that you're coming tonight, I'm slightly put off that my current slump was the draw for you," Kace deadpanned.

We all laughed again as we picked up her bag and blanket, then started to walk with her to her apartment, keeping our promise to Mary that we would walk her home.

"I can swing by and pick you up around five," I suggested as we made our way onto the sidewalk across from the park.

"Actually, I'll meet you there if that's okay. The underground train goes straight there, right?"

It did, but I was hoping to pick her up. "Yeah. A block from the stadium. I'll meet you right out front at 5:30." I wasn't going to push her and I honestly understood her wanting to just meet there.

As we approached the door to her building, Ali stopped walking and turned to us. "Thank you both, for walking me home… even though it was literally across the street. And despite my incredible confusion when you two first showed up, I'm so really you did. This was fun."

"Yeah, we suck," Kace joked. Then he reached toward her and laid his hand on her cheek. A string of panic coursed through me every time one of us touched her. It was a trigger that we didn't quite understand yet, so I was worried we would scare her away.

Thankfully, she didn't seem fazed by Kace's touch. "Maybe you will be my lucky charm tonight."

My favorite color reappeared on her cheeks and I didn't even care that I wasn't the one that put it there, just glad I got to be there to see it. Ali leaned into his hand ever so slightly. "Just don't think I won't be the first one to *boo* if you swing and miss."

Kace lowered his hand, the smile on his face so big it looked like it hurt. "I may do it on purpose, just to hear your voice."

I took my turn and grabbed her hand, intertwining our fingers and squeezing. "See you tonight."

When we started walking off, Kace spoke without even looking at me. "What are we doing, Cam?"

"No clue."

But that was a lie. I knew exactly what we were doing.

We were going after the same girl. And the craziest part was, I wasn't mad about it.

ali

I CANNOT BELIEVE how quickly I agreed to hang out with Nick. Cam. *Ugh.*

It's not like I was mad about their little name game, but I was embarrassed, and a little worried I would call them the wrong thing. Learning they were athletes made sense, though. Their bodies screamed *athlete* and Atlanta was a huge sports city. Everywhere you went, sports were the focus of the crowd, and working in the sports bar on campus should have helped me know who Cam and Kace were—but it didn't. I just never made the time, or effort, to concentrate on football and baseball.

My college days were spent grinding at work and hitting the books. Since leaving college, my focus had been on my writing career, and just plain survival.

After getting home from our impromptu picnic, I started to Google Cam and Kace, but before it could load, I shut my laptop closed. Kace's words, about getting to know me without me already knowing everything about them meant something to him —them. It made me want to get to know them organically, the way they wanted.

When Cam asked me to go with him to see Kace, it felt kind of weird. Not that we were going on a date, but going with one guy to see the other play seemed like trouble. Kace's eyes were excited, though, and I could tell he wanted me there with Cam.

After spending my afternoon catching up on my day job, I showered, got ready for the game, and headed down to the underground train. It was five in the evening and crowded. I imagined most people were headed home from work, but I noticed quite a few people wearing their Kings gear, most likely headed to the game, as well.

The train took twenty minutes to get to the closest station to the stadium and I exited in a mass of hurried people. I wasn't sure which direction to walk so I decided to go with everyone who wore Kings shirts.

As I elbowed and bumped my way out of the middle of the group, I was grabbed by my left elbow and pulled backward. Fear immediately took over and I raised my right hand as I turned around, attempting to swing at whoever felt it was okay to touch me.

But before my hand made contact, I recognized the face.

"Nick!" I screamed. I was both scared and relieved it was him.

"Wait, wait… come this way." He pulled me out of the group of people and off to the sidewalk where a bench and a few trees were. Once we were away from the crowd, he let go and I placed a hand over my heart to calm my nerves.

"Fuck, I'm so sorry. I didn't…I forgot…shit, just wanted to grab you before you made it too far," he explained, taking his hat off and running a hand through his hair.

"You scared the shit out of me. And geez, *I'm* sorry."

"For what? That punch didn't land."

"Calling you Nick. *Cam* is going to take me a minute to get used to."

He smirked and put his Kings hat back on. "Actually, that was the perfect time to use Nick. Had you yelled 'Cam' we may not have made it out of there as quickly as we did."

"What the hell are you doing here? I thought we were meeting at the stadium?"

"We were, but I got here a little early and thought I would meet you here so we could walk together. I just didn't expect you to be in the middle of four zillion people." He looked around at all the people that had exited the station and were lingering around. "Let's get out of here."

He took my hand, intertwined our fingers like he did that morning, and walked away from the crowd. "Everyone else went that way. Shouldn't we?"

"The stadium covers quite a few blocks. This way will keep us away from the crowd. Plus, we will be entering the player and family entrance, and it's on the south side of the stadium."

Once my heart rate had returned to normal, and we were strolling at a normal pace, I was able to register how amazing my hand felt in his. Something about touching him and being around him made me burn. He was wearing khaki shorts and a polo shirt with a Kings logo on the left upper chest area. The look was a little preppy and with his hat turned backward and his sunglasses on, I wanted to stare at him all day.

He squeezed my hand when he realized I had been looking for a while, which made his forearms flex and made me groan with obvious weakness.

"You all right over there?"

"Just trying to figure you out," I lied. I didn't need to figure him out, I needed to check him out.

We rounded the corner of a building and I stopped and gasped when the stadium came into view. It was bigger than I imagined. I had seen the stadium from afar as I traveled on the train, but I had never been up next to it. The magnitude of the number of people that could fit into the seats was overwhelming.

There were people everywhere. Vendors selling Kings gear.

Someone passing out flyers. Food stands. There was even a drum line playing music, and people dancing in a commons area. And we hadn't even made it into the actual stadium.

Cam gave me a minute to take it in, and then pulled my arm toward a glass window with an older woman sitting behind the pane.

"Hey, we have two tickets waiting under Kace Jackson," Cam spoke lightly, leaning into the hole in the window to keep his voice from going anywhere but to the woman. She pushed some keys on her computer, asked for an ID, and slid two tickets under the window.

Cam held onto my hand the whole time as the atmosphere took over and I was on cloud nine. How could anyone not love being there? It was like a huge pep rally with eight shots of espresso.

Cam led me to a smaller gate than the one everyone else was entering. The sign above the gate read Players and Family Only. He gave the guard our tickets, they did a quick scan of my bag, then nodded to Cam. "Mr. Nichols, please let us know if there is anything we can do for you to help you have a relaxing time tonight, sir."

"We will be okay, man," Cam assured him, shaking his hand. "Thank you."

"What was that about?" I asked as we walked away.

"Sometimes it's hard to watch a game down at field level without getting asked for an autograph a few hundred times. He was just letting me know I could call them if I needed help."

"Is that how it's going to be tonight?" I was kind of worried.

"Doubt it, I have my disguise on." He said and lifted his sunglasses to waggle his eyes at me.

"A hat and sunglasses?"

"No. A woman," he smirked. "You're my disguise because I have never brought a woman to a game before."

Those words made me feel special, but I shook that feeling

off. The night was about having fun. *Friends*. This wasn't the time, or place, to get in my head about whatever I was feeling toward Cam.

We navigated the people flowing through the corridor, stopping long enough for Cam to grab us two beers and a box of popcorn. Once we went through the opening that led us to our seat section, my breath was taken away. It was amazing. So big, with people everywhere. Lights and sounds were all over the stadium adding to my amazement.

Cam led the way, no longer holding my hand so that he could carry our beers, and walked down the steps toward the field. The Kings—who were easily identifiable thanks to the names across the front of their uniforms—were spread out on the field doing several warm-ups.

I wasn't a complete baseball novice. I knew the basics. So, I recognized what I was seeing, and instantly started shaking with nerves and excitement. A group of players were stretching along the right-field foul line. Another group near the wall of fans were signing autographs. Some were taking batting practice. And a large group in the outfield were playing catch.

Cam filed into the front row behind a netting that protected the fans from foul balls and set our beers down. The first three rows of seats were blocked off and guarded by a security officer. They were also cushioned and more spacious than the rest of the seats behind them.

But I hadn't even made it that far.

I was still ten rows up, completely frozen. My eyes started darting around the field again looking for Kace. I didn't know what number he was or what position he played, but I was still glad I didn't Google his name. The thrill of discovering everything firsthand was overwhelmingly poignant.

My eyes caught Cam, who was standing in front of our seats looking up at me, hands in his pockets, and a smile on his face, enjoying my fascination. He took his hands out of his pocket and held up two fingers on his right hand and an "o" with his left hand. From where I was, facing him, it looked like he was telling me 2-0.

I started to scrunch my forehead and mouth *what?* But then it hit me. Kace was number twenty and Cam was helping me find him. My eyes darted back to the field, and I scoured the jerseys looking for number twenty, until I found him. His back was to me, his legs were crossed, and he was leaning with one arm on a bat like it was a cane. The tattoos that wrapped around his arm were on display from the short sleeves of his uniform. He was watching someone else take batting practice and probably talking, because the other player was nodding as he listened to whatever Kace was saying.

I stared, unmoving, making a few people have to navigate around me to get down to their seats.

After about five minutes, Kace turned around and eyed the seats where Cam was—still standing, but alone. Cam motioned his finger upward, letting Kace know where I was.

When his eyes caught mine, a smile spread across his face and he dropped his bat, walking toward the wall where the netting wasn't blocking the seats—right in front of the aisle I was standing in.

I realized he was coming toward me and instinct took over. I jogged down the steps toward him—adrenaline and excitement fueling my sudden lack of inhibition. He held his arms up, silently suggesting a hug, and I walked right into his hold.

"You made it!"

"I did, this is incredible, Kace."

He leaned back, still holding me tight, but looked into my eyes. "My name on your lips sounds so good. My real name."

"Could have been that way for weeks if you weren't such a liar," I teased.

"Touché, *Allison*."

"Not even the same thing," I laughed, then swatted at his shoulders as he backed up a little more, loosening his hold.

Before he could say anything else, a swarm of fans came down the steps I had just run down, and started to scream. "Kace! Kace! Please! Can we get a pic and an autograph? Kace!"

It was instant madness. I didn't know how many there were, or who was saying what, but I was thankful for the guard—who I had apparently run right past—holding them back.

"Look what you started," Kace joked.

But he probably wasn't too far off base. Once I ran past security, maybe everyone else wanted to try. "Shit, how come he didn't stop me?"

"Cam took care of it," he mentioned. "He knows you're okay down here."

Cam!

I was supposed to be there with Cam, and instead, I was throwing my arms around Kace.

I knew this was trouble.

I looked over to Cam, but he wasn't even watching us. He was in a conversation with an older man, maybe in his 70s, who was dressed in an expensive suit and tie.

"Hey," Kace grabbed my attention. "I gotta get out of here before Hank—the security guard up there—kicks my ass for making his job harder than it has to be. Do me a favor?"

I nodded, acknowledging everything he was saying.

"Stay."

Stay where? I didn't ask out loud, but I was sure my face expressed my confusion.

"The whole game. Just stay. Please."

"Kace, they may have to drag my ass out of here when it's over."

"Good, then I'll see you after the game." He grabbed my hand, running his thumb along the back of it, and bit his lip. "Wish me luck."

Then he left, jogging toward the dugout and disappearing into the side closest to where I was standing. I was physically swooning, and burning in the spot he rubbed his thumb.

Meanwhile, the fans behind me disappeared as quickly as Kace did, uninterested once he was gone. Hank looked relieved.

I slid down the row of seats toward Cam, who was laughing at the old man, but stood and took my hand the second he noticed my approach.

"Mr. Brumer, this is Ali. Ali, this is the owner of the Kings, Mr. Brumer." I shook the old man's hand with my free hand and exchanged pleasantries with him just as Mr. Brumer got a call and had to leave.

The need to apologize to Cam was overwhelming, but he didn't seem upset, or fazed, at all that I spoke to Kace. In fact, he handed me my beer and asked, "Kace seem like he's planning on swinging at the air again, tonight?"

"Ha. I um…have no idea. He had to cut it short for poor Hank up there." I spoke like I knew Hank and like Cam knew Hank, and we were all just a big group of pals.

"There were a lot of girls after Kace," Cam laughed while he watched the field being transformed from a practice area to game ready. "Hank probably enjoyed it."

Only then did I realized just how many of those fans were female, and a little jealousy flared up in my chest. Cam must have sensed it and looked my way, but I schooled my face and tamped it down. I had no right to be jealous over a man I barely knew because of women that he didn't even know. I prided myself on being a rational woman and there was no need to stop.

"Did you know you are the first woman he's ever given tickets to? A lot of firsts for Kace these days." He was still holding my hand, but easing my jealousy over someone else, which made my cheeks burn with embarrassment.

"Same here," I said quietly.

"Yep, same here," he added.

Hoping I could tell him without words, how special I thought he was, I squeezed his hand tighter. Cam had to be one of the best guys I had ever met. There was no way he would classify as one of the guys I would put on my "most guys" list.

Not even close.

kace

ALI REALLY WAS my lucky charm because I played my best game in weeks. Or maybe it was just the endorphins from having her at the game.

It was surreal and intoxicating.

When I took the field, I found her standing and clapping. When I got a hit at my first at-bat, I looked her way to see her on her feet, yelling with excitement. I hit a home run in the sixth inning, and as I crossed the plate, I looked up and saw her jumping and cheering with Cam. I ran close to the netting, and they held up their hands for high fives. I gave them each one, but kissed my fingers before touching them to hers.

At the end of game, I made the last out on a diving play. My teammates swarmed in to congratulate me, but I looked to her. She was hugging Cam, and they were jumping with excitement.

I waited for the jealousy to spark in my gut, but it never came. Not when she was with Cam. In fact, I was relieved. There was no doubting that I felt something strong for Ali, but knowing Cam was with her when I couldn't be, made it easier to breathe.

After I showered and changed, I ran to the waiting area where I was sure Cam would be, hoping Ali would stay with him. But when I rounded the corner and entered the room, I was finally bitten with the jealousy I had been waiting for.

Cam was nowhere to be found, but I did see Chase, standing entirely too close to Ali, with a look on his face that told me he was trying to hit a home run "off the field."

Over my dead fucking body.

I started to march toward them—navigating the crowd, ready to kill Chase—when Cam popped out of the bathrooms in the back of the room, and instantly inserted himself between Chase and Ali. He put his arm around her waist, silently letting Chase know to back off.

And I was... relieved.

Chase put his hands in the air, surrendering and Ali looked more at ease. I realized I needed to take a deep breath before I did something I regretted, and waited for Chase to just leave, entirely.

When I finally made my way to them, they noticed my approach and Cam dropped his hold on Ali. She jumped into another hug, much like she did before the game, and I held tightly to her tiny frame.

"You didn't swing at air!" she squealed, making me shake in laughter. Cam was also laughing over her shoulder.

"Dare I say you were my lucky charm?"

"Dare I say you finally listened to me, and stopped pulling that front foot up before you swung?" Cam added.

"Yeah yeah…" I trailed off, loosening my hold on Ali and joining them in our circle of three.

"This was the most fun I have ever had." Ali was clapping her hands together, unable to hide her excitement.

"She is a pro, Kace. Best ballgame sidekick ever." He looked at her, his eyes warm with adoration.

"Oh, and look what Cam got me!" She turned around and I finally noticed she was wearing a jersey.

My Jersey.

Jackson. 20.

"That is the sexiest thing I have ever seen." I looked at Cam, thankful once again for our friendship. I wanted him to know that high. I wanted him to play, knowing she was watching.

"So today was your first baseball game. How about Sunday being your first football game?"

Ali's eyes got big, and she looked from me to Cam a few times before settling on Cam. "You play Sunday?"

"I do. First preseason game."

"And I was going to go. So how about we both go?"

"I would love that!" Then her face fell, "But I have to work Sunday."

"Ali, you say the word, and I can make sure you don't work Sunday." I could call 678, request a flamingo, and they would come through for me. She may have needed the tips, she may have needed the work, and I respected that. But it was worth a shot.

"Actually," she said, "I'll call in. They can deal for one night without me."

"And you will be okay missing the day?" I didn't want to suggest she needed the money, but I wanted to give her the chance to reconsider just in case.

"Yes! They will be fine! This will be amazing!"

Cam was smiling and clapped his hands together, rubbing them with a buzz. "Seats down by the field, or in the box?"

I looked to Ali, letting her make the decision. "Oh, we need to be near the field. My first football experience needs to be legit."

Nodding to Cam, I agreed, and he pulled his phone out to text whoever he usually did when he put names down for ticket requests.

The room was starting to thin out, most of the team and their families leaving already.

"Let us take you home, sweetheart," Cam suggested when he slid his phone back in his pocket.

"That actually sounds better than being on the train this late."

Cam pulled his keys from his pocket, and we started to walk toward the parking garage. Ali was between us and we both made a move to guide her with our hands on her back, which resulted in us laying our hands over each other.

We withdrew our hands and Cam looked past Ali to me and laughed. "Get your own body part, fucker."

I flipped him off and chose to take her hand instead. She didn't resist, nor did she resist Cam's hand going back to the small of her back. She did, however, giggle. "Y'all are ridiculous."

We walked, just like that, all the way to Cam's truck. It felt good and natural to have my best friend and my girl with me.

Wait, my girl?

Apparently at some point I decided that her being mine was the end game. I guess the truth was, she was ours. I wasn't willing to stop this thing, whatever it was, and I wasn't willing to come in between whatever Cam was feeling either.

The way I saw it, Ali would eventually understand that we both liked her, a lot. She would have a choice: me or Cam. I would have to make peace with however she decided to handle us both wanting her. In the meantime, I was going to enjoy getting time with both of them, together.

Cam had a lot of cars, but he had chosen his truck. His really, big ass truck. Which suited me just fine, except it was impossible to find a parking spot in downtown to accommodate its size.

After circling Ali's building twice, looking for a parking spot, she finally sighed, "Guys, I can walk, ya know? You don't have to park and walk me, just drop me off." She had insisted on the backseat but had scooted up in between the middle console of the front to chat with us on the ride to her apartment.

Cam and I both shot her a *hell no* look. Not a chance we were letting the night end by kicking her out of the truck at the sidewalk and wishing her well.

On the fourth pass, we spotted a parking spot next to the area of the park where we had picnicked, and Cam pulled in before it disappeared. Then we all three sat quietly in the truck, no one making a move to get out.

I didn't want her to go. Cam didn't want her to go.

Thankfully, before it got awkward, Ali moved and slid toward the door on Cam's side. Cam jumped from the truck first, and helped her down the sidestep, holding her hand naturally. Something I knew they did all night during the game.

Again, the jealousy never came.

Instead, I shocked everyone, me included, and took her other hand as the three of us walked from the park to her door, hand in hand.

"I don't think you have any idea how amazing this day was." She was looking down at her feet as we approached her building. I lifted the hand I was holding and kissed her knuckles.

"I bet I do." I lifted the hand I was holding and kissed her knuckles softy.

She looked to me smiling, then looked to Cam. "Thanks for this fancy shirt."

"Number 20 looks good on you."

She didn't get why he said that... yet.

But I did.

She dropped our hands and started rummaging through her bag, looking for her keys. She pulled them out just as Cam was handing her his phone. "Can you put your number in here? We should have done that already."

She took it and added her number to Cam's phone and handed it back to him. I wondered if she ever found my number that I had slipped into her back pocket the other night at 678, but I didn't ask, I didn't have to. Thirty seconds after she gave Cam his phone back, mine and Ali's phones pinged with a text. I checked it and realized he added us to a group message, so we all had each other's numbers.

"See you Sunday?" she asked me.

"Yes, ma'am. I'm going to pick you up, though," I said to her, pointedly. "The game is a lot later than tonight's, and I would feel much better scooping you up myself."

"I would feel better too, it gets wild down over there at night. Kace can park under the stadium and keep y'all safe," Cam added.

She looked torn at first again, but easily agreed. "Okay."

After unlocking the building door, she put a hand on our chests. She looked from each of us, and then leaned into me, kissing my cheek. Then she leaned into Cam and did the same to him. "Goodnight."

Cam and I backed away, and waited until she was in the building, to turn and leave. We walked back to his truck in silence, but when we got into the cab of the truck, Cam sighed loudly and hit his head against the headrest. "We're doing this, aren't we?"

"Looks like it."

"You're not fucking around here, are you, Kace? Your normal MO is to talk to a woman long enough to dip your dick into her and move on."

Ouch. But he wasn't wrong. Except for that time.

"Cam, I would do anything for you. And if I could back away from Ali, I would. I know how you feel about her, I feel the same damn way. But if I didn't, I wouldn't do this to you. I would relent, Cam. You know I would."

He sighed again and rested his forehead on his steering wheel. He was silent, mulling over what I said. He knew I was being honest, he just didn't know how he felt about it. "I think this is the part where I'm supposed to be mad and jealous," he started.

"But I'm not. I just keep thinking how you finally have a woman you want to pursue past pussy, and she's the same damn woman I can't seem to stop thinking about."

"Fucking ironic, right?"

He smiled and rolled his head over to face me. "I just need to know we are good? That we will always be good."

"Better than good," I assured him.

Knock, knock.

CAM

Who's there?

ALI

Who's there?

Friday.

ALI

Friday who?

CAM

Friday who?

Friday is one day closer to Sunday.

CAM

I cannot believe you're my best friend.

ALI

I rolled my eyes, but would be lying if I didn't admit I was excited.

I smiled, looking at her response in our group message. It was Friday morning, and I was determined to lay in my bed until the very last second before I had to be at the stadium for the game. Cam had dropped me off and decided to go home instead of crashing at my place—something he often did when we were in the city late.

Cam had a house in an actual neighborhood, twenty minutes outside of the city, with bushes and driveways and neighbors that walked their dogs. It was a house fit for a family of five, but he lived there alone. Cam was always meant for family life. He had a back porch with a grill and a grassy yard. The house had been decorated to feel home-y. My penthouse was a little more bachelor-pad.

My phone dinged again with another message.

CAM

I have practice today, I won't be at the game.

I know, fucker. I'll see you Sunday.

ALI

Another game? Don't you get a day off or something?

Once a week. Usually Mondays. Sometimes Thursdays. One or two Tuesdays. It just depends.

ALI

Geez, I didn't even play last night, and I'm exhausted today. The adrenaline made me crash hard.

The fact that watching a baseball game gave her such an adrenaline rush made me smile. Baseball was a slower sport, and didn't get the credit football got as far as intensity. But it was no less exciting.

CAM

What are your plans, sweetheart?

ALI

Me?

He has never called me sweetheart.

ALI

Never know with you two. ;-)

CAM

True. ;-)

ALI

I'm working, then I am going to work.

Sounds… complicated. lol

CAM

Double shift?

ALI

Ha… no. 678 is not my real job. I'm just helping
Mary, remember?

So, you have another job?

ALI

Yes, I'm a freelance writer for a publishing
company.

CAM

WHAT?

How did we not know that?

ALI

It hasn't come up.

CAM

I don't think I thought to ask because I assumed
you just worked at 678.

ALI

I haven't thought to mention it, either. But yes, writing is my actual job. lol

Why is that so fucking sexy?

CAM

I have a librarian image in my head, maybe some glasses, and a pencil between your lips. Yep, I'm with Kace. Sexy.

ALI

Okay, once again, you two are ridiculous. And I have terrible, terrible news for you.

Uh oh.

ALI

I work from home, so no librarian look. It is more of a drunk, stay-at-home-mom of two boys, forgot to shower, and may have the flu look. Everyday. It isn't a very glamorous job.

CAM

FUCK, that's even better.

I groaned. That woman could be in a potato sack and would still be the sexiest woman I had ever seen. There was also something sexy about knowing she was a writer. It added a level to her I didn't know yet—depth I wanted to dig into more.

Pic, or I don't believe you.

ALI

LOL. You first.

CAM

image sent

Cam sent a selfie of himself sitting in front of his locker, his nameplate shining in the background. He was wearing shoulder pads but no shirt. He had yet to be on the field, so he wasn't sweaty, but it looked like he was about to get his jersey pulled on over his pads for a morning practice session. That shit took a team of professionals to get on—shit was tight.

I held my camera up, put one arm behind my head to prop up a bit, and took a shot of myself lying in bed, relaxing.

image sent

ALI

Gah. Okay. Okay.

I laughed out loud, loving when she played along with us. Instead of being annoyed or confused... she was... my phone dinged before I could finish that thought.

ALI

image sent

Another groan fell from my mouth. Ali sent a picture of herself, in her pajamas—a t-shirt that said: "I'm Great in Bed, I Can Sleep for Days." No make-up and her hair was up but falling around her face in tendrils. Her chin was resting on the back of one hand and her elbow rested on the desk next to a laptop and a coffee cup. It looked like it was straight out of a magazine.

The best part of the picture, though, was the pencil she had put between her lips.

I shut the phone off and tossed it on my bedside table, then threw the covers back and climbed out of bed. I didn't feel like resting anymore. I needed a cold-ass shower.

ali

ONE SECOND I was trying my hardest to stay away from, well…everyone. And the next I was deep into, whatever it was, with two sexy athletes who sent tingles down my spine just by being in their eyeline.

Thursday had been amazing, and surprisingly it wasn't awkward—at all. Kace and Cam—I was getting used to their actual names—didn't "fight for my attention" the way they both said they would. Instead, they were just happy, always smiling, joking, and being good to me, and one another.

The picnic and the game started a friendship among us that I hadn't seen coming. And thanks to our very active group text, we learned a lot more about each other as the days passed.

Both their moms were teachers. Cam had three older sisters and Kace was an only child. I told them more about losing my mom, about my dad that lived two hours away, and a little more about my writing.

"Pics, or it didn't happen" became our new game. But each time the guys sent a pic my stomach coiled, and my heart raced with excitement. I had to pinch myself that those two were both so invested in whatever it was we had, even though I knew it could never be more than what it was.

Sunday finally came and Kace had sent a new pic sitting in front of his locker, much like Cam's in his first picture. He was wearing his jersey, had eye black under his eyes, his hat was on backward, and the scruff on his face made me want to rub my cheek on it. His lips were full, and a bright shine was in his crystal blue eyes.

KACE

See you tonight, gorgeous girl. First, I have to kick New York's ass on the ole' ballfield.

Cam's pic came in after that. He was high on a balcony with the city of Atlanta in the background. He had told me that the team stayed at a hotel close to the stadium the night before games, so I imagined that was where he was. He had no shirt on, and I could see his bare chest from his pecs and up. It was the first time I'd seen his bare chest, and, just like Kace's picture showed me on Friday, he was perfection. He had the body of an athlete, no doubt about it. Not overly huge, but hard in all the right places. I still didn't see any tattoos, but he had mentioned he did have some. I was going to die one day wondering where, and of what. His hair was a mess in the picture—very un-Cam-like—and he held a cup of coffee in his hand.

CAM

Gameday mode. See you both tonight. ;)

I flopped back in my bed, my clit throbbing and wanting me to touch myself to their pics. I was too flustered to be creative with my picture, so I held the camera over my face as I laid on top of my made bed and snapped a quick pic.

Playing hooky today. If anyone asks, I am so sick. *cough cough* ;-) See you later.

I went downstairs around six-thirty to wait on Kace. He had texted me after his game telling me he would be a little late, but not much. I figured I would be waiting for about thirty minutes but at six-thirty-five, as I looked into the window of the sandwich shop and read the menu I already knew by heart, I felt arms gently wrap around my midsection. Kace slowly squeezed my waist while nuzzling his nose into my neck. His breath tickled and I squealed, but not from fear—from giddiness.

I knew it was him because of how soft his touch was, and how the air around me had started to sizzle as he neared me. It didn't even dawn on me to be jumpy, or freak out, but he noticed.

"You didn't jump ten feet away," he whispered.

"I knew it was you."

"Yeah? How so?"

"I just knew." I turned around to face him, a smile spread wide on my face as I leaned in to hug him.

"Ready?" He took my hand and guided me around the corner to a silver Audi A5 parked along the road.

"Wow, yours is smaller than Cam's," I joked.

"Careful, Ali, I may have to prove you wrong," he winked.

I blushed, feeling like I lost that game.

He opened the passenger door for me and I slid into the soft leather seat then waited for him to round the front of the car to join me. When he slipped into his seat, both of our phones chimed with a text. *Cam.*

CAM

Tix at will-call. See ya later. Have fun, Ali!

I looked over to see Kace texting back.

I loved being in their circle. They were amazing friends and I knew I would always subconsciously measure my future friendships with the "Kace and Cam-o-meter."

Question 1: Do you cheer me on in all my endeavors?

Not that I was great at having friends. I had been friendless for so long that I started being more comfortable being alone.

But I was becoming comfortable being with Kace and Cam. Talking to them. Joking with them. Laughing with them. I wasn't sure how I was ever going to be okay with not being around them, but I knew that would happen. The attraction and tension we all had would explode, and since I was the odd player in our little game, I would be the one left friendless again.

And I was okay with that. After all, I had only recently gotten to know them. I had no business being too attached, and I needed to steel myself for when that day came.

Which would probably be soon if they didn't stop being so damn irresistible.

Just enjoy it, Ali.

The ride had been relatively quiet, but as we approached the stadium, my jaw dropped. Like the baseball stadium, I had passed the football stadium on the train, but I had never been that close. I was in shock and pure amazement at its massive size. Unlike the baseball stadium, it was a dome. I remembered reading in the newspaper as they built it a few years ago that the roof was an architectural phenomenon, and up to one-hundred thousand people could fit in the seats.

Kace took a turn out of the traffic and into a driveway that led under the stadium. There, we checked in with security before finding a parking spot next to several expensive vehicles.

We walked hand in hand to the small will-call booth that had a sign over the top of it: Player Tickets. Kace requested Cam's tickets, and we made our way past another security guard, and into the corridor of the stadium. There were so many people. More than at the baseball game. They were all extremely spirited —like being at a really big party.

Kace led me through a large hallway, a light shining from the end and as we neared the light, the entire stadium came into view.

Once again, I was stunned into silence, and froze. The magnitude of the atmosphere was unmatched. I had been to concerts and political debates that held less weight than the preseason football game Cam was about to play.

Not even Kace's baseball game was this hyped.

Every seat was filled, fans were yelling at the top of their lungs, and the lights around the stadium were spinning. I felt dizzy as I took in the scene.

"Give me two minutes. Stay here," Kace said.

I nodded, not sure where else I would go, and not wanting to be anywhere else but there anyway.

Staying true to his word, Kace was back in less time than it took me to read the scrolling words around the second level of the stands. He held a bag but quickly ditched it into a trash can after pulling out a red jersey and holding it up for me to read.

Nichols. 20.

It was Cam's jersey, and I just about melted from Kace's excitement as he told me to put it on.

"Cam is going to love this."

"Thank you!" I said as I pulled it over my t-shirt.

"Yep, number 20 looks good on you," Kace winked. "Ready?"

Kace had his head lowered and was walking down the steps toward the seats closest to the field. If he was hoping no one would recognize him, it worked. Though I imagine his only saving grace was that no one expected him to be there, so they were not looking.

He was no longer holding my hand, but still leading the way

for me to follow. I was praying I wouldn't miss a step and fall so I held onto the handrail and kept my eyes on my feet. But every time I looked down, the crowd yelled, and I looked up. What were they yelling for? The game hadn't started, the teams were not even on the field.

We finally made it to the first row and slid in, past a few people, and into two plush seats. They reminded me of the seats at the baseball game—seats you only got if you knew someone, or had a billion dollars. Despite being in the front row, we were so high up and away from the field. The drop from our seats to the field below was probably ten feet.

The crowd directly around us was not as enthusiastic. Most everyone looked to be calm, and in conversations with one another, not paying any mind to the field.

Kace and I sat down and he started filling me in on the activity in the stadium. "Cam and the Jets will come out of that tunnel." He pointed to our left where an inflated tunnel had been erected. "The other team comes out over there." Again, he pointed to a tunnel, but on the right side of the field. "The cheerleaders stand here, in the middle, get the crowd pumped up and excited for the game."

"Doesn't look necessary," I murmured as I looked around again at the already "pumped up" crowd.

"This is an area reserved for family and friends. We have our own servers, our own bathrooms, and our own food menus. Keep your ticket in your pocket because if you need anything, they will check and scan your ticket every time."

I slid the ticket into my back pocket, taking note of everything. Once he finished filling me in, I leaned back in my seat and looked around. I felt like I could look and look for days, and still find something new to look at.

Signs were everywhere and a video board above our heads played videos of the players talking about getting ready for the season. After a minute, Cam came onto the screen. "Tradition. Domination. Winning. A new season starts today."

I'm sure his words were part of a bigger video, but I heard nothing else but him.

"Remember when I came to 678 and Cam called from work and chatted you up just to annoy me?" Kace leaned in and whispered.

I laughed at the memory, and at how matter of fact Kace was about Cam annoying him. "Since that was only a week ago, I remember it well."

"That was one of the things Cam was working on. He had to do his portion of the stadium vids. Shit is boring, and poor Cam was stuck here for days."

I loved that insight. I remember thinking that night that I wanted to ask what Cam did for a living, what Kace did, but we got sidetracked and I never found out. *I wonder if they would have told me the truth?*

I swallowed down the thought as another one popped into my head. "I told him my favorite number was 20."

"Yeah, you did, we thought for sure you were saying that on purpose."

"No, I just remember being little and my parents saying, 'you can do that when you're twenty,' so it stuck, I guess."

"Cam and I have the same agent so when we both came to the pros, we told him to negotiate our jersey numbers. We didn't care what the numbers were, just as long as they were the same number." Kace looked sheepish, "Pretty lame thing to negotiate but we thought it would be cool."

"I think it's—"

The announcer interrupted my response to let everyone know the Jets were making their way to the field. A video played showing the team walking in a group, down a corridor, toward the tunnel.

They all wore their helmets and looked ready for war. As the shot panned out, number twenty came into view. Cam was leading the group of players to the field. Through his helmet, I could see his eyes and he looked focused. His hands were fisted at his sides, his arms barely swinging as he walked.

My hand went to my chest, my heart attempting to beat out of my skin at every pulse point on my body. I had to look away just to stop tears from falling down my cheeks.

Why was I emotional?

I was embarrassed by my irrational reaction, so I kept my head lowered, hiding my pooled eyes. Kace squeezed my hand and rubbed my fingers with his thumb. If he knew how I was feeling, he didn't let on. He just stood next to me, cheering as the announcer introduced the team onto the field.

I peeked up and saw them running out of the tunnel, fire blazing, and smoke filling the tunnel. It was exhilarating. Even more so as I spotted Cam jogging to the sidelines while he looked up at the crowd. His eyes scanned for a minute before stopping on Kace and me. He took his helmet off and smiled at us, winked at me, and then threw his helmet back on and headed to his coach.

Kace and I cheered Cam on, held hands, and high-fived. Every time Cam got hit by the other team I gasped, only to have Kace assure me he was fine.

"Funny how you, and all these tattoos and weird t-shirts, play the quieter sport. And Cam and his perfect hair and collared shirts plays the wild sport."

"Hey, baseball is downright dangerous," he laughed.

"Not once did I see a 300-pound man shove you into the ground."

"Fair enough."

After the game ended, I was relieved. In fact, I wasn't sure I could watch Cam get pummeled too many more times. On top of that, the Jets had lost and I assumed Cam would be in a sour mood after such a rough night.

I was wrong.

By the time we made our way to the family and friends waiting area outside the locker room, Cam was already there, freshly showered, and a huge smile on his face. He was talking to a group of women and laughing at something they had said. I eyed the sight long enough that Kace leaned in and whispered, "Easy tiger."

His words made me realize I was more transparent than I thought. I was jealous, which made me mad at myself, considering I was holding hands with another man. It was like being at the baseball game all over again.

Kace whistled for Cam to get his attention, and when Cam finally looked our way, his smile grew impossibly big. His hair was still wet from his shower, as if he had thrown on clothes and run from the locker room as fast as possible. He widened his arms, probably reading the expression on my face, and I ran to hug him. I wrapped my arms around his neck, and he lifted me slightly in the air. "How was it? Did you love it?"

"No," I shook my head adamantly as he lowered me back down. "No, I don't think I loved it. You looked like you were getting killed, and as it turns out, I'm not a fan of watching you almost die."

He barked a huge laugh as Kace caught up behind me. "Only my ego over the loss is bruised. Swear." Then he nodded at Kace. "Any crowd probs?"

"Nah, pretty easy night. Although she's not lying," he thumbed at me, "she ended up covering her face every offensive play."

"Let's get outta here," Cam suggested.

We followed Kace to his car and did the same routine as we did the night of the baseball game—me in the back, Kace driving, Cam in the passenger seat. Kace told Cam everything he did wrong, Cam agreed, I swooned. It was all very much similar to before. The only difference was finding a parking spot was easier in Kace's small Audi.

The guys walked me to my door, I kissed their cheeks, we said our goodbyes.

It was perfect.

The night was perfect.

I was so smitten.

Shit.

cam

FOOTBALL SEASON WAS OFFICIALLY UNDERWAY, and baseball season was in the prime of their playoff contention. Kace and I were busy, one, or both of us, either out of town, or practicing. Which was normal for us, it's what we did and what we were used to. And we loved it.

But that was before we had met Ali.

Now we jonesed to be in Atlanta, spending time with her. It had been two weeks since we had last seen her, but neither Kace nor I had intentionally stayed away. In fact, I wished Kace could go to her, maybe take her out, show her we were still interested.

Video chats helped. Sometimes it was just us Ali and me. At other times, it was her and Kace. On a few occasions, we managed to get all three of us together. Our conversations always flowed, and those led to an amazing, flirtatious friendship. The more I got to know her, the more I wanted to be around her again—touch her... kiss her. Fuck I wanted to kiss her.

Once, when it was just us on video chat, I teased her. "Do you know that the next time I see you, I'm going to kiss you?"

She turned that gorgeous shade of pink, easy to see even through the screen. "Kace said the same thing," she added an eye roll and laughed it off. It was something she did when she thought we were just playing games with her.

But I was serious, and I knew Kace was, too.

Fucker.

On top of video chats, we also kept our group text active. Ali liked to send us random things, Kace liked to joke around, and I liked to add my two cents.

I sat at my locker, thinking about how we had just lost our third preseason game in a row in Dallas, when my phone chimed.

ALI

Image sent Look at this! TMZ Atlanta has a poll on you two... Who would you rather go on a date with, Kace Jackson, or Cam Nichols?

ALI

How did I never notice this stuff before I met you two? This is cracking me up!

KACE

Whoa babe, that's a legitimate question. What was your vote? Asking for a friend. ;)

I started to text back, but then stopped when I heard a commotion on the other side of the locker room. Derreck, an offensive lineman—and a huge reason I got sacked four times that night—barreled through the door.

"Boss Man." I think they call me Boss Man because I was bossy, they swore it was because I was the team leader. Either way, I had learned to answer it.

"What's up?"

"I got a girl I want to introduce you to. She's good friend of my lady here in Texas and since we don't fly back till tomorrow, I thought you may wanna...ya know...join us." He waggled his eyebrows, trying to entice me to tag along.

I tilted my head, trying to find his motive just by looking in his eyes. He probably didn't have one, the guys were always trying to hook me up with someone, and I trusted Derreck—aside from watching my blindside. But I wasn't feeling it. Meeting someone wouldn't be fair to whoever she was.

Because she wasn't Ali.

"Sorry man, I'm uh, kinda seeing someone," I said, sheepishly rubbing the back of my neck. I wasn't even sure if it was true. Was I seeing Ali? I had only taken her out once—to the baseball game. All the other times I had spent with her was shared with Kace. Even the baseball game was shared with Kace.

We hadn't talked it over with her, other than letting her know we were interested, but I knew I would be devastated if Ali dated someone else other than Kace or myself. We had kind of put ourselves out there. She knew where we stood.

I think.

"What?" Derreck asked, unbelieving. "You've never mentioned seeing someone, and fuck off if you tell me it's Jackson."

"No, her name is Ali," I laughed. He knew how close Kace and I were. "It's new, man. I haven't said anything because there isn't much to tell. I'm feeling it out."

Derreck nodded, accepting my explanation. Despite being in a testosterone-filled locker room, no one gave me shit for anything, even my feelings. I figured I could do just about anything I wanted, and they'd be agreeable so long as I stayed the number one quarterback in the league.

And despite losing three games in a row, I was the best.

"You do you, Boss Man. But if she doesn't work out, Cyndee is fiiine." He laid on the words, driving his point home, and then left with a wave.

I looked back down at my phone, hoping I didn't miss too much of Ali and Kace's texting.

ALI

I voted for the third option. Neither. :)

KACE

Was that really an option?

ALI

ha-ha no.

KACE

Oh, thank God, my ego couldn't take the results
of that.

ALI

I'm sure your ego would survive.

KACE

So....??

ALI

??

KACE

Picture this...Cam and I both wanna take you
out... Right, Cam?

I know he's reading this....

CAM!

ALI

He just finished his game, maybe he's busy.

KACE

Probably still trying to get all that dirt he ate out
of his face.

I'm here, you fucker. Patiently waiting for Ali to
say "I'd pick Cam" so I can come scoop her up
for our date.

KACE

Ha... no... so Ali... Here's the scenario....

God, Kace was a persistent little fuck. Braver than I was, that's for sure. I was cringing just reading the thread as he put Ali on the spot.

ALI

I would stick with neither. No thanks.

KACE

No thanks? I didn't even give you the scenario.

Okay now my ego is slightly bruised. And to think, I would do anything for you.

That was an understatement. Ali got under my skin before she ever spoke her first words to me—I'd already do anything for her.

KACE

Same. ;-)

Kace's reply came quickly, but Ali didn't text back right away. She was either typing a lot, or bailing on the conversation. I hoped she knew I was just teasing again.

Finally, her name popped up.

ALI

Same.

I smiled at her perfect answer. Until she sent the rest.

ALI

But still—neither.

Neither.

Neither.

Inflection, cadence, lilt. None of those existed in a text. I had no way of knowing, based on her words alone, if she was playing with us. But for some reason, in my gut, I knew she was driving home a point. To us, and to herself.

Neither.

That sounded worse than another word that had been bouncing around in my head—*both.*

I decided at that moment that I wanted to get back to Atlanta as soon as possible, see Ali, and let her know in exact words where I stood. No more teasing, no more games. But it didn't feel like a good idea without Kace, so I opened up a private message to him.

> Getting on a plane tonight to ATL. The word neither isn't sitting well with me.

> It's ending, huh? We had some fun getting to know this woman and now what?

> I just can't do this. I know we were joking around, but I want more.

> Me too.

> But I love this, too.

> Then get on a damn plane tonight, meet me in ATL, and let's change the word neither to both.

After texting with Kace, I called one of the team assistants and had him book me on the next flight out of Dallas. I never heard back from Kace, but I knew he would be there. As different as we were, we were also alike, so when I landed in Atlanta at eleven that night, I wasn't shocked at all to see him leaning against a pole near baggage claim.

As I approached him, he smirked at me and got in step with my quick stride to baggage claim. But neither of us spoke as I waited for my bag. We even ordered an Uber in silence.

We rode together in silence.

We got out of the car and stood on the sidewalk in front of her building, all without a word to each other.

There were two apartments on the sixth floor and we didn't know which was hers, so as we stood at the panel to buzz her apartment, we had to take a guess. Starting with 6A, we buzzed a few times and got no answer. Switching to 6B, we finally got someone to reply.

"What the fuck do you want?"

Kace and I looked at each other, confusion all over both of our faces. I cleared my throat to speak but didn't get the chance.

"Leave me the fuck alone! It's almost midnight you mother-fucker! Come in this building and I will shoot you between the eyes, you hear me?" The voice was female, but most definitely not Ali.

Too raspy, too colorful.

Reminded me of Mary, but probably much older.

6B was the wrong apartment.

"Sorry, wrong number," I shrugged as Kace rolled his eyes. What else was I supposed to say?

"She must be 6A. Did she mention having to work? I know she gets in well after midnight sometimes," Kace mentioned.

"She didn't to me, but she could have. The pic she sent us of the poll was from her apartment, so I assumed she was off."

"What do you want to do?"

"Wait."

Kace nodded, shoving his hands in his pockets. "Yeah, me too."

We laid our suitcases down along the brick wall of her building and sat on them, settling in for however long it took.

"Now that we have a minute to chat it over, what's the plan?" I had a plan, but I wanted to know what Kace was thinking.

"I liked your plan. Both is better than neither," he replied simply.

"Think we can pull something like that off?" I leaned my head against the brick and looked up between the tall buildings, looking for the stars but unable to find them. People passed by every so often, but it was late, and on that side of town, not many people were out and about.

"I think if anyone can, it's us."

I agreed with a quiet hum. The past weeks of knowing Ali had been amazing and part of that was because Kace had been there, too. But it kept things from moving forward. It was kind of hard to be amorous with your best pal staring you down. Nonetheless, the moments have been priceless.

I just knew I wasn't going to be able to sleep until things were settled. I couldn't go the whole season, tiptoeing around a relationship with Ali because Kace was in the picture. He couldn't do it either. I should have known the circumstances would lead to this.

We met her at the exact same time.

We felt the exact same feelings.

We wanted the exact same from her.

We were both being drawn in by some weird, invisible pull that neither of us had felt before.

I wasn't a betting man, but I would have bet my entire career that Ali felt the same way about both of us. She thought because Kace and I were friends that her feelings were a losing battle. In her eyes, she would only ever have our friendship because she wouldn't be able to choose between us.

When she was with Kace, I saw how she really felt. I wasn't blind. Nor did I get jealous. I related to those feelings because she and I were the same way. And having the resolve to share her with Kace made me want to see her as soon as possible.

My foot began to tap with anxiety as thoughts ran through

my head. I was usually the patient one, but it was Kace that shoved my leg and told me to knock it off and calm down.

The clock was going on two in the morning, and Ali still wasn't home. I had moved from being nervous to being worried and started to buzz 6A again in the off chance she didn't hear it the first time.

Five more minutes of buzzing her apartment and I still got nothing so I pulled out my phone. While I was daydreaming, Kace had already texted her a few times in our group text.

No answer.

Kace and I both started to pace and I was two seconds away from having the cops drive to 678 to check on her when I heard her sweet voice behind me.

"Hello?" She sounded shaky and a little scared so I turned quickly, only to see her clutching her bag and backpedaling.

Then I realized I was wearing a hoodie, pulled low over my eyes and sunglasses, even though it was pitch black. *No wonder I couldn't see the stars.*

Kace was dressed the same way.

We flew a commercial airline into one of the busiest airports in the country—that was how we got through it all without being stopped by fans. But in our haste to get there and our mindfuck over sharing Ali, we forgot to lose the disguise.

At that realization, and in an attempt to ease her fears, I dropped the hood down and threw my $700 Ray Bans to the ground in record speed.

Kace opted to pull his hoodie off completely and had lost his sunglasses with the motion.

Neither of us gave a fuck. Especially after her face turned from fear to excitement. She squealed a sigh of relief and bolted toward us, jumping into my arms and wrapping her legs around my waist. Ali was a jumper and jumping *into* my arms was something I was sure I would never get tired of.

I held on to her tight and rocked her back and forth. I didn't know if she was that happy to see me, or relieved I wasn't an axe murderer lurking outside her apartment, but I soaked her in regardless.

After only a minute, and without her feet even touching the ground, she lunged from my arms and into Kace's. He did the same as I did and soaked in the moment, squeezing her tight.

It had been two weeks since we had last seen her—since the night she and Kace went to my game. Since she kissed our cheeks and left us reeling with emotions.

And a thirst for more.

Having her leap into our arms made the flight and the wait worth it. She seemed equally excited to see us. Or so I thought.

After a few minutes in Kace's arms, she hopped down and started raining her fists onto on his chest, pounding, and then turned and did the same to mine.

What the fuck?

ali

AROUND TEN O'CLOCK, on my night off, Molly had called to tell me the bar was slammed and begged me to come in to help. She had covered for me a few times and I owed her one. And she wasn't wrong, the bar was packed, no one else was even being allowed in.

Pretty wild for a Sunday night.

Molly and I worked together in the same section, covering twice as much ground in half the time. The night flew by, but the last group didn't leave until two in the morning—Tony had to force them out.

I had never been more relieved for a night to end. Although nothing happened, I had been getting strange vibes all night making shivers ran down my spine. And not the good kind I got from Kace and Cam.

Something was off, like I was being watched or followed. I couldn't even put my finger on it, but once it was time to go, I practically ran the few blocks home not even bothering to turn my phone back on and check my messages.

As I approached my building, I slowed to a walk but came to a complete halt when I noticed the dark figures in front of my door.

On a whim, I called out, "Hello?" After the words left my mouth, I thought about what a stupid idea that was. I should have detoured until it was clear. I tried to tell myself that just because two people were wearing dark clothes, hoodies, and sunglasses at two-thirty in the morning, didn't necessarily mean they were up to no good. But thanks to once being attacked in an alley by someone I thought loved me, my fear stood in the forefront of my brain.

At my call, they turned quickly and looked at me. There was no time to run before they immediately started shedding their sunglasses and hoodies.

Cam.

Kace.

What the heck?

A combination of relief and joy overcame me, and I ran toward them, jumping into Cam's arms.

I missed him.

I missed them.

I was also glad they *were* them.

Without even putting my feet on the ground, I reached for Kace and wrapped my arms around him, as well. He grabbed me from Cam, and I locked my legs around his waist. I felt like a toddler being passed around, but that was just a testament to how big they were.

After the relief and happiness started to wane, it sunk in how scared I had been. How scared they made me. Why didn't they warn me they would be there?

I jumped from Kace's arms and immediately started pounding his rock-hard chest with my fists. I was nowhere near strong enough to hurt him—not that I was trying—but my mind was spinning, and it never occurred to me I could use words like a normal adult.

I saw Cam in my peripheral and turned to give him the same fist jabs until he grabbed my wrists to make me stop. "What the hell are you two doing out here? Trying to scare me senseless?"

Kace placed a hand on the small of my back and I immediately calmed down, leaning into his touch. I huffed a few big breaths, trying to calm myself more.

"Breathe, baby. Breathe," Kace whispered.

Kace said the words, but it was Cam's face I was looking at and another shiver ran down my spine at his use of the word *baby*. Something he had never called me before but felt like a declaration of sorts. It rolled off his tongue so easily, I wasn't even sure he knew he said it or if he knew what it did to me.

Cam knew, though. He was staring right at me. He saw my pupils dilate, my mouth open, and my look of desire as Kace intimately whispered in my ear and rubbed my back.

Cam let go of my wrists and reached out to touch my cheek. I instinctively leaned into his touch as well and let his palm caress my cheek as his thumb skimmed my bottom lip. "You okay, now, Angel?"

"What are y'all doing here?"

"Can we go inside? We need to talk. But here," he looked around and motioned to the street, "may not be the best place."

Needed to talk? That didn't sound good at all. I started replaying our conversations in my head, trying to make sense of what could have happened between then and now that would have them there at an ungodly hour, needing to talk.

As we walked up to the 6th floor, and toward my apartment door, Kace groaned under his breath. "Um, we may need to send the lady in 6B some flowers or something…"

"Miss Jensen?" I questioned.

"Is that her name? We need to remember that for her apology flowers."

"What the heck did you do?"

"Buzzed her apartment until she threatened to shoot us

between the eyes. No biggie. Also, that is how we found out you are not 6B." Kace shrugged.

I laughed out loud as I unlocked my door. "No, you didn't."

"Yeah... but that was at midnight or so, she's fine," Cam added.

As I opened my door, I switched on the light. "Midnight? How long have you two been out there?"

Cam was the last one in and shut the door, locked it, and leaned against it. "My plane landed at eleven."

"What's wrong?" I no longer felt like laughing, something felt wrong. They seemed off. Was that what was bothering me all night? Did I subconsciously sense something?

That seemed implausible, but I didn't discount the idea—stranger things had happened.

Cam pushed off the door as Kace leaned against my bar top. It was a small space, and with the two large men in there, it felt even smaller. I had closed the curtain hiding my bed earlier, so the only thing visible was my couch, TV, and kitchen area.

I motioned to the couch, silently asking if they wanted to sit and they both nodded as they walked to the couch. Kace took my hand and lead me to join them.

As I sat at the end, against the armrest, Kace sat beside me on the couch and Cam opted for sitting on my coffee table so that we created a small circle.

Cam ran a hand over his face before speaking. "Look, baby," there was that word again, "Kace and I want to get something out there, something off our chests."

I was scared, but I just nodded for him to continue.

"Earlier, when we were talking about who you'd pick, we were just being us and joking around, but..."

"Oh my God. I know, I know. Please don't tell me you flew all the way home for that? Guys, I knew it was just a game. It's *always* a game. That's what you do!"

"Wait, I know you know that, but..." Cam took a deep breath and looked at Kace, who encouraged Cam to keep talking. "Ali, us being attracted to you has never been a game. We may have played around, but we always meant what we said about how we feel about you."

Cam stalled and Kace took over the conversation. "I think we were trying to see how long we could stand to just be your friend, but we don't want to be your friend, neither of us does."

"We want more," Cam added. "We want you to be one hundred percent honest about where you see this going." He motioned between him and me and Kace and me.

Of course I wanted more from them but the problem was still the same. I wanted it from both of them and choosing one of them over the other was impossible.

Did they want to know who I was feeling more? That was an unanswerable question and I was speechless. They were right, though, it was time for honesty.

"Cam," I whispered, trying to talk and be strong. A look of resignation came over his face as if he was preparing himself for my denial. But that wasn't what was happening, not really, so in the same tone, I looked to Kace and said his name. "Kace."

They each took one of my hands and I felt like I was in the twilight zone again. How did I attract the attention of not just one but two of the hottest men in Atlanta—the world?

I had learned just how popular they were and paid attention more when I heard their names on TV. I watched their games and interviews. I asked more questions when we talked and when I talked to Mary. They could have any woman they wanted, but a part of me always knew they felt something more between us. It was only a matter of time before the fantasy of us all being friends and them never being with other women—because I couldn't handle the thought of that—crumbled.

I wasn't going to choose between them, though.

Never.

"I don't think my attraction to you two has ever been a secret. I may not have said the words, but I'm sure my eyes and face speak very loudly. I thought this was something I could keep on a friendly level, but you both know, and I know, that isn't what this is anymore. Probably never was. I understand your need for more, I want it too, but I will never, ever be able to choose between you two. I meant what I said—neither. Even if you two weren't friends, I can't have either of you, because I don't think I could just move on with one, knowing how I felt about the other."

Kace started to speak but I cut him off. "Please don't try to convince me otherwise. Someone loses, no matter what. Let it be me. You two have been friends forever and I always knew I was the third wheel."

"Ali," Cam whispered while stroking my hand that he was holding. "That's no longer an option, sweetheart. Neither Kace nor I can just shrug this off and be okay with it. We both fell for you the second we laid eyes on you, I don't even feel like this is a choice, anymore. I cannot walk away."

"I can't either," Kace whispered.

Tears pooled in my eyes and I stood up, angry. How could they ask me to choose one of them, right in front of the other no less? We weren't in some dumb ass episode of the Bachelorette, I wasn't handing out roses. My whole body started to shake with anger and frustration. I turned to walk to the front door, planning to open it and beg them to leave before our conversation went any further.

But Cam caught up with me before I made it that far and grabbed onto my waist. He slowly pulled my back into his hard chest. His breath tickled my neck from behind and it was all I could do to get a word out— "Please." It was the only word I could manage, and I didn't even know what I was begging for.

Mercy?

Kace stepped in front of me, but with my eyes on the floor, I could only see his feet. He took a deep breath before his hand came to my chin, gently tilting my face up to look at him.

Once our eyes met, I knew what was about to happen. It was written all over his face. He had told me it was going to happen the next time he saw me. He even promised.

He gave me a minute to back away, to make my own decision, but I didn't.

I couldn't.

I was lost in Kace's intense stare, Cam's hands on my hips not forgotten. I felt like they were trying to tell me something, but I couldn't make sense of what.

But I knew Kace was about to kiss me, and I was about to let him.

With Cam watching.

There was no backing away. I was lost as Kace leaned in closer, his breath a whisper on my lips. I didn't move, I didn't close the gap. I wanted it to be on him. He was the one that had more to lose—mainly Cam—and I didn't want to make that decision for him.

Finally, he closed the small space between our lips, gently pressing his to mine. The motion was slow, soft, and hesitant. But it ignited something in my heart that seemed implausible.

Love?

Our first kiss was too soon to fall in love, but I knew that love was inevitable. If I didn't run away, I would fall hard and fast for Kace Jackson.

It wasn't just a kiss, it was a statement. He flew home late, waited outside my apartment, and didn't waste a lot of time before kissing me. He needed it as much as I did.

Neither of us intensified the kiss, though. As much as I wanted to wrap my arms around him and slip my tongue into his mouth, I hadn't forgotten that Cam was standing behind me.

Kace backed away, his lips still puffed from our kiss as he looked behind me, to Cam, and then back to me. The emotion on his face never changed.

Without warning, Cam turned my hips so that I was facing

him. I expected him to be mad, that Kace had just kissed me right in front of him, but he wasn't. He had a smile on his face and lifted his hands from my hips to hold my cheeks. Slowly using his thumbs, he caressed the edges of my lips where I still had traces of Kace's kiss all over them. The motion made me feel like he was debating on whether or not to wipe them clean.

I wanted Cam to kiss me, especially since I knew it would be the last time I was with them. But just like with Kace, I wanted it to be Cam's decision.

Everyone was silent, except for my small gasp as I felt Kace take hold of my hips from behind. The high I felt with them both touching me was intense, and I felt a safety I never had before.

Taking advantage of my parted lips, Cam leaned in quickly and gave me what I wanted.

What *he* wanted.

His lips sealed over mine, harder than Kace but not invasive. Just enough to give me a tremble and let me know that he was also a man I could fall in love with if I wasn't careful.

Kace's hands tightened on my hips, making me groan into Cam's lips. I realized at that moment that Cam never wiped Kace off my lips—a decision that felt intentional.

The thought had me groaning again, turning me on, and tempting me to push things farther. I wanted to beg one of them to be with me, to give me the release and satisfaction they were both eliciting inside of me. But that thought halted me because I couldn't have that.

I couldn't have *them*.

If I told Cam I wanted to be with him, I would mourn for Kace. If I told Kace I wanted him, I would mourn for Cam. Backing away and shaking my head, I was holding back tears. I held my hands up to keep Cam from coming forward. Then I tried to shake Kace's hands from my hips.

This was the worst of all their games. None of us could win.

Kace wasn't letting go of my hips, though. He tightened his

hold and brought his mouth to my ear. "You don't have to choose Baby."

I froze and processed.

My stomach flipped and flopped as his words sunk in. Turning around, I looked at Kace, then turned back to look at Cam. My eyes were wide, and my mouth was dropped. No one said anything for entirely too long.

Cam leaned in quickly and kissed me again, only that time, the kiss was far from chaste. He deepened the kiss and I let him, opening my mouth to welcome his taste. Kace ran his lips along my neck at the same time, gently kissing me from my shoulder to ear. My libido shot through the roof; my knees began to weaken.

When Cam tore his lips from mine, Kace's replaced them. He gave me as much as Cam did. Deep and ravenous, holding my neck, like a starving man eating his first meal. I moaned into his mouth as Cam kissed my wrists and took my fingers into his mouth, give them a small nip.

It was three in the morning and I was convinced I was dreaming, because I had dreams just like that—not having to say bye to one of them over the other.

But that wasn't believable. That wasn't how things worked in the real world. So I broke the kiss and stepped back from Kace, allowing Cam to keep my hand in his since I didn't trust myself to not fall from weakness.

Once I felt steady, I walked away, toward my bed, and ran a hand down my face. My back was to them because I knew my brain didn't function properly when I looked at them. I stood for a few minutes, trying to process what it all meant and I had a million questions, yet no voice to ask them with.

With my eyes to the ground, I began to pace like a caged tiger. Both guys waited patiently, knowing I needed to think things through, and they were allowing me that moment.

Then I stopped my pace, looked up to see them both standing

on the other side of my small apartment, hands at their sides and looks of determination on both their faces.

Kace and Cam were larger than life—perfection. They were both all-male with hard muscles, tall physiques, and gorgeous faces. A girl would be stupid to not take their offer and jump. But too many questions swirled in my mind, and once I found my voice, I couldn't stop them from spewing.

"Why me? Have you done this before? What do you expect from me? What if you get mad at each other? What if you get mad at me? What if I ruin your friendship? Are you two really gay? Oh my god, probably bisexual? How—?"

At some point in my rant, the guys had moved closer and Kace lifted me into his arms, cutting me off. He sat down on the couch with me in his lap and Cam sat next to us, taking my feet into his lap.

"Calm down, Ali," Kace said gently.

"We don't expect anything from you," Cam added. "You navigate this however you need. All we wanted you to know is that if you can't choose one of us, then choose *both* of us. Kace and I have never felt anything for the same woman before, so no, this has never happened. Also, for the seven hundredth time, we are not gay."

I laughed at Cam's deadpan statement, loosening the tension I had in my gut. Kace even laughed before adding, "I promise we didn't really plan this. We just both want you and want you to be happy."

"This doesn't feel real," I whispered.

Kace began to rub my back. "Nothing has to change. Let's take things slow. You set the pace. You're in control."

"It's late," Cam said after a few minutes of silence. "I know we overwhelmed you tonight. We just couldn't sleep until you knew where we stood."

I wasn't going to be able to process it all in that moment, Cam was right, I needed sleep. But I didn't want them to leave. "Stay here tonight."

Still in Kace's lap, I laid my head on his chest and tried not to think about everything that had happened. The day had been long, and I was suddenly overwhelmed with exhaustion as I waited for them to answer me.

But nothing came.

No words.

I had been so at peace in Kace's arms that I drifted off to sleep before their responses were ever voiced.

I woke up at five in the morning, still tired after only two hours of sleep. I sat up in my bed, not even remembering going to bed. The last thing I remembered was asking Cam and Kace to stay, then I fell asleep. I was still fully dressed in my work clothes, minus my shoes, so I assumed they had laid me down in bed.

It was dark and I needed more sleep before I started my day, but my mind couldn't rest. Kace Jackson and Cam Nichols kissed me. Really, really kissed me. My heart was beating hard just thinking about it.

Deciding that I would sleep better with my shorts off, I pulled them off and tossed them to the floor then started to lay back down and close my eyes. But before I squeezed them shut, I realized my eyes had adjusted to the darkness and there was someone else in my apartment.

There was a small light next to my bed and I flipped it on quickly. Kace was on the couch, shirtless but with his jeans still on. His arm was over his head and I had the perfect view of his chest. His body was a piece of art.

Then I saw Cam on the floor next to the couch, in between it and the coffee table. He was on his stomach, his head on a couch pillow. He wasn't wearing a shirt and with the view of his back, I suddenly saw that tattoo he mentioned he had.

They stayed.

I asked them to stay and they did, but they weren't in the bed with me, they didn't undress me, they didn't even have blankets. I felt awful and moved to tears at the same time. Sliding off my bed, in just my panties and a t-shirt, I walked to my closet and pulled a blanket out. Then I gently covered up Kace.

Poor Cam was on the hard floor with just a pillow so I gently rubbed his shoulder, stirring him awake. "Cam?"

He barely woke up but managed to lift his head off his arms and look at me. "You okay baby?"

"Come get in my bed, you have to be miserable down here."

"I am okay, sweetheart." His voice was full of sleep. "What time is it?"

"Only five."

"Go back to sleep."

"I feel bad. I asked you to stay and you are on my floor."

He let out a small, tired laugh. "Kace has a game tomorrow... today... he needed the couch."

"Well my bed is a king and there's plenty of room." I was almost begging but it did the trick. He put his hands under his body and lifted in a push-up motion.

Once he was standing, I took his hand and led him to my bed then laid down and got under the covers, while he climbed on top of the covers next to me.

He was back on his stomach, his arms up under the pillow, and he looked up at me with a smile. "Sleep angel."

When I smiled back and closed my eyes, I knew that whatever I had to discuss with myself about being with them both was pointless.

I didn't have a damn choice.

My mind and heart—and body—wanted to see it through. I

knew eventually something would go wrong, but I was going to have to face that when the time came.

Meanwhile, I thought that maybe it wasn't their worst game ever.

Maybe it was their best.

kace

I WOKE up to my alarm blaring and I blindly tapped around on the table for my phone. Normally, I kept it on my bedside table, but I couldn't even find the bedside table.

Then I remembered… I wasn't at home. I was at Ali's apartment, on her couch.

I sat up and grabbed my phone off her coffee table then looked down, noticing Cam wasn't on the floor anymore.

It was nine in the morning and light was streaming in through the curtains behind Ali's bed. I stood up and saw her curled up tight under the covers, sleeping soundly. Cam was next to her, still in his jeans on the outside of Ali's blanket. I decided not to wake either of them. I had to meet with the team trainers at noon, and had a game later that night, but Cam had the day off.

Searching for my shirt, I threw it on and then snuck up as close to Ali as I could. Since her bed was shoved tightly into an alcove, there was no way to walk next to the bed. But that didn't stop me from leaning over her from the end and kissing her cheek—it paid to be 6'4.

She stirred just a little and although I wasn't sure if she could hear me, I whispered, "Good morning beautiful, see you soon."

Then I grabbed my shoes and bag, and quietly let myself out.

I decided to just walk across the park to get to my place. It wasn't far and gave me time to stretch out my muscles. Sleeping on Ali's couch was probably not my best idea, but there was no way in hell I was leaving when she asked us to stay.

Despite my achy muscles, I couldn't believe how light I felt. Free and happy, with an added bounce in my step.

Ali had fallen asleep so quickly last night, a mixture of working late, dealing with Cam and me, and adrenaline from what we had suggested. And while she didn't exactly agree with what we offered; I knew she had as little choice as we did.

I opened my apartment door and I saw my housekeeper already in for the day, going about her business. I gave her a quick wave and headed straight to my room. The shower was calling my name and I took a minute to let the hot water hit my shoulders and run down my body. As I replayed the night before in my head, my cock started responding, growing harder.

Kissing Ali.

Watching Cam kiss Ali.

Ali gasping into Cam as I gripped her hips.

Fuck.

I grabbed hold of my cock and stroked, easing the throbbing the best I could. It had been a long time since I got myself off, but I no longer wanted a quickie in a bar bathroom. I wanted Ali.

I pictured her wide eyes, and the way her lips looked after being kissed by Cam. I imagined how wet she was, being pressed between both of us as we warred with kissing her. Fuck I wanted inside her so bad, but I was determined to do exactly what I told her I would do—go slow. So I squeezed tighter and let my hand bring me pleasure—for now.

CAM

I left Ali sleeping. Fuck, I didn't want to even leave.

KACE

Me either. You're off today, though, why did you leave?

CAM

I don't know. I thought about waking her up, but I just didn't want her to feel pressured to talk.

KACE

How you feeling about last night?

CAM

Better. Relieved. Hard.

KACE

Fuck Cam, leave some shit out.

But, me too.

CAM

I'm gonna watch some film on the team we play next week, and then head to your game. Need anything?

KACE

Nah.

CAM

Try to catch a nap. Y'all have to beat Pittsburgh tonight.

KACE

Trust me, after I leave this appointment with the trainers, I am headed into a dark corner of the locker room until game time.

ALI

Hey

I know I'm supposed to work tonight, but I just called in sick and bought a ticket to the game instead.

Is that okay?

Thirty minutes later.

ALI

OMG, of course it's not okay. I'm so sorry. I just don't know what to do here.

I don't know how to act.

I want to see you play again, but I definitely understand that this is an awkward situation.

Fifteen minutes later.

ALI

The ticket wasn't too expensive. I'll give it away later. I called the bar and told them I felt better.

Sorry.

Wow. Now I sound like a lunatic. Not even sure I'm ME right now. ha-ha. okay. bye, guys.

See ya around.

Two hours later.

CAM

Ali, baby. I'm so sorry. I've been in the film room. My phone was on silent.

Kace said he was going to take a nap until game time.

I know we kinda left everything in a weird place, but you never, ever have to worry about us not wanting to see you at a game… or anywhere… ever. Only you don't have to buy your own tickets either… perks of knowing the team's all-star! ;)

Let me pick you up on my way.

Ali, please answer your phone.

Another hour later.

KACE

Hey! I passed out hard, about to get ready and get to the field.

You two coming?

CAM

I still haven't heard from Ali. Gonna stop by her place, and 678 if I have to, on the way to the game.

KACE

Shit, okay.

I have to put my phone in my locker, see ya tonight.

I took the field that night, knowing I would see Cam and Ali in the stands, and it fueled me. I was high from the path we laid out for all of us, and when I saw her texts, wanting to come to the game, I knew she was willing to give it a try. We needed to make sure she never doubted herself when it came to us, though. As far as I was concerned, she was welcome anywhere I was no matter how unorthodox our relationship.

Less than twenty-four hours before, I had been sitting in my hotel room in Chicago, bullshitting with Ali over who she would choose between Cam and me. She gave the exact answer I was prepared for.

Neither.

When Cam suggested we change neither into both, a swarm of relief and contentment had come over me. We all knew that was the only way we could be happy.

Unfortunately, by the fourth inning, I still hadn't seen them in the stands. And by the seventh inning, I saw Cam show up, but not with Ali.

He saw me staring at him from my position at short stop, and it felt like a million miles of space was between us. I should have been focused on the game because, at that point, a line drive hit my way was going to knock me out cold.

Cam ran a hand down his face, then lifted his hands in the air, and shook his head. The whole movement showed me how stressed he was and answered my unasked question. He didn't know where Ali was.

With one out, a runner on second base, and a two-ball count to the batter, I stood up out of my ready stance and yelled, "Time out!"

Time outs were saved for the coaches, pitchers, and catchers. A middle infielder never called time out. Which was why the umpire looked at me like I was nuts, and Ethan Jones, the pitcher, stumbled off the mound in confusion.

But I didn't have a choice.

The umpire looked toward the dugout, unsure if he should grant my request, but I was already walking off the field. As I pass the mound, my team met me there and Chase spoke up first.

"What the hell, Cap?"

"Sorry guys, I gotta go."

My teammates started stressing their questions, one right after the other. Why and what being something I couldn't answer for them yet. I'd fix it later, but I needed to go find Ali first.

After jogging off the field, I told my manager to send out a replacement, and nodded to Cam to meet me outside. He bolted from his seat before I got into the dugout.

I didn't bother changing my clothes.

Dirty uniform, cleats, and all, I ran through the locker room and out to the parking area where Cam always parked. When I hopped in his already running car, he hit the gas and I punched the dashboard. "We have to find her."

cam

I HAD SPENT the entire afternoon trying to get ahold of Ali. I called, I buzzed her apartment, I even got past the main door at one point and knocked directly on her apartment door.

No answer.

Ali never struck me as an irrational woman, but a part of me worried that after her texts went unanswered, she changed. I slammed that thought down the second I had it, though. She may have been uneasy and awkward in her texts, but she wouldn't ghost us because she thought we were ignoring her—she wasn't like that.

When I went to 678 and asked for her, they told me she had never shown up for the shift that she had decided to work. That was when panic set in and I was no longer worried she was simply avoiding us. Something felt wrong, seriously wrong.

I didn't know what else to do, though, so I made my way to Kace's game, knowing he was probably wondering where I was. When I got there without Ali, I could see the concern on his face from my seat. He only made it one more pitch before the distraction was too much. When he called a time-out in the seventh inning, I already knew why.

"You sure about this?" I asked him when we pulled out of the parking garage. An uninjured player leaving mid-game was going to catch the attention of every media outlet that covered sports. Analyzing why he left and where he went.

"Something doesn't feel right," was his only answer.

I started to call Ali's phone over and over again from the car, hoping we got through to her somehow. Then after a dozen tries, it started going straight to voicemail.

Pulling up along the park near her building, we both jumped from my car and walked quickly to the door. We buzzed and buzzed until someone finally came out and we grabbed the door to let ourselves in. Instead of going up to her apartment though, we went to the second floor, where we knew Mary lived.

Faced with the same problem we were faced with the night before, we started knocking randomly on 2A hoping that was where Mary lived.

"What the fuck?" she said as she opened the door.

"Mary!" We both yelled at the same time.

"Boys? Oh my God, what are you doing here?" She took note of Kace still in his uniform and pulled him into her apartment, looking around to make sure no one saw him. "I was just watching the game and you fucking left the field, what the fuck? You're gonna get yourself mobbed if you walk around like that!"

"Have you talked to Ali?" Kace asked, not worrying about the truth Mary had just dished.

"Ali? No, but she's probably working tonight."

"She never showed up. And she's not taking our calls. She's not home," I told her.

"Did I miss something?" She looked between us calmly.

"We stayed over last night, not like that, though," I added, so Mary didn't have to ask. "We got in late, told her we wanted to see her, and ended up crashing at her place."

"She was going to come to my game, but we didn't answer her

texts, so she backed out," I added. "But now she has been MIA since about one o'clock this afternoon."

Mary grabbed her cell and tried Ali without another word. After a minute, she tried again with no answer. "Hmm, straight to voicemail."

"We've gotten to know her well enough to know that this isn't normal."

"You're right, it's not." Mary set her phone down and started pacing. After a few laps, she grabbed her phone again and dialed another number. "Phillip? Hi, its Mary!...Yes, yes I'm well, thank you. Look, have you heard from Ali?" A moment of silence passed and then Mary added, "I don't think anything is wrong, no, but she's not home, and not answering her phone, so I just wanted to be sure she didn't go to your place for a few days."

Kace and I looked between each other, not sure who Mary was talking to.

"Of course, I will, Phillip, and you do the same." With that, Mary hung up the phone. "That was Ali's dad. He hasn't heard from her, and also got her voicemail when he called earlier."

"This is our fault. What if we made her feel like she needed to escape?" Kace started pacing.

"How the fuck would this be your fault?" Mary asked.

"We've both been chasing her, Mary. We're both crazy about her. Last night, we were all in a group text and we mentioned her choosing one of us." I shrugged to play off the significance of what I was going to say next. "When she said she would never choose between us, we told her she could have us both."

Mary didn't even flinch, just stood there nodding like that entire statement made sense. "So, you think you scared her into running away?"

"I guess so," Kace answered. "What other—?"

"Fuck that!" Mary shouted and laughed. "Ali is a lot of things, but weak isn't one of them. It would take more than you two goons to make her drop off-grid. Besides, she isn't stupid either. And only a stupid woman would turn you two down."

"So, what the hell else, then?" Kace was exasperated and unconvinced. "We just want to make sure we didn't fuck this up, Mary. We need to know she's okay."

"Honestly, she probably got caught up somewhere, her phone died, and she's working her way home. Give her some time, don't panic."

"I'm gonna go check her place again, and then wait for her." There was no way I could heed Mary's advice and not panic.

"Here," Mary handed me a piece of paper. "This is my number. You boys call or text me when she shows up."

We knocked, yelled, and waited. Two hours later, and Ali still wasn't home.

Kace was sitting on the floor, leaning against her door and I was back to pacing the hallway. It was creeping up on midnight, and real fear had taken over. What if something happened to her? She didn't have a car, but I still scoured the accident reports from the afternoon—I was *that* manic.

After a few more paces, Kace leaned his head off the door and turned to put his ear against it. "Cam… I think I heard something."

I didn't believe him, but I got quiet and joined him.

After a few seconds, I heard what he heard.

A moan, a cry?

Someone was in there so I started banging again, begging Ali to open the door. "Baby. Please."

"Sweetheart, it's Kace, please open up, we've been worried about you."

We kept it up for a few minutes before Kace made the best decision of his life. "Back up, I'm kicking the door in."

ali

I WOKE up that morning to an empty apartment, but a note left from Cam on the coffee table.

Gonna miss you today. See you soon, Angel.

I was already gone for them, and couldn't wait to see them. With Cam having the day off, I figured he would go to Kace's game, so I spontaneously bought a ticket.

Then I freaked out.

Later, I laughed at myself because I knew he would want me there. But I had already called work again and told them I would be there after all. I didn't want Cam and Kace questioning where I stood, though. I wanted them, and had decided I needed to see everything through, no matter how much it would hurt in the end.

My new plan was to work a little, then fake not feeling well again. I'd head straight to the stadium and try to catch their attention. Faking sick wasn't a good idea, it would bring bad karma, but I was willing to risk it. A girl had to do what a girl had to do.

Before work, I slipped on some clothes and went down to the street to get a sandwich at the shop. It was mid-afternoon and the streets were busy with people looking for lunch. As I waited to order at the shop, I regretted leaving my phone upstairs since it could have distracted me from the long line.

Soon, though, I was bouncing out of there with a turkey sandwich, and a smile plastered on my face. When I rounded the corner that led to the building door, I saw a man in a hoodie, sunglasses on, and bent over looking at a phone.

Cam.

Kace was working and only those two guys would wear hoodies and sunglasses trying to stay low key on the sidewalk. He hadn't seen me yet, so I decided I would get him back for scaring me the night before and pretend I didn't see him.

I unlocked the building quickly and started up the steps, smiling to myself as he followed me. When I approached my door, I thought of something snarky to say to him and twisted around putting my back against my door.

That was when my world stopped.

When the entire world halted.

"Miss me?" His words made me want to vomit and I almost fell over from shock. "I bet you thought I was your boyfriend, didn't you?" I was frozen, completely unable to move. I stayed silent while he removed his sunglasses and kept talking. "Or should I say boyfriendssss?" He laid on the 'S' like a snake. "I gotta tell ya, Ali, I thought you'd at least look at my face before letting me follow you up here. What kinda dumb bitch are you?"

"Alan," I finally whispered in disbelief. Why was he there? Why did he even care? How did he know where I was? How did he know about Cam and Kace?

He read my questions in my eyes and held up one finger. "Don't worry, love, I will answer all those questions for you. But first, open the door."

I started to shake my head, denying his demand, but he knew I would say no and instantly jabbed something into my side.

"This is a gun, Ali, and I will fucking use it." He jabbed it harder, bruising my ribs. "Open. The. Door."

I would rather die in the sixth-floor hallway than I would let him in my grandma's apartment. I shook my head again, resolve written on my face. *Kill me.*

Luckily, or unluckily, he didn't want to kill me. He wanted in my apartment. So, he slammed me against the door, jerked the key from my front jeans pocket, and used his body size to hold me in place while he opened the door.

I didn't even think to yell or scream, it all happened so fast. Before I could even register what he was doing, we were inside, and he was pushing me onto the couch.

"Bitch!" He locked the door behind him and stalked toward me. He lifted me by the hair and forced me against the wall.

There was a small amount of light streaming through my curtains and I could make out just enough of his face to see that he looked eerily the same. He had discarded the sunglasses and replaced them with familiar black frames. He had a clean look, but slightly disheveled, and I wondered what he had been doing with his life for the past two years.

He didn't appreciate me scrutinizing his face, though. Rearing back, he used the back of his hand to smack me across my cheek. Then, he changed, and went from scary to scarier, but not in a menacing manner. He got giddy and happy. A smile crossed his face and his voice got almost...perky.

"I think you're wondering how I knew where to find you, am I right?"

I didn't respond as I held my cheek, tears streaming down my face.

"Well, that's a super fun story." He nodded, his eyes never leaving mine. "I spent six months after you left trying to find you because you were *mine*. But it seemed you had disappeared into thin air. You left everything you owned in that apartment. Your clothes, your furniture, your entire kitchen. You left it all for me to clean up, by the way. Bitch move." He shook his head and tsked. "What a pain in the ass that was after I had gone through all the trouble of making sure you could move out of that dump, and in with me. I mean, you left everything, Ali." He paused and thought of his next words. "The only thing missing was your car. I spent months looking for that car. And guess what? I found it."

Again, his jovial attitude was scaring me. I tried pushing him away, I had heard enough. And I knew if I didn't try to run, he would hurt me again. But he just got more forceful and slammed me back against the wall.

"Wait. You haven't heard the best part. The car was a dead end. The new owner was an 85-year-old woman who told me she paid cash for it. But you already knew that part. And I'm not a monster, Ali, I left that dumb bitch alone. She didn't know shit anyway."

Mrs. Bertie. I met her through a friend of my dad's. She really shouldn't have been driving at all, but she paid cash, and I handed her the keys, never looking back.

Alan pushed on me harder and I moaned.

"Shut up and listen," he demanded. "So where was I? Ah yes, well once the old lady was a dead end, I gave up. I didn't really have time for your shit, Ali. I had a life to live. And I was fine with that life because I was positive yours was worse. After all, you had nothing. But then... then I saw this." He held up a sheet of copy paper with a picture printed small in the top left quadrant. It was a little blurry, and a little dark, but because I was there when the picture was taken, I knew exactly what I was looking at.

Me. And Cam. And Kace.

That night I spilled drinks at the bar.

Cam was holding my arms and leaning his forehead toward mine. Kace was standing in front of us, a protective stance with his fists clenched. He looked like he was ready to fight anyone that dared to come near Cam and me. That night, I hadn't been able to see Kace's face since I was behind him. But the pic made it clear he was almost looking for a face to punch.

My eyes left the picture and went back to Alan. He was smiling like my reaction to the picture was exactly what he was looking for. Then he shoved the picture in my face again.

My eyes widened in confusion. "I...I..."

I didn't realize at the time that people were taking pictures at all. But now that I knew who Cam and Kace were, it shouldn't have shocked me to know there were pictures from that night. I had yet to Google them, but I bet if I did, I would find that picture somewhere.

I then started thinking back to being in the park with them, and going to the games with them. How many more pictures were there of us? Why didn't I think of that being an issue?

I let my guard down. They made me forget.

I never would have imagined Alan wanting to track me down. Two years had passed, and although I still lived with the scars he left in terms of fear, I had no longer thought he was a threat.

God, I was so stupid.

I had a million questions but didn't want to ask.

Filling in the blanks, Alan kept talking. "I could tell by the apron you had on that you worked wherever the picture had been taken. The reporter that posted the picture mentioned it was taken at 678. He did the work for me. I've spent the last few nights watching you, trying to decide how I was going to handle this situation."

That explained the feelings I was having of being watched.

He paused and took a deep breath, and when he started talking again, the chipper tone he was using was gone. "The way I see it, you owe me, bitch. And now I know you can pay up."

"What do you mean?" I started shaking my head. I didn't owe him anything.

"I got you out of that dingy bar and cheap apartment. I did all that for you. And you thanked me by leaving without a word. All that took a lot of time and money. Money that I want back."

"I don't have money," I cried.

"I followed you home last night, thinking I would have a nice, calm chat with you." He seemed to disregard my statement and continued. "But what happened, Ali? What the fuck happened? You want to tell me, or you want me to explain? You were there." I then registered Alan's hoodie and the sunglasses he had discarded. It wasn't a coincidence, was it?

"You jumped right into their arms, invited them upstairs, and they never fucking left," he yelled, finishing the last part at a tone I had hoped my neighbors could hear.

"I don't have money," I repeated.

That was all I got out before the first blow to my stomach. He had slid his gun somewhere and chose to use his fists, pounding my abdomen three times before he kept talking. "You are a fucking whore, you little bitch."

Another punch.

"I bet you can get one of those two pussies to pay up on your behalf."

Another punch.

"I don't even want a fraction of what I know they can afford."

Another punch.

"Five million."

Another punch, this time higher, my breast being his target.

Tears were streaming down my cheeks at his physical onslaught. I was weak and began bending at the waist. Unfortunately, Alan was able to hold me up with one arm and continue his assault on my body with his other hand.

"I won't kill you, Ali. I'm not a fucking monster." In his delusional world, beating me wasn't monstrous behavior as long as he didn't kill me, but after the tenth hit, I would have rather died— the pain being too much to handle. "Tell them, five million, or I find you again and make this worse. The games have just begun."

He started using his knee between the legs, mimicking the motion a woman would use to *knee* a man. After ten or so times, he stopped and held me close, my body limp and wanting to succumb to the pain. "They don't get *my* pussy for free so now its unusable. They have until it heals to pay up." Then he leaned closer to my ear and dropped his voice to a whisper. "I've had this pussy before. Trust me, they'll pay me whatever I want to keep it fit for use."

He backed away, laughing, and I fell as I heard him open the door to leave, locking it on his way out and taking my key with him.

Moaning in pain was all I could do. I couldn't scream or run—two things I swore I would do once I was free from his hold. Not only was I was too scared he would come back if he heard me move a muscle, but I was in too much pain to move.

At some point, I blacked out, and when I opened my eyes again, the room was pitch black, indicating it was dark outside. I still didn't move, though. I closed my eyes again and prayed for the pain to go away and for my emotions to settle.

Exhaustion.

Adrenaline.

Fear.

Confusion.

Anger.

I would call the police tomorrow. I would fix it tomorrow. But at that moment, I was frozen.

I opened my eyes again to the sound of someone knocking on my door.

Alan was back, it was all I could think of despite him having a key. I laid still and quiet, not wanting to let him know I was awake.

Once the knocking stopped, I waited a little longer until I was sure he was gone again. Then I moved onto my back and started peeling off the jeans I was wearing. They felt too tight against my swollen skin and I wanted them gone. It took a lot of effort but eventually, I got them off and tossed aside.

My shirt was an old button-up, long sleeve men's shirt—something I often wore at home for comfort while I worked. I decided to keep it on but take the bra off that was constricting my swollen breasts.

Once released from my clothing, I laid back over and curled into the fetal position. I knew I needed to call the police, but I was still disoriented and didn't know where to even begin to find my phone.

Suddenly a wave of embarrassment washed over me. *How did I let this happen? Why was I not more careful?* Cam and Kace were going to hate me for bringing drama in their lives—their very public lives. They didn't owe anyone money, either. Especially not Alan.

He was *my* problem, and I refused to involve them.

The only thing I knew to do was remove them from my life. Alan would have to accept that he couldn't use them for money. He could find some other way to punish me, or get his way, but I could handle it as long as it didn't affect anyone I cared about.

After what seemed like several hours of contemplating what to do, I stood on shaky legs and decided to start the healing process by taking a shower, forgetting about calling the police. When I made it to my bathroom and turned on the light, and was directly in front of the mirror, I was able to lift my shirt and see the damage Alan had done.

Tears started streaming down my face again and I let out a cry. All in the blink of an eye, my life was changing again. My relationship with the guys was ending before it could ever start.

My body was in pain and bruised beyond belief. My fear, that I had learned to suppress, was back at the forefront of my brain.

I gave myself a few more minutes of tears to let it all out, then, from out of the blue, I heard banging on my door again.

"Baby. Please."

"Sweetheart, it's Kace, please open up, we've been worried about you."

Relief that it wasn't Alan washed over me, but the reality that I had to deal with Cam and Kace before I could steel myself, sunk in. I wasn't ready. They would break me. I needed more time and I needed to be in better shape.

They can't see me like this.

I started to inch my way toward the door, pain racing through my legs from Alan's punishment. There was no sound plan, maybe faking sick and telling them to leave until I was better and not contagious. I wasn't sure. Nor did I get the chance to worry about that. Before I made it three steps out of my bathroom, my apartment door flew in.

I screamed at the violent sound the wood made, crunching under the foot of Kace. Cam came running in behind him and they both immediately made their way toward me.

Again, the tears were back. Instinct made me want to run into their arms, but they couldn't touch me. The pain my body was in was half the reason why; the lack of will power I had when they touched me was the other.

Before they could reach me, I thankfully found my voice.

"Stop!" I yelled in fear and determination, and unlike Alan, Cam and Kace heeded my words and stopped, unwilling to do anything I didn't want. That alone was indicative of how different they were.

"You okay?" Kace asked as he raised his hand toward me, like approaching a wild animal. I guess in a way, I was wild. None of us, not even me, knew what was going to happen next.

"We have been so worried about you," Cam added.

There was no hiding that I had been crying. And I thought that was why Kace's eyes got wide and he was suddenly shaking where he stood. But there was something I forgot about, something that the pain in my body had forced me to forget.

"Ali," Kace's voice was low, almost lethal. "Who the fuck did this to you?"

I lifted my hand to the cheek Alan had backhanded and pressed, causing me to wince from the bruising.

The guys started to move toward me once again and I held my hand up to stop them. "Please don't," I begged.

Cam's face was as deadly as Kace's and I had no doubt they could tell someone had hit me. And by the look on their face, Alan would be dead at their hands if he was there.

Kace dug his phone from his pocket and I assumed he was calling the police since I clearly hadn't done that myself. But instead, he barked orders to whoever answered the other end of his call. "Get a team who can fix a door asap. And new locks." He rattled off my address before hanging up quickly.

"We have been calling and texting. We drove over to 678, we buzzed your apartment, we banged on the door," Kace explained. "We've been sitting outside your door for hours, and when I heard you, the door had to go."

"Kace left his game, that's how worried we've been." I noticed Kace was in his uniform, with his jersey unbuttoned and untucked. His blue undershirt was still tucked in, and his baseball pants were smudged with dirt. He was still wearing cleats, his hat was on backward, and if I hadn't been mentally fucked, I would have melted just by looking at him.

Cam was wearing his usual jeans and Henley, but had a leather jacket on that made him look more menacing than I knew he was. His hair was normally in place, but he had clearly been running his hands through it all night.

I realized how worried they really were, and how much of a toll it took on them. And they didn't even know the half of it. I wasn't sure how much truth I could manage, but I wanted to give them some explanation. They deserved that much.

"Please talk to us," Kace begged as he inched forward. "What happened?" I held my hands up once again and Kace stopped, adding, "You have all the power. I won't move. Just please tell me."

Cam agreed with a nod and I felt it—the power they gave me. They made me feel alive, wanted, respected. I needed to push them away and save them from my mess but when I opened my mouth to tell them to leave, the words didn't come.

"I need to tell you something," I whispered instead.

They froze, not willing to risk any movement or action that may cause me to get scared and stop talking.

Hesitantly shuffling my feet toward my bed, my plan was to sit so my legs would stop shaking. But sitting sounded painful so I stayed on my feet until I was ready to tell them I was hurt more than they could see.

"It's a long story," I started.

kace

WHEN I KICKED the door in, I didn't expect to see Ali disheveled and disoriented. The need in me to know what the hell had happened was taking over my entire body. The longer it took her to talk, the more I wanted to approach her and force her to tell me everything. But her arms were still up, asking us to stay back, and I had meant what I said, she had all the power.

Cam and I stayed completely still as she started talking.

"Um, I'm going to tell you something, but first, I need you to make me a promise that you cannot break, under any circumstances."

Cam nodded then looked at me, making sure I was going to agree as well. "I promise, Ali. Anything you want."

"Anything," I confirmed.

She took a huge gulp and inched to standing directly in front of her bed. She looked over my shoulder at the broken door and then back to me. We had closed it the best we could, but the frame was damaged. She had nothing to worry about, though, because a damn SWAT team couldn't have gotten past us to reach her.

"I need you to promise, that no matter what I say, you will not come near me."

The fuck?

"You cannot take a step in my direction. Please promise me."

We nodded again to agree, but that was the hardest promise I ever made.

"Two years ago, I left my boyfriend after the first sign of abuse. I didn't hang in there and pray he got better, I left. Without a word. Without anything." She started to wring her hands in uneasiness. "I found out he had been paying his sorority brothers to harass me while I worked at a bar on campus during my senior year. His end game was to scare me away from the bar, and I was constantly grabbed, groped, and touched by strangers that did his bidding to scare me. I didn't know why at the time, but like I said, I later found out it was him all along. When I confronted him about it, he hit me with the back of his hand, knocking me out. When I came to, I was alone in the alley. So I ran."

She paused, but I was visibly fucking shaking. Her jumpiness and fear of people reaching for her started making sense. I didn't know who the guy was, but I knew he was going to fucking die.

"My grandma left me this apartment," she kept talking, "and he didn't know about it, so I quit college, sold my car for money, and hid here until I got a job. Thankfully it was working from home as a writer because I never, ever, wanted to go back inside a bar. But then Mary needed me, and she didn't know anything because I let it become my past. It had been two years though, so I decided to get over myself and help her."

Tears started pooling in her eyes and I wanted to lunge toward her, but Cam's big hand grabbed my arm and held me back, like he knew what I had been thinking. Cam was much more levelheaded, and I needed him to keep me in check. But I felt him shaking too, taking his anger out with the hard grip he had on my bicep.

I let him. The pain grounded me and reminded me what I needed to do—nothing.

Once Ali was sure we were staying put, she was able to keep talking. "That night that I spilled the drinks, well, apparently there were pictures taken of the scene." *Oh no.* "He saw a picture online and was able to determine where I was working."

No, fuck no.

It was the picture Cam had been worried about. The picture I had *not* told her about. The sole reason I stopped at 678 all those weeks ago to check on her. Guilt started eating away at me and I felt ill, but somehow managed to keep myself upright.

"He, um…. today… he… he… found me," she finished on a whisper.

Cam fell to his knees, and I grabbed his hand, knowing he was feeling as guilty as I was. We should have told her, warned her. We were so caught up in being *regular* guys that we selfishly kept it to ourselves.

"Did he…?" I couldn't even finish the fucking sentence as bile rose in my throat and I fought to suppress it with a swallow.

She gently touched her cheek and nodded, more tears streaming down her cheeks. I dropped Cam's hand and started toward her, but again her arms came up, stopping me.

"You promised!" she cried.

I did, and I stood by that promise, but when I looked down at Cam and saw the tears in his eyes, I realized he was no longer going to be able to help me keep that promise. I was on my own, and had to keep my own level head as he battled with guilt and anger.

"Please let us make this right," I begged.

"This isn't your fault," she cried, her hands covering her mouth while the tips of her fingers wiped the tears away.

Cam huffed, but didn't speak. I laid my hand on his shoulder, assuring him I was there.

Before anyone else spoke, a knock came on the broken door.

Ali jumped back, but I recognized Cam's handyman, the one I called to fix Ali's door. He poked his head in and let us know he was ready to work, but I couldn't let him.

"Out!" I yelled.

"Yes sir," he responded.

Despite being on his knees with his head down, Cam was still more rational. "Javy! Wait!"

Javy poked his head back in and looked at Cam, who never looked back. "Find a very quick way to secure that door tonight, then come back tomorrow and replace it."

"Yes, yes, I can do that! Right away!" Javy came in, never looking too long at the scene we created as we all stayed in place. He worked quickly, adding metal latches to the door and the wall that folded over one another and locked. Fifteen minutes later, no one saying a word, he was done and silently showed me how to lock the door before vanishing.

I backed up toward the door and locked it tight. The frame was still a mess, but it was more secure than it was before. I wouldn't have been able to kick the door down if it had that lock on it before.

The time that Javy had been there had given Cam a moment to compose himself so he stood and took a deep breath.

"We knew about that picture, Ali," he confessed, clearly still angry with himself. "I knew, and I sent Kace to check on you at the bar that night he came alone. We were so fucking selfish, worried you would find out who we were. We didn't fucking tell you."

Ali gasped but started shaking her head 'no' as she considered his words.

"Had we been honest, you would've been prepared. Informed. Safer," Cam added. "Being with Cam Nichols and Kace Jackson is never a private and safe decision."

"You didn't know about, Alan, though." I took note of his name—Alan. "I didn't tell you because I thought it didn't matter. I never got upset with you for not being upfront about who you were, so I'm not going to get upset about that now. I'm more upset with myself for not considering Alan was still a threat. For naively carrying on, going to your games and putting myself in a position to be found. I made those decisions after knowing who you were. I was an idiot, and in turn, I've pulled you two into something you don't deserve to be a part of. You don't need this in your life."

"You're not pushing us away," I growled. "Don't even think about that. We can all figure this out together."

Ali just shook my words off and broke out into fresh tears. "There's more…."

cam

I WAS GROVELING in self-hatred over the pain that our lie had caused Ali. Had we been honest, she could have protected herself. Maybe she wouldn't have ever told us about Alan, but she would have known who she was associating with when we were around.

"He didn't know from that picture alone," Ali kept talking. "I mean about being associated with you two. Last night, he, um… he said he followed me home, watched me invite you two in, and waited for you to leave."

"We didn't leave," Kace groaned.

"You didn't leave," Ali repeated. The importance of those three words were weighing heavily between us. "It just fueled his anger, I think. Confirmed we were more than just that picture."

I began shaking my head in disbelief, again.

"He told me to tell you two he wanted five million, or he would come after me again." I didn't even give a fuck about the money. I made more than that on a weekend. Kace too. Money was no object, and we would pay him double, or triple, to keep her safe.

"I'll give him whatever he wants to keep you safe. But we also need to call the police." I was talking, but still not able to look at her.

"I know. I should have, I just…I haven't been…awake. But, there is one more thing."

Ali was no longer crying; she had somehow hardened herself. I looked up but could barely look her in the face.

"Look at me!" Her voice was demanding, cutting through our self-abhorrence.

I snapped my eyes up to hers from the sternness of her voice and gave her my undivided attention. Kace and I created a wall, the way we always did, standing shoulder to shoulder with our arms at our sides. Our bodies were steel-like with strength as we both stood before her, waiting.

Slowly, she took her hands to the top buttons of her shirt and began undoing it slowly, methodically. Under any other circumstances, I would have been instantly hard and turned on from watching her undress.

After she worked the buttons to the bottom, she kept the shirt closed until she was ready. I started to stop her, not sure why she was exposing her body at a time like that. But before I spoke, she eased the shirt open and let it fall from her shoulders to the floor, knocking the wind from my chest again.

Her naked body was bruised and battered. Her breasts were swollen, and her ribs were black and blue. I thought the first time I saw her body that I would ravage her, make her feel good, show her how much I cared for her. Instead, just realized why I couldn't touch her.

"It hurts," she whispered as her hands rested over the lower part of her white panties. "And he kneed me here over and over again. It hurts."

"I'm going to kill him," Kace said, eerily calm and frank. He meant it and I was right there with him.

Before we scared Ali, before we did something stupid, I dialed

911 and gave them Ali's address with a brief description of what was going on.

Kace took his jersey off and started walking toward Ali. She trusted that he knew she was in pain and wouldn't make it worse.

Gently, he wrapped his large, dirty jersey over her small frame and started closing a few buttons. He looked into her eyes, inches from her face and then leaned in to gently kiss her lips. "Police are coming. And we aren't going anywhere, do you hear me?"

Ali nodded then rested her forehead onto Kace's chest and I knew it took all his strength to not wrap his arms tightly around her.

He looked over to me and I nodded at his unspoken words. She was ours, and no one would ever lay another hand on her as long as one of us were around.

ali

I COULDN'T BELIEVE I told them everything. But when I realized they thought it was their fault, I had to clear the air. I couldn't let them think I blamed them. Once I knew who they were, I continued to step out into their world, giving no thought to Alan, or his willingness to find me. They made me feel normal, made me forget, and as much as I wished Alan hadn't returned, I didn't regret the freedom their presence in my life had created.

The police arrived not long after Cam made the call. Both officers recognized Cam and Kace—especially Kace because he was still in his uniform. They even asked him about leaving his game and why. It was like they were accusing him of hurting me and had proof. "Social media blew up when you walked off the field, Mr. Jackson. Finding you here seems a tad suspicious, if I'm being honest."

The cop's comment didn't even make sense. He was digging for something that didn't exist, and Cam shut him down, telling him to do his damn job. I had been clinging to Kace the whole time, why would he think I would cling to the one that hurt me?

They weren't convinced Alan was the problem and that scared me. It was like two years ago all over again.

After Cam escorted the cops out, he explained to me that Kace walking off the field was going to be the center of sports news until answers were given. Even the cops wanted to be the ones that broke that news story. I was scared it was going to be public in a matter of hours, but they assured me they had people that would make sure it stayed as contained as possible.

I was finally able to gently sit on the couch after everything was settled. Cam disappeared into the bathroom and Kace took the seat beside me. He grabbed my hand and kissed my knuckles, making me smile a little.

We agreed to keep the attack from Mary—my choice—since she was dealing with a lot already. The guys did text her, though, letting her know I had been asleep all day and was okay.

Cam came out of the bathroom and gently pulled me to a standing position in front of him. He began unbuttoning Kace's jersey that and slid it off my shoulders. Goosebumps formed over my skin as his fingertips skimmed my shoulders.

Earlier, I had shown them my body, wanting them to see what Alan had done to me, but it wasn't in a sexual or provocative way. I knew Cam's intentions weren't supposed to be sexual either, but I could finally breathe again, and I couldn't help but feel aroused by his gaze.

Carefully, he leaned over and swept me up into his arms then walked closer to Kace.

Kace stood from the couch and kissed me, then whispered, "I'll be right back, baby." Concern flashed in my eyes so he added, "I need to grab me and Cam some new clothes but I promise I'll be right back. We're both staying here tonight." Then he kissed me again, put Cam's leather jacket on over his uniform, and left.

Cam turned and headed to my bathroom where he had drawn a bubble bath for me. He didn't take my panties off before easing me into the warm water. But once I was submerged in the bubbles, he reached down, under the water, and slid the panties off my legs.

His attempt to handle me with respect was noble, but I'd be lying if I didn't admit that I wished he'd look at all of me. Maybe even climb in the bath with me.

I bet he could make me forget Alan ever existed.

He sat on the edge of my bathtub, slowly soaping a washcloth, then he reached down and gently bathed my battered body, taking care to not press hard on my bruising. With each passing of his hand, my breathing got more and more erratic. I wanted him to touch me with his bare hands so bad that I thought I would combust if he didn't.

Grabbing his wrist, I stopped his movements across my stomach. He took his focus from his mission and looked at me with confusion. Using my other hand, I took the washcloth from his grip and splayed his hand across my lower stomach. Slowly, unsure what was driving me to be so bold, I started pushing his hand lower.

"Ali, baby…what are you doing?" Cam was breathing harder, warring with himself about what the right thing to do was.

"Please, Cam," I begged, downright pleaded. No shame, no fear, I just wanted him to touch me. I *needed* him to touch me.

He squeezed his eyes shut and angled his head toward the ceiling, fighting off the urge to give in to me. When his eyes returned to me, he wore a mask of resolution. "Trust me, I want nothing more than to make you feel good, to make you forget, to remind you how much I care about you. But you're hurt."

"It won't hurt," I whispered. In the warm bath, it was easy to forget the pain I had coursing through me.

"I'm not going to be the reason you're in more pain. The first time I touch you, I don't want you to be thinking of anything but me. No pain. No Alan. Just me."

"What about Kace?" I asked, eyeing him through my thick lashes.

He cracked a knowing smile and shook his head. "When I touch you, Kace won't exist either."

It felt good to see his cockiness back, and his ego still intact, after such a trying day. And, he had a point. The first time he touched me, I didn't want there to be any barriers of pain and distress, so I let go of his hand.

He stood and made quick work of grabbing a towel and helping me up; immediately wrapping the towel around me and scooping me back into his arms. When we were back in the main room, he went down to his knees as he helped me step into new panties, and I held onto his shoulders to keep myself steady. Before he stood back up, he ran his hands up the outside of my legs and I could see how much desire he was fighting. Finally, he slid a t-shirt over my head and I climbed onto my bed just as Kace returned with a bag slung over his shoulder, wearing a t-shirt and gym shorts.

Cam took the stuff Kace brought and changed, not bothering to hide as he did. He pulled his shirt over his head and his jeans fell to his ankles. For a moment, he was in nothing but his boxers and I groaned from the need in my body. Maybe it was the endorphins or the adrenaline, but I didn't know how I was going to survive all night without *something*.

Anything.

I rubbed my legs together, trying to find friction as Cam shook his head at me, knowing what I was thinking. I was drunk on them, losing all inhibitions and regard. I thought that maybe I could just take my hand down...

"Fuck!" I cried out in pain as my hand pressed between my legs. The guys had been frozen, watching me, but my cry made them both spring back into action and they were lying beside me in a flash. Tears sprang into my eyes and I held my arms over my face, embarrassed that I had even tried.

All I wanted was a little relief and all I felt was pain. Throbbing. I moaned from the bruising and frustration. I wanted to *feel* despite Alan's assault, but I was realizing he did exactly what he wanted to do and took away my ability to feel pleasure.

"I didn't want him to win," I cried quietly. "He said he was making me…unusable."

"Just heal," Cam whispered, though I could hear the venom in his voice.

Kace slid my arm off my face and kissed my cheek, taking away the tears that stained them. I turned to him and he enveloped me into his arms making me feel safe as I snuggled into his t-shirt.

Cam started to move behind me, getting off the bed, and I jerked up to see where he was going. "Just going to the couch," he explained, running his hand on my legs.

I shook my head and looked at Kace for help. It was unconventional, a lot to ask, and probably not what they meant when they said I could have them both. But I wanted to keep them both close and was willing to beg if I had to.

Kace nodded to him to lay back down. "Whatever she wants, remember?"

Cam scooted up to spoon me and rested his hand on my hips. Then he kissed my neck. "Sleep. We got you."

I had never felt safer, or more cared for, in my entire life and I never wanted that feeling to end. There was just one more thing I needed to tell them.

"I was going to say yes."

kace

THE NEXT FEW DAYS, we made sure one of us was always with Ali. We knew she wanted to stay home, and would tell us she was fine if we asked her to leave, so we brought clothes over and stayed the night.

Most of the time, only one of us could be there, which was usually Cam since I had a game every night. But I went straight to Ali's after my games and stayed with them. Then Cam went off to practice in the mornings and I would hang around quietly as Ali worked on her day job.

Cam had called 678 to request a few days off for Ali. It may have been an extreme overstep but she needed time to heal. Cam and I decided we would cover whatever expenses she was losing, but she took us by surprise when she said she was putting everything she made at 678 away for Mary. Of course, Mary didn't know it, but Ali wanted to make sure she didn't suffer financially on top of battling cancer.

Ali said she did well with her writing career. Not enough to pay off Alan, but well enough to take care of herself.

Cam and I had been hounded by the media about my sudden disappearance from my game, but we both agreed to keep it short and simple, explaining that a family emergency had come up. My coach didn't like the answer, though, so unfortunately, I told him the truth—my girlfriend had been attacked. I left out the part about it being Cam's girlfriend as well, but he accepted what I told him even though he could tell I left something out.

By Friday, I was tired and drained after our game had gone into extra innings—making for a long night. But I was ready to get to Ali's, where I had started to feel like I belonged. Her little place was magic when we were all there together.

With the new door and locks in place, Cam and I each had a key so Ali never had to open the door and risk it not being us. Since it was so late, I slid my key in quietly, expecting Cam and Ali to be asleep.

"Surprise!" I heard before they jumped from behind the bar in the kitchen.

"What is this?" I smiled, and took note of the food, the cake, the candles. Then I thought of the date and it definitely wasn't my birthday.

"Ali wanted to have a late dinner with both of us, so I cooked." Cam motioned toward the spread and scoffed, "You know how hard it is to keep Beef Wellington warm without overcooking it?"

Beef Wellington was my favorite. Cam knew that and I felt a tug in my chest, my heart swelling with contentment.

"I made the cake when you hit the walk-off home run," Ali added. "I wanted to celebrate!"

I felt another tug in my chest, thankful to have found her and to have Cam with me. Ali fixed three plates and brought them to her small, circular table. Candles were lit and soft music played as I chatted briefly about the game. Then Cam filled me in on his practice and Ali complained about a piece she was writing that she couldn't get right.

It felt so easy and right.

Once dinner was cleared and Ali had served her cake, she started to squirm. Cam and I watched her as she worked something over in her head, until she finally pushed her shoulders back resolutely, and spoke.

"I have a question?" She started, eyeing Cam and I back and forth. "How does this work?" Her question was vague, so Cam and I just continued to stare at her.

"Sex," she finally blurted.

Oh shit. I was extremely far from being a prude, but I had never discussed logistics of sex either. If I wanted sex, I had sex. The end.

But this was all new to me. Ali was not a normal girl. I wanted more than sex from her. Not to mention she was also speaking to Cam. And then add in her injuries. I didn't know what to do.

"Can you be more specific?" Cam seemed more levelheaded, of course.

Ali rolled her eyes, but then straightened herself again, and spoke like the woman we knew she was—strong, down to earth. "Guys, I'm a woman who's found herself with two hot boyfriends. No matter how unorthodox that is, I still want to be with you, intimately. Both of you. So I need you two to figure out who's gonna have sex with me, and do it already."

Well, okay then.

"Who do you want to have sex with baby?" I couldn't believe I asked that question. It was more my instinct to scoop her up and fuck her senseless at the mere request. But again, she wasn't a normal girl, and it wasn't a normal situation.

I made quick peace with the fact that if she said Cam, I would kiss her goodnight and head home. Our sleepovers had worked thus far because being intimate was off the table. But she was almost healed and we were both itching to touch her.

Then her eyes darted between Cam and me, her face turned a beautiful shade of pink, and I knew what she was about to say before she said it.

"Both. I want you both."

At the same time? I didn't ask that out loud because, of course, that was what she meant. I knew by both of us sharing Ali, that it may become a possibility, but I honestly figured we would both be intimate with her on our own time. For as close as we were, Cam and I had never shared a woman in bed.

That's not to say I wasn't 100% on board. I had no problem fucking Ali in front of Cam. I'd fuck her in front of everyone if she wanted me to. Cam was a little more of a traditional romantic, though. I was sure he wanted to share their first time alone, so I turned to him and raised my eyebrows, waiting for him to answer her.

"I told you," he hummed, "that you can have us however you want. I'm not taking that back. I can't wait to show Kace how wet I can make you, Angel."

My cock started throbbing at his words. The thought of having Ali, and watching Cam have Ali, was almost more than I could take. Ali's eyes caught me adjusting myself and she smiled, like we were waving a bright green go flag. Standing up, she walked to Cam and straddled his lap as he pushed his chair back from the table.

"I'm ready," she whispered. "I need to feel something. Please make me feel something."

She started kissing Cam and he wrapped his hands around the back of her, grinding her along his cock, through his jeans. He was testing her, pressing into her bruising, and she moaned a little in pain. But she didn't stop moving, and Cam didn't stop kissing her.

Without undoing my own jeans, I palmed myself to ease some of the need I had, and let out a groan while watching them. Their kiss was deep and sinful.

Intimate.

Peeping wasn't really my thing, but I was wanted there. They expected me to watch and I knew I was invited to join them when I felt the time was right. The time was always going to feel right, though. Ali didn't want to bounce between Cam and me, she wanted us both in every sense of the word.

"You sure about this?" Cam asked her, then chanced a glance at me, looking unsure for just a second—until Ali pleaded.

"Please."

He growled and stood up from the chair with her in his arms. She wrapped her legs around his waist, and he carried her to her bed. I had no idea what kind of lover Cam was because I had never actually seen him with someone. But it was like once she said please and he stood up, he was no longer the good little quarterback. He was possessed and self-assured. Dominant.

He laid Ali down on the bed then backed away a few steps. He was wearing a dress shirt, and started unbuttoning it slowly as Ali watched.

She looked needy.

And relieved.

I stood from my chair to get a better view while still rubbing myself over my jeans. Ali groaned as Cam slid the shirt from his shoulders. He was as big and toned as I was, with a tattoo on the back of his shoulder that we got one night after celebrating being brought to the big leagues. I could see his muscles flexing below the ink.

"I'm not fucking you tonight," he hissed, surprising both Ali and me. "You just cried in pain, and I told you before that I won't do anything to add to that pain. I'll lose my goddamn mind if I start fucking you, and I don't trust myself not to hurt you."

Ali was frustrated, her eyes wide with confusion and anger. But Cam didn't take his shirt off for no reason. He wouldn't have teased her just to turn her down. I may not have known what kind of lover Cam was, but I knew what kind of human he was, and he was going to make Ali feel everything he could without risking her more pain.

Ali didn't know that, though. She looked over to me as I stood off to the side, my hand squeezing my dick. Her begging expression asked me if Cam wouldn't fuck her, would I?

I silently shook my head no, agreeing with Cam on this—I wouldn't risk hurting her. But I wasn't going to leave her hanging, either. "Cam's right. Let's take it slow. But I promise he's gonna make sure you get everything you need tonight."

"We all get what we need tonight," Cam grunted.

"Take your clothes off—undress for us," I commanded as I stepped up next to Cam. She wasn't as high as she was the other night when she tried touching herself right in front of us, so she clammed up a little with shyness.

To encourage her, I pulled my own t-shirt over my head, making a show of undressing for her. Soon, she did the same, and was in her bra and panties, laying on the bed with her hair fanning out around her. She looked like a fucking angel.

A lot of her bruising had faded, but there were still signs that it was there. It reminded me of how bad I wanted to kill Alan once the cops finally found that fucker.

"Stop!" she demanded, noticing the change in my face. "Don't look at me like that."

I couldn't see Cam's face, but I knew it mirrored mine as Ali leaned up a little and told him the same thing. "Not now, Cam. I'm okay!"

He wiped a hand down his face and cleared his train of thought, then immediately got back to business, kneeling at the foot of the bed and rubbing his hands up Ali's legs.

Once his thumbs met up at the apex of her thighs, he used them to rub her clit over the outside of her panties. The tease was enough to make her fall back onto the bed and look to the ceiling.

Keep your eyes on me," Cam ordered. Ali responded quickly to his tone and her eyes shot down at him. He peeled the panties down her thighs and her legs fell open, giving me a first glance of her wet pussy.

Cam and I both started swearing under our breath in desire. I had never been a quick trigger, but I was in danger of coming in my jeans, right here, without even being touched.

I took a step forward and ran a finger through Ali's wetness before bringing it to my lips to taste. Fuck she was a goddess. Knowing what she wanted, asking for it, and somehow creating a moment Cam and I never even dreamt of.

Cam and I have shared beds and clothes.

We've shared food.

We've shared laughs.

We have a history that dates back to our childhood and we've shared our dreams and goals.

But now we were sharing Ali. And I knew it was going to be the best night of my fucking life.

CHAPTER TWENTY-THREE

Cam

WATCHING Kace taste Ali almost single-handedly ended my night. I had to close my eyes and tamp down my urge to come like a fucking teenager. My interest in Kace's dick was zero, but I had a vested interest in his happiness—and he looked damn euphoric.

He and I both shed our jeans together and stood naked in front of Ali. Instead of my original plan, to devour her pussy with my mouth, Ali sat up quickly and got on her knees at the end of the bed.

With one hand on Kace and another on me, she ran her nails up and down our chests, tracing the lines and cuts of our bodies. "I think I just died and went to heaven."

"Is this your heaven?"

"I have the quarterback, and the Allstar, at my fingertips, Cam. This is every girl's heaven."

Before we could say anything else, she wrapped her small hands around both of us and stroked our cocks, keeping her fists tight and strong. Kace and I were hissing and moaning, not just from watching her stroke us, but from watching each other, as well.

Then she licked her lips and got closer to Kace, and I moaned as his precum dripped onto her tongue. "Oh fuck," I exhaled.

"Ali?" Kace's voice was strained with desire. "I swear on baseball that I want nothing more than you wrapping your pretty little mouth around me, but I won't make it, baby. I will come right down your throat, and you're not ready for that. *I'm* not ready for that."

Before she could even back away, I reached down and pulled her legs from under her so that she flipped onto her back. I spread her pussy open and ran my tongue between her folds, anxious to taste her. Then I sucked on her clit, teasing the tight bundle of nerves while Kace went for her bra and removed it with a flick of his wrists.

I kept my eyes up on Ali's reactions, trying to learn what her body wanted and what she responded to as I kept my tongue on her. But I always watched as Kace leaned down and kissed her lips, her neck, and eventually her tits, latching on to one of her nipples. With us both tasting her body, she started to squirm, making it harder for me to keep my tongue where I wanted.

Grabbing her thighs, I used my strength to hold her legs open and her ass still, then returned my mouth to her. Within seconds, her body was convulsing and she screamed from the mixture of pleasure and relief. Kace had pulled back from her, watching her, as the pent up tension in her body faded under my tongue.

When I was sure I had every last drop, I crawled up her body, careful to keep her cum on my tongue. I wanted to kiss her and make her taste what I had just done to her. To show her she was mine.

"Give me those lips, Angel," I whispered, before closing my mouth over hers and pushing my tongue between her teeth.

Kace took my place between her legs and used his finger to quickly rub her clit, trying to get her back to the edge. Once he had her shaking again, he pulled away and ran his tongue up her slit the same way I had.

When she moaned, I pulled away and looked down, watching Kace in a way I never had before. His eyes were closed and he wasn't just teasing her, he was tasting her, working his lips and his tongue to bring my girl more pleasure. Devouring her so much, that just watching him made me start stroking myself, unwittingly.

"You taste so good... fuck so good." Kace had looked up at us, seeing one of my hands pinch at Ali's nipple while my other hand worked my cock. "I can even taste Cam. The taste of his tongue that still lingers on your pussy. Proof he was here before me."

He growled his last words, and then pushed his tongue inside her, making sure she knew that I may have been there first, but it would be his mouth that lingered on her body long after we were done.

I could live with that.

The three of us were made to be together. Sharing Ali with my best friend, taking turns worshipping her body, getting to watch her every move while he took charge and made it his mission to make her come.

Looking down at Kace again, I saw him doing the same thing I was, stroking himself just enough to ease the pain. He may have been the one with his mouth on Ali, but I knew I could use my mouth as well.

"Kace is out of control," I whispered to her, loud enough that Kace could hear me too. "Stroking himself while he eats you like a fucking meal. I have never seen him come before, baby. See what you do to us? How much we want you?"

"Kace!" She screamed, trying to watch him the way I was as her body took over. Kace had to stop touching himself long enough to keep her legs open and push her through her release.

When she started to come down a little, I couldn't take it anymore and pumped my cock harder. My dry hand was no match for what I imagined Ali's mouth or pussy would feel like, but I was too far gone to shove myself between her lips.

My spine tingled, my knees buckled, and I roared like a goddamn lion as I came all over Ali's chest. Ropes of my cum ran between her tits and it felt like I could keep going forever. Kace straddled her legs, and watched me make a mess of Ali's chest before finishing himself off as well. His eyes locked on hers, and he grunted as his cum mixed with mine, running all over her body. It felt like we owned her.

I knew she owned us.

While Kace and I tried to catch our breath, Ali took a finger to her chest and gently mixed the cum we left on her body. Her hum of satisfaction made me feel like a King, and I looked up to see Kace with a similar expression in his eyes.

When he looked up and caught my eye, I tried to ask him if we were okay. Was all of it okay? His eyes were always easy to read, and I immediately knew he was more than fine. But he also nodded, and I nodded back to let him know that I agreed—we were okay.

He motioned for me to grab Ali and then hopped off the bed toward the bathroom. Ali was limp but I scooped her into my arms and walked her into the bathroom. Kace had started drawing her a bath, so I set her down, standing between us.

Kace took a towel to her chest and wiped our cum away. Then, without warning, she lunged at him and pressed her lips to his. She wrapped her arms around his neck as I stood behind her and ran a hand down her spine.

When she turned around to kiss me, I scooped her back into my arms and lowered her into the warm, bubbly water. We sat near her as she bathed, then each took a shower when she was done. For the entire time, none of us spoke. Words didn't feel necessary. Sweet looks and soft smiles were all we gave, and it felt like more than enough.

Kace and I had both gotten used to sleeping in Ali's bed, with her between us. It wasn't even questioned anymore. We even had preferred sides of her bed. Which was where we were when Ali disappeared back into the bathroom.

"I could get used to this," Kace sighed.

"I think I already am."

"Is this crazy? How good it feels?"

I laughed and shrugged; it probably was crazy. But I didn't care. I had a feeling that night was the beginning of something amazing.

Saturday night, I had to stay in the team hotel, and Kace had a game. It was the first night we had left Ali alone since her ex returned, and I was close to freaking the fuck out.

Ali seemed okay, though, telling us she was fine, and not scared. Mary had agreed to go sit with her and watch Kace's game on TV so she wasn't alone, then Kace would head straight there after the game. Mary looked at us suspiciously when we asked her to go hang out with Ali, but she didn't ask much.

I knew we were being overprotective, and probably irrational, but Alan was still MIA which made him a continued threat. Despite having cops close, and always scouring her apartment area, I felt like we were the only ones that could protect her. It felt like our job, way more important than playing our games.

But that wasn't the way it worked. We had to play.

I watched Kace's game in the bar area of the hotel, hoping that having some of my teammates around would help distract me. But I was annoying the shit out of everyone as I tapped my fingers on the table and begged the pitcher to speed up.

Ali had been looking forward to her time with Mary, so I didn't call her to check in, but I did send a few texts throughout the night. When the game was almost over, a few fangirls found their way to our table, and started asking for pictures and autographs. I politely obliged but was way too anxious, so I got out of there as quickly as possible.

I made it to the lobby, and I thought I was free, but I heard my name being called before the elevator opened. "Cam! Wait! Cam!"

It was one of the fangirls. She had seen me heading to my room and probably wanted me to invite her up—that happened often enough that it no longer shocked me.

The doors to the elevator opened and I climbed in hoping they would close before she got to me, but she put her arm in the way to stop it, right before it closed.

Instead of coming in with me, though, she stood in the doorway and kept the door held open. She huffed a breath out and handed me a piece of paper before stepping back, and letting the doors shut with her on the outside.

The letter had been taped together so I couldn't tell what was inside, but I assumed it was her number. A lot of women really thought by giving me their number I would be like, *"Cool, I will call this chick."*

I didn't play those games.

I shoved the note into my pocket, intent on throwing it away when I got to my room but by the time I walked in and sat on the bed, my phone started to ring and I forgot about it.

Kace.

Relief washed over me knowing that if he was calling, that meant he was out of the locker room and headed to Ali.

"You out?" I answered the phone without any pleasantries.

"Yep, the longest game of my career."

"No shit, I was losing my mind." I heard him shuffle around in his car instead of answering me and after a few seconds, curiosity got the best of me. "What the hell are you doing?"

"Trying to find a note a fan gave me tonight. All taped up and shit. Probably her number so I want to toss it before I get to Ali's. I'd rather not put that shit in her face, ya know?"

"Yeah, the same thing happened to me a few minutes ago. I need to toss it before I—" I pulled the note from my pocket without finishing my thought. It was all taped up, just like Kace's. Coincidence?

"Hello?" Kace interrupted my thoughts.

"Did you open that note?" I asked as I flipped mine through my fingers.

"No, fuck Cam, I'm not kidding, Ali is it for me. I can't even fathom calling some random chick, right now."

"Mine is taped up too..." I trailed off, barely hearing what he had to say after *No*.

I tore the tape off my letter and opened it quickly.

Five million or this goes public.

Attached was a picture of Kace, Ali, and I in bed together. Thank God we were just sleeping but we both have our arms around her and its obvious who we are and that we are sharing the affections of one woman.

It was taken from behind us as we laid in Ali's bed, meaning someone had to have been on her fire escape in the past week that we had been staying the night. There was only a small crack in her thin curtains and the shot was aimed in that exact spot.

I felt rage. Someone—most likely Alan—had been on her fucking fire escape. What would he have done if we hadn't been there? Pictures are nothing compared to what he could have done. We secured the door with new locks, but not the window.

"You there?" Kace finally asked.

"Open your letter," I demanded. I needed to know if his letter was the same as mine.

"Why? What are—"

"Open it," I repeated, my voice not leaving room for him to argue again.

He shuffled with the paper and after a minute, his words confirmed my fear. "What the fuck?"

"Take her to your place tonight. Get her away from her apartment until that fucker is found."

"We need to call the cops again. I'll get her to my place, but we need to tell her about this and call the fucking cops."

Ali was going to feel violated, just like I felt. Another picture of us threatening her once peaceful existence. I was almost scared she would try pushing us away, either to save herself, or to save us. But then again, the new picture wasn't a fan picture. It was intentional stalking, and an invasion of privacy. Not to mention, it made it obvious that the three of us were in some sort of relationship together.

That didn't bother me.

A part of me wanted to parade Ali around, show her off, and tell the world she was mine—and Kace's. I gave zero fucks what the world thought about us being with the same woman.

But that was not how it would go for Ali. She would be the villain—made out to be something she's not, and the target of everyone's backlash. No one would understand. Hell, we barely understood it ourselves. We were just navigating things one day at a time, slowly. But those pictures would make whatever we were trying to build impossible.

"You tell Ali. I'll call the cops," I decided. "I'll tell them you got the same thing and they can meet you at your place if they need to talk. Send me a picture of your note." I wiped a hand down my face, worry dripping off me in waves.

"Yeah, I will. Want me to FaceTime you when I tell Ali?"

I wanted to say yes because I wanted to be a part of that conversation. I needed to have some sort of control and idea over the outcome. But, I trusted Kace to handle it and I had to call the cops. "Just be with her."

"I'll text you and keep you posted. You worry about playing Seattle tomorrow."

"I'm seriously close to pulling a 'Kace' and walking out of this hotel tonight. There is no way I can play with my head not in the game."

"Well, you can't do that. You're gonna have to rest easy knowing she's not alone. I'll be with her all night."

That did make me feel better so I took a deep breath and let out a final sigh. "I know."

"Good. I just parked at Ali's. I'll text you an update later. Let me know what the cops say."

I hung up and immediately dialed the detective that had come to Ali's the night of her attack. He agreed to meet me discreetly in the lobby and I filled him in on the notes. Just as I had anticipated, he wondered about the nature of the picture, but I just shrugged him off with a half-truth: *"She's a very good friend of ours."* He knew I was not being completely honest, but the nature of our relationship wasn't relevant to finding Alan.

After he left, I dragged myself back up to the room and shed my clothes. I needed a shower and sleep, but first, I needed to send Kace a quick update.

I sat on the bed and started to open the text app when my phone started ringing.

Video Call from Ali.

ali

ENTERTAINING MARY WAS INTERESTING. How the guys got her to hang out with me all evening, and not tell her about Alan, was a mystery I didn't question. Since the night he came into my apartment and hurt me, I hadn't wanted to leave. Ironically, I didn't feel safe anywhere but home.

The guys made it too easy on me. I was able to stay put and never leave. But eventually, I had to get back to work, for Mary if not for anything else. She thought I had just been on vacation, and I guess in a way, I had been. Not even 678 knew the real reason I took time off.

I wasn't exactly sure what Cam told them when he called because I hadn't been in the right headspace to care. As the week went on, I forgot to even ask. Now that I was sitting there with Mary, I was curious.

When the baseball game ended, Mary told me she was going to stay until Kace got there. We had watched the game and eaten frozen pizzas, laughed and told stories. The night really was amazing time spent with my only friend. But I was getting tired, Mary was tired, and the zest we had earlier in the evening had worn off when the game ended, so until Kace showed up, we yawned and watched the local news.

Mary never questioned what kind of relationship I had with Cam and Kace, nor did I bring it up. The guys told her they both put themselves out there to me, and based on my reaction to the baseball game, Mary.

It was hard not swooning when Kace went up to bat. When the camera zoomed in on him, or as he took a lead off first base, when he bit his lip. When he dove to catch a line drive, I think I moaned out loud while he dusted the dirt from his uniform. After the game, when they pulled him over for a quick interview, I scooted to the edge of my couch and hung on his every word. Mary had to have seen how bad I had it. It was good Cam wasn't on there too because it probably would have gotten awkward for her.

The lock on the door clicked open and I jumped out of my thoughts. I knew it was Kace because I made sure he and Cam had keys while they were staying with me. But Mary must have figured the same thing since she started sliding her shoes on to leave.

"Honey, I love ya, but since Kace is back, I'm headed to bed," Mary yawned the whole sentence.

"I don't blame you. I'm going to bed, too!"

"Yeah, sure ya are. Good luck getting sleep with that stud nearby," Mary said as Kace stood in the doorway. "Good game tonight, Kace," she added as she passed him to head out the door.

"Thanks, Mary. Let me walk you downstairs."

"The fuck? I have two fucking legs and I'm not so old I need an escort... for fucks sake," Mary lashed at Kace, who just laughed at her.

"Okay, fair enough!" Kace relented as he continued to laugh. "Thanks for keeping my girl company tonight."

Mary winked at him as she turned to leave but before closing the door, I heard her say, "Cam said the same thing."

Kace grabbed a few slices of pizza, asked me about my night, but he never changed his clothes, took his shoes off, or even leaned back to relax.

He was tense and I wanted to ask him what was wrong, but I didn't want to seem pushy. Maybe he was just tired, and that was how he dealt. We were still getting to know each other, and I didn't know his cues or what he needed. I wanted to learn, though, so I made sure he knew I was there for him.

Crawling into his lap and straddling him, I leaned in and rubbed my nose against his while my hands rubbed the back of his neck. "You okay?" I whispered.

He shook his head *'no'* as I continued rubbing my hands on him. I gently kissed his lips, and then leaned back to look him in the eyes, not saying anything else. It was his turn to talk, to tell me what he needed.

So, I waited.

And waited.

His eyes focused on mine, his hands rubbed my backside, and he bit that damn lip again—the same way he did on TV.

Finally, he spoke. "I need to tell you something, and I need to show you something. But I need to know you are going to be okay when I do."

I leaned back, nervous.

"Shit, I suck at this," he groaned.

"You can't do this, can you?" I was convinced that he had finally come to his senses and decided he couldn't be with me while Cam was, as well. It was the only thing that seemed to ignite fear in me. After being so intimate the night before after what I had asked them to do, I shouldn't have been shocked.

After all, Kace was always the wildcard. He was the one that couldn't do *relationships*. How could I ask him to finally do one and include Cam? Even if it was their idea, it was too much.

Kace seemed confused about what I was asking, so as tears fell from my eyes, I tried to tell him it was okay. "It's been a weird week and now that everything is settling down, it's all coming to light. Sharing a relationship, no matter how close you two are, is not easy. Especially with all my additional baggage. You two signed up to be boyfriends, not bodyguards." I wanted to say more, but I was choking up and I didn't want him to feel bad.

Kace stopped my tears in an instant, though, by taking my face in his hands and kissing me, hard. He invaded me. A kiss so passionate, I forgot why I was upset. Instead, I got so turned on, I subconsciously started moving on his lap, trying to find any type of friction I could.

When he pulled away, he smiled, knowing his kisses made me needy.

"Baby girl," Kace started, shaking his head softly while still holding my face in his hands. "I'm not going anywhere. Apart from the circumstances with your ex, this has been the best week of my life. I'm here, Cam and I both are in this. Don't. Worry. About. That." He punctuated each word with a kiss to my lips.

"Then what's wrong?"

"Here." He handed me a note that looked like it had been taped up but was ripped down the side. I unfolded it and gasped, dropping the image, and the note, as my hands started shaking. Kace took my hands in his and tried to calm me down. He filled me in on Cam getting the same thing, both being handed to them by a random fangirl. Cam was calling the cops. Kace was taking me to his place.

I didn't even put up a fight. I packed a bag and was ready to go within minutes. I didn't feel safe, I felt violated. Alan had been on my fire escape while the three of us laid in my bed. Who knows what else he saw, or had pictures of?

"Just a few nights," Kace had said, knowing how much I loved being in my grandma's apartment.

We locked up as tight as we could and drove the short distance to Kace's penthouse. The underground parking was secure, the building was secure, and Kace's floor wasn't even accessible without a special key for a private elevator. Not to mention we were on the 64th floor—seemed unlikely Alan would be outside the windows taking pictures that high up.

As I walked inside and took in my surroundings, I felt better, lighter.

Kace's place was huge. His kitchen was the size of my entire apartment. It was an open space, with leather couches, and huge windows along the far wall. He showed me the two extra bedrooms—one being the one Cam always slept in when he stayed over. He also had a gym and a games room. There was a loft that was fairly empty, but had a few oversized chairs, and more windows. I could picture myself working up there in the light and clean space.

Finally, he walked me into his room. "You're staying in here with me."

Once I was settled in, I climbed into Kace's huge bed. He took a shower, then walked into the room with nothing on but his athletic shorts, and I practically panted. I was never going to get tired of seeing his body. The tattoos down his arms and chest. The muscles and abs. The way his arms flexed every time he moved them. I had seen him like that every night that week— sometimes with even less. I knew what he looked like, but I still got butterflies thinking of all of him being mine.

When he climbed in the bed next to me, he took me by surprise when he asked, "You wanna call Cam?"

Hell yeah, I did. But I still wasn't sure what was appropriate between them. *How did I navigate this?* Kace and I were alone, but Cam never left my mind. *Was that okay?*

I nodded and grabbed my phone, but hesitated before dialing. "Is this weird for you?"

"No, he and I always FaceTime."

"You know what I mean," I laughed, then rolled my eyes.

"No baby," he tucked me under his arm, "it's not weird. Hell, I wanna call him, too."

I pressed call on my phone and it didn't take long before it started connecting to Cam. I wondered what he would think when he answered and saw me in bed with Kace, while he was across town.

"Thank God," Cam answered with relief. "I was worried he wouldn't get you to leave your place."

"I don't want to be there right now."

"She didn't put up a fight," Kace added.

Cam ran a hand through his hair, his bicep flexing when he did. "I spoke with the detective. They think he paid the girls to deliver the notes, but that they weren't involved. Technically, he said someone paid the girls, didn't say Alan, but whatever."

"They were supposed to be outside her place keeping an eye out for him. What the hell is their deal?" Kace asked with anger.

"I'm so sorry," I cried. "This isn't something we should have to be dealing with. You two have become nothing more than my babysitters."

"Hey," Kace laughed. "I'd like to think we've done more than babysit you."

I started to blush and turn my head but Cam spoke. "Ali, he never would have found you if you weren't with two guys who live in the public eye. We are the ones that should be saying sorry."

"We weren't together then."

Kace rolled his eyes and laughed. "Baby, we've been with you since the moment we laid eyes on you."

I swallowed, silently agreeing how true that statement was. It felt like the first night we saw each other was the moment we were together. "I miss you tonight, Cam."

"Miss you too."

"I thought, for a second, that Kace was ending this tonight. He came in so out of it, and I knew something was wrong."

"Your first thought was that?" Cam asked.

I shrugged.

"Never," Kace leaned in to kiss me on the side of the head.

Cam laid back on the bed and used his free arm to prop himself up. The image made me want him; everything made me want him. All I could think about was how much I wanted them. There I was, being threatened by Alan and his little games, and all I could think about was sex.

"What are you thinking right now, Angel?"

Oh he knew, he definitely knew. Even through the screen he could see where my mind had gone. I tried to hide against Kace's chest, but he stopped me and tilted my lips up. He kissed me twice, two short pecks, then almost made me drop my phone as his third kiss consumed me.

"You need out of your head?" Cam moaned. "I bet Kace can do that for you."

I pulled away from Kace and looked back at the phone. "Maybe I need out of my head, or maybe it's been two years since I last had sex and I suddenly find myself with two boyfriends. Both being sexier than any one man should be, and unwilling to touch me in case I break. I'm only human, ya know?"

Cam laughed while Kace started kissing my neck. I tilted my head to give him better access and closed my eyes for a second, just to soak it all in.

"You're telling me it's been two years?" Cam asked.

Our eyes connected and I realized his arm was no longer behind his head. I didn't want to have to lay it out for him, but I wanted him to know exactly what I meant. "Apart from last night, it's been *two* years."

Cam's huff told me he connected the dots, and the way Kace bit at me said he did as well. Alan was the last person I was with and I wanted to forget that part of my life.

"Kace?" Cam moaned. Kace took his mouth away from me and looked at Cam through the screen. "Wipe her memory away."

"Wanna watch?"

I whimpered and almost dropped the phone again.

"Fuck yeah. I want to see her face when you make her come."

I realized Cam was unabashedly stroking himself below the screen.

Kace's voice came into my ear, as he tugged at my tank top, but my eyes didn't leave Cam's face. "Hold the phone up for Cam. Let him see you."

I held it up higher so Cam could see Kace pulling my top down below my breasts. They were being pushed up and together by the collar of my shirt. Cam moaned again and stroked faster. Kace moved down my body and spread my legs, taking my shorts and panties off in one swift motion. When I looked down at him, he stopped moving and pointed at the phone. "Eyes on Cam."

I looked back at Cam and told him what I needed. "Lower the camera."

He did and I felt myself get wetter when I saw his shorts pushed down just far enough to release his cock from the waistband. He was slowly stroking himself and biting his lip.

Kace's mouth found my clit and I almost came on the spot, making him back away with a tsk. "This one's for Cam, Baby girl. You're not coming until he does."

Watching Cam stroke himself was torture with Kace in charge of my pleasure. He was gently licking and nipping at me, causing just enough shocks to make me moan but not enough to push me too far.

When Cam tilted his head back, I was sure he was close. I begged Kace to take me over the edge. "Please, Kace, please!"

"Only when he says so," Kace growled.

"Please!" I cried.

I grabbed onto his hair and pushed myself against him. I almost threw the phone to use two hands, but I didn't want to miss a second of watching Cam. His eyes were open, his mouth parted. He scrunched his forehead just a little and started mumbling profanity.

"Let her come, Kace. I can't—" His words were cut off by my scream as Kace heeded Cam's request and used his tongue to make my body explode. Cam's cum was all over his stomach. I wanted to touch it, taste it.

When I was able to focus again, I looked at Kace and saw his mouth was glistening. He looked pleased with himself, and I wanted to kiss the smirk off his face. Cam who had covered his eyes with his arm, was still trying to calm himself down.

"I miss you, Cam."

He laughed and uncovered his eyes to look at me. "Miss you too, baby. Now I definitely have to take a shower, and sleep."

"See you tomorrow?"

"Of course," He gave me a sweet smile, then spoke louder. "Take care of my girl, Kace."

Kace answered by licking my sensitive clit again and making me shudder, which was a good enough answer for Cam.

We hung up and I wanted to cry. How did I become attached so fast?

Kace didn't let me wallow. He kissed his way up my body and took my top off over my head, leaving me completely naked. Reaching over me, he turned off the light beside the bed, and pulled me against him. His hands roamed my body as his kisses landed everywhere he could reach.

"I need you, Kace." He propped himself over top of me with one arm, and let his free hand slide lower. He ran his fingers between my legs, making sure I was ready, and wasted no time lowering himself, sliding into me gently.

"Tell me if I hurt you."

It wasn't wild or drawn out. No crude or lascivious acts.

He hovered over me, thrusted in and out of me, while staring into my eyes. He kissed me with reverence. A part of me wanted to see how much of a savage Kace was capable of being in bed, but in that moment, he gave me exactly what I needed—intimate, impassioned, and downright romantic.

It didn't feel like just sex.

It felt like a declaration.

kace

I WAS ADDING to my list of firsts by the second.

First relationship. Check.

First time having a woman in my apartment. Check.

First time sharing my bed. Check.

First time making love. Check.

The first time getting a woman off while she video chatted with Cam. Double-check.

In the past week, so much had changed. Not just in my life, but inside me. The playoffs started in two weeks, and all I cared about was ensuring Ali was safe and happy.

She was in my arms, naked, with a smile on her sleeping face. I hadn't wasted any time getting inside of her. There wasn't a lot of need for pretense. We were both desperate for each other, and after making her come for Cam, I knew she wouldn't be able to take too much more. But she gave me exactly what I needed when she came as I spilled inside of her.

We never spoke another word, just fell asleep in each other's arms.

"Good morning," I whispered to ease her awake.

"Mmmm, good morning." She blinked her eyes open and

looked up at me, a smile still on her face and a look of content-ment in all her features.

"Sleep well?" I tucked the stray hair from her face and kissed her cheek, she pushed her tits into my chest.

"Better than I have in years. Do you think Cam will be mad?"

I took my focus from her tits, and back to her face, at the abrupt question. "Why would he be mad?"

"Were we supposed to wait on him?" She flushed with embar-rassment. "I mean, shit, there's no handbook for this."

I couldn't help but laugh, she was so cute when she was nervous about things I could control. "Baby, Cam knew exactly what was happening here last night. Hell, I let him watch half of it."

Honestly, I don't think I had ever been as turned on as I was last night, knowing Cam was watching her face and getting himself off.

"I just wish I didn't have to worry every time I was with one of you." She buried her face in my chest, hiding as she spoke.

"You don't," I said simply as I rubbed her back. "Cam and I know the score, Ali. We have said it before, and I'll say it again. You can have us however you want us. But I am glad I got to spend last night alone with you. I'm glad I got the chance to cherish you alone."

That brought a smile to her face, and she looked into my eyes, "Me too."

She brought herself over top of me, and straddled my waist, the sheet falling as she moved. She started grinding down on my cock as I threaded my hands into her hair. I had been hard since I woke up, but her climbing on top of me sealed the deal.

Pushing up from my waist, I warned her I was about to be inside her again. She lifted slightly on her knees, making it easier on me, and I slid between her folds. Both of us looked between our bodies and watched as we connected, gasping from how good it felt.

Her tits hung in my face, so I took one of them in my mouth, massaging the other with my hand as she started moving. She was riding and rubbing me, using me however she wanted, and I let her.

But I knew if I let her keep going too much longer, I was going to finish before I'd even had a chance to start. I lifted her off me and flipped her over, then positioned myself behind her. On her knees, I pulled her ass up to me and made my way back inside her. Harder. Quicker. Rougher than the night before.

Our first time, we made love. I was slow, sensitive, steady, and careful not to hurt her. That wasn't the case anymore. I was rabid, reckless. I kept a menacing rhythm while I reached my hand around to rub her clit, using my other hand to pull her hair, letting her know I was in control. I was getting off on testing her trust in me. After everything she had gone through, I knew she was getting tired of being treated so delicately, but to what extent? I wanted to push just a little, and see how far she'd let me take her.

She gave as good as she got, and before long, she was coming, screaming my name so loud I actually wondered if my housekeeper had already come in for the day and could hear us. Not that I cared. I gritted my teeth and clenched my jaw, making her scream one more time as I came inside her.

We both collapsed onto the bed, breathing hard and shuddering in the aftershocks of pleasure. Then she turned over to me and smiled. "I needed that."

"Me too."

I climbed from the bed with a buzz that I was sure was better than any drug, and carried her to my shower. I cleaned her up, then promised her breakfast while she got dressed. My housekeeper hadn't got in yet, so I was rummaging in the kitchen looking for things that I had no idea where to find. Ali came in dressed in holey jeans and a tank top. Her hair was still wet and hanging down her back.

"Let's go to Cam's game." That was a suggestion I didn't see coming. "I'm so tired of being trapped inside. What kind of trouble could Alan cause in such a big place, and with you with me?"

I thought about it for a second. I didn't want to take any risks, but at the same time, I wasn't holding her hostage. She was free to come and go as she pleased—I just knew I would panic if she left alone. So, she had a point, why not go?

"Let's do it. We can surprise him."

"Yes! We can be his groupies!" she squealed.

The game was an afternoon game, so we ate breakfast, and didn't have to wait long to get ready and head out. I wanted to take her to the box seats with Cam's family, but she insisted on the same seats we had before. She didn't want to meet Cam's family, for one—not without him. She also loved being close to the field.

I didn't argue, but since we were surprising Cam, I had to call around a bit to secure Cam's tickets without him knowing.

Ali wore her Nichols jersey and the same holey jeans she had on earlier. She was more relaxed than her last game, but kept telling me over and over that if Cam got hurt, she was going to cry. She had watched the last couple of games on TV, so she knew how it was going to go.

She still didn't like it.

When the Jets ran out of the tunnel and took the field, she cheered loudly for Cam.

The plan was for us to yell for Cam as loudly as we could until he heard us, but that seemed impossible because the noise level was so high. He was throwing with the backup quarterback near the sidelines, his helmet off so I nudged Ali, letting her know that was our best chance.

We cupped our hands, laughed, and started yelling. "Cam!" He didn't even flinch. We tried ten more times, but he never looked our way. I could barely stop laughing long enough to try again. I knew almost everyone on that field personally. I knew I could get the attention of anyone, and they would get Cam's attention for us. But this game we were playing was way too much fun.

With one last effort, Ali changed things up, "Nick!"

I was bent over, laughing harder. She was laughing at herself, but the joke was on us because that caught Cam's attention, and he turned our way.

I don't think I had ever seen him smile as big as he did when he realized we were there. He dropped the ball without an explanation, and jogged to the edge of the field, as close as he could get to us. There was still a ten foot drop from our seats, but Ali leaned over as far as she could, and reached for Cam's outstretched hand, as I held her other hand.

"Good luck!" she told him.

He kissed her hand and winked, not saying a word, then backed away and grabbed his helmet. He was switching back into game-mode.

I knew we were going to end up in random pictures again. Ali knew it too. Especially after getting Cam's attention and him coming to us. The cameras followed him everywhere in that stadium. So, we spent the whole game making sure everyone knew we were friends, and that was it. I was itching to touch and kiss my girl again.

The lead was slim, so they kept Cam in the game well into the fourth quarter. With four yards to go on a third down, they called for a quarterback draw where Cam ran the ball up the middle himself instead of handing it off. Once he declared himself a runner, though, the defense saw blood. He made the first down but was smashed between two defenders who probably had wet dreams about taking out the best quarterback in the league.

Ali gasped, and when Cam didn't get up, she panicked. I waited two more minutes until the trainers helped Cam off the field, and grabbed Ali's hand to lead her up the stadium stairs. We ran down the corridor, took the stairs down two levels, and pushed through the door to the family waiting area, looking for someone who could get us in to see Cam. I knew Cam was fine. He always got shaken up, but showing Ali that Cam was okay felt important.

It paid to be me, sometimes, because the first person we came across opened the locker room, and we made our way in. I knew the locker room well and led Ali through double doors at the end of a row of lockers where I knew they would have taken Cam. He was lying on the medical table, surrounded by team trainers, when they heard us come in.

"That is gonna leave a bruise, Boss," one of the trainers said as we approached.

"Cam!" Ali cried.

He turned to see her approach and sat up, wincing a little from the movement. I could tell Ali wanted to throw herself into his arms, but she refrained, afraid she would hurt him.

"Hey, Angel!" He pulled her in for a hug and buried his face into her neck. I nodded to the trainers for them to get lost. When it came to Cam, I had that kind of power, and they knew it.

Once they were out the door, Cam pulled Ali into a kiss. He was still wearing his shoulder pads and uniform, but that didn't stop him from inching her even closer to him.

Ali began to fall into Cam's kiss but then pulled back quickly. "Are you hurt?"

"Are you worried about me?"

She hit his good shoulder but winced, the pad stinging her hand. "Yes, I was worried. So was Kace!"

I started shaking my head. I was never worried; I just knew Ali was. I kissed her stinging hand and told her as much. I wanted to show her how it worked with Cam, where they took him, and what went on down there.

And honestly, I wanted to get away from the crowd so I could kiss her myself. I inched up behind her and turned her head my way, finding her lips for a minute.

"I needed that," I said as I backed away, mimicking her words from my bed that morning.

Cam motioned for me to help him get his pads off. Injury or not, that was a two-man job, and I had pulled him out of his pads a million times.

As I did, Ali groaned, "I think I need therapy. You guys are turning me into someone I barely know." She shook her head and bit her lip. "Kace Jackson undressing Cam Nichols is the sexiest thing I have ever seen."

Cam stood up, his football pants still on but his jersey and pads discarded. He strode over to Ali and leaned down so they were face to face.

"You mean to tell me you spent all night in Kace's bed, and *him* undressing *me* is the sexiest thing you've ever seen?" He tsked like he was disappointed.

"I bet every woman in this world would kill to be me right now, Cam. This is all very heady," she joked. Or maybe it wasn't a joke. She looked a little pained at the thought, which was why we tried keeping *us* quiet in the media. But she was blushing again, holding strong with her raillery.

Cam closed the small gap between them and kissed her. She wrapped her arms around his bare shoulders, and he picked her up, wrapping her legs around his hips.

Unfortunately, Cam had taken a beating on the field and groaned from the pain that lifting Ali caused in his ribs. She quickly responded and jumped from his arms. "Oh my God!"

Cam being Cam, he laughed it off. I knew he would rather weather the pain than not have Ali in his arms, but the trainers were inching back into the room. He needed precautionary X-rays and to be wrapped for compression. So, he let her back away and motioned for them to come back into the room.

cam

IT HAD BEEN a week since Alan sent the note, and the cops still had no idea where he was. I knew as time went on, and we didn't pay up, there was a chance he would get more aggressive, but the detective told us it wasn't a good idea.

I could reason that he was right, but I was starting to doubt the police even cared. It was like they were playing a game, and everything somehow came back to Kace and me. We weren't being truthful enough, as far as they were concerned, and that was true, we weren't, but they didn't need to know the nature of our relationship with Ali to find Alan.

The pictures.

Kace and I sat on his balcony while Ali was working and talked about how much those pictures would harm us if they found their way online. We couldn't think of an issue big enough to make us care. Except one.

Ali would be a target. Not just by Alan, but by everyone that chose to judge her, or attack her out of spite and jealousy.

She said it herself, and even though it sounded egotistical, it was true, any woman would kill to be her. I didn't care if the world knew how Kace and I carried on in our private lives, we signed up for that when we became part of the public eye. But Ali didn't, and being with us shouldn't force her to face the scrutiny of the world.

Ali had returned to working at 678 after the week was up. Kace and I couldn't be with her the whole time, it was impossible. But she wouldn't risk Mary's job anymore, now that she was better. She had to go back.

On top of making sure the cops were always close, Kace and I greased every palm of every bodyguard and bouncer there was at 678, encouraging them to keep an eye on her as well. Even when they gave us a weird look, we added another hundred and told them that we insisted.

We had no shame when it came to keeping her safe.

Ali thought we were insane, but she didn't stop us. Except when we suggested hiring her a personal bodyguard. She wasn't having any part of that. Though she did agree to taking a private car service to and from work, with a driver we had hired before and trusted.

At night, we were all still staying at Kace's penthouse, with Ali in bed between us. Had I always known Kace's bed was so comfortable, I would have told him to scoot the fuck over years ago, instead of taking his guestroom when I stayed over. He laughed when I told him as much, but suggested it was just because Ali was there. He may have been right.

My place was in John's Creek, a suburb, and not close enough to 678. I had gone home a few times to grab clothes, and things I needed, but I only had interest in sleeping where Ali slept.

The Friday following my brutal exit from the game, Kace left for few games out of town, and I was preparing to leave Saturday for the same reason. We were both nervous about leaving Ali, but we had to trust that we had put enough measures in place to ensure she was safe. She even agreed to stay at Kace's apartment without us there.

With it being just her and me on Friday though, I wanted to

surprise her with something different. Ali had called and told me she was getting cut from the bar at nine pm, wondering if I would be at Kace's when she got there. I told her I would be, but then called the car service and canceled her ride, wanting to surprise her myself.

I pulled up right at nine and saw her eyes searching for the black luxury car that was supposed to pick her up. Fear was in her eyes as she stood alone and exposed in a place where Alan could easily approach her, and knew to look for her.

I hopped out of the car and waved, not caring that I had traffic backing up behind me. Relief flooded her face when she saw me and a smile replaced the tension and fear.

With a skip in her step, she bounded toward my car and hopped in. Before she buckled up, she leaned across the console and kissed my cheek. "This is a surprise!"

"Decided to change things up a bit. I missed you too much to hang around waiting at Kace's."

"What about the car?"

"I canceled it. I have a surprise for you."

"Yeah? Tell me, tell me."

It wasn't the grandest surprise ever, but it was a surprise nonetheless, so I shook my head *no* with a smirk on my face.

Small conversations filled the car as we drove toward the outskirts of Atlanta. We talked about things like how my practice went, and how work went for her, plus how my bruised ribs were doing.

I knew when my phone starting ringing it was Kace, so I answered while Ali stayed quiet as a mouse.

"Hello."

"Hey," Kace's tired voice filled the car, causing Ali to perk up. "God tonight's game was brutal. I got hit by a pitch right on my fucking arm. Stung like a mother fucker."

"Welcome to the bruise-brigade," I joked dryly, referring to the fact that we were all healing. "Who was on the hill?"

"Johnson. He's such a fucking tool. He either hits me with a pitch, or I take him over the fence. I guess I should expect it by now." *I hated that guy.* "Look, I just wanted to check in really quick. I wanna go call my girl before I pass out. Everything good there?"

"Yeah. Ali actually got off early, so I planned a little surprise for her."

"Nice. I won't call her then; just tell her I miss her."

"She can hear you."

Ali giggled and sighed. "Miss you too."

"Ah… love that sweet voice." Kace was instantly in a better mood. He took a minute to ask her about work, just like I had, but I cut in when I knew I was closing in on my location.

"I have a surprise for Ali in four minutes. Can she call you back in seven?"

"You two enjoy the night. I'm going to soak in ice and go to bed."

"Okay man."

"Call me in the morning!" Ali added.

"Night baby, I will."

Ali took a deep breath after the call ended, catching my attention as I put my blinker on to turn down a neighborhood street. "Everything okay?"

"Of course. I just can't believe how easy you two make this on me. Kace seemed happy."

"He is." I was never going to make her feel bad for how she felt, but I really couldn't wait until her insecurities over Kace and me were gone. We were unusual, I got it. Hell, I was living it. But the only thing we could do was just prove to her, over and over, that we were okay. We would keep reminding her every chance we got if that was what it took.

The gate opened to my multi-million-dollar home and we made our way down the driveway. There was a winding road that was surrounded by trees, and led to a clearing where the house sat.

The house was big without being overly ostentatious. The lawn was perfectly landscaped with a circle drive taking up most of the front yard area. Five steps led up to huge double doors, and a garage sat off to the side.

"This is your house?"

"This is Home Sweet Home." I pulled around the circle drive and stopped directly in front of the doors. I wasted no time getting to Ali's side of the car and opening her door, taking her hand to lead her toward the house.

"Wow! You and Kace are like night and day." She was right. In some ways, we were complete opposites.

"There are more garages around back, a guest house to the side over that way," I pointed into the woods to the right, then motioned for her to walk up the steps. "And this is the door."

I rarely entered through the front, opting for the garage entrance. But I wanted to bring Ali in the first time through the front since I was showing her my home, and showing her more about myself.

Pushing the door open, I escorted her through the foyer and into the living room. The house was homey with pictures of my family, soft leather couches in front of the fireplace, and a TV above it in the main room. It was big, but nothing was overdone. I liked using my home for living, and since it was just me, I never worried about how it looked to anyone else but me.

But I wondered what it told Ali about me.

"Cam, this is amazing!" Ali was looking everywhere, but a wall of pictures caught her eye and she walked over to them. "Is this you and Kace?"

"Uh, yeah," I said, sheepishly rubbing my neck and feeling kind of embarrassed about the display of me and my best friend. Pictures of us playing baseball, and swimming in the lake. More of high school, and on the day I was drafted to the NFL, Kace being right there by my side.

Ali stayed silent as she looked at all the pictures and I glanced at her face to see if I could read what she was thinking. All I saw was a lone tear falling down her face.

"What's wrong?"

"Oh my gosh, nothing." She laughed at herself and waved me off. "This just puts context to what you two have told me, about growing up together, and how close you two are."

I slid my arms around her waist from behind and looked at the pictures with her. "Yeah, these are some of my best times. All of them having Kace right there with me." I turned her to me and brushed my thumb over her cheek then pecked her lips. "Some things never change."

I spent the next ten minutes showing her around—the extra rooms, the kitchen, and the gym. I showed her the pool, the office, and where Kace usually stayed when he came out here. Then finally, we made our way to my room.

Like the rest of the house, there wasn't too much going on in there. Very plain and manly. A bed with black sheets and a thin blanket, a dresser, a chair, and a sliding door that led to a balcony overlooking the backyard. But having Ali in that space made it light up.

She ran her hands over my dresser as she made her way to the windows. I stayed by the door, watching her every move.

After another minute, she turned to me with that smile I loved so much. The one that said she was about to say, or ask, something that would probably embarrass her, but she was going to do it anyway.

"How're your ribs?" She turned a slight shade of red and bit her bottom lip. I knew what she was asking, and it was the exact reason we went to my bedroom that night.

I wanted her so bad. I needed her. She had been too easy with me all week, nursing my bruises the way I had hers the previous week. I told her a million times that I was fine, that it happened all the time. But she was in a constant state of worry.

So, I let her dote and coddle me. I settled for kissing her and tucking her safely between me and Kace for the night. But it was just us now. And as much as I loved having Kace around, it was my turn to show Ali exactly how I was feeling.

In my bed.

Without answering her, I closed the distance between us in a few strides, and pulled her to me. My mouth found hers and she melted into my hold.

Within seconds, we both got ravenous; tearing at each other's clothes while keeping our lips firmly against each other. I backed up toward my bed and stopped when my legs hit the side.

Ali had started undoing my jeans and working them down my legs, and once I was in my boxers, I used every finger I had to peel the shorts off her body as fast as I could.

It wasn't how I pictured things going. I wanted to draw her a bath, fix her some dinner, and make love when we made our way to bed.

That wasn't happening.

At least not yet.

I was getting inside her before we did another damn thing.

When I had her fully naked, I sunk down to my knees. I knew how she tasted, and I wanted more, so I spread her legs and placed her hands on my shoulders to keep her steady. With one quick peek up at her eyes, I ran my tongue between her folds, reveling in the sounds and motions she made as I did.

I kept at it for a bit longer, driving her to the edge of an orgasm and then stopping. But in doing so, I got wild, losing all sense of control, and I snapped.

I lifted her off the floor, threw her to my bed, and was inside of her before I even got my boxers all the way off. Both of us cried out in pleasure, and it took one full thrust inside her for her to fall apart. She was spasming around me and testing every level of willpower I had not to come as well.

Once she came down, I gathered my control and pushed again, hard, my eyes on her eyes, and my hands on her hips. There wasn't too much romance going on. My jaw was locked and my body hard as I kept my pace. It was all I could do. The relief of being with her—in her—was too much.

I tried loosening my arms on her hips, but she protested and urged me to grip tighter. "Harder, Cam. Harder."

Relief spread through my body at her words. She was asking for the one thing I knew I could give her. I held tight and pounded into her, hard enough I thought I may hurt her, until once again, she came. Her eyes rolled back in her head, and she took hold of my wrists as her body shook in pleasure with her breathing going hard and choppy.

Watching her come was the best thing I had ever seen, and that was coming from a man who had won three Super Bowls. I would trade that Lombardi trophy to watch Ali come any day.

All three of them.

I finally allowed myself my own release—roaring like a goddamn animal. The sensation in my legs and tingles down my back seemed to last forever. My body was stiff, and I could feel blood pumping in every vein I had.

Ali watched as I came inside her, still holding onto my wrists. I could feel her squeezing, encouraging me to keep going, but I was drained. I could have fallen on top of Ali and slept for days, but I also wanted to take care of my girl.

Staying inside of her, I leaned onto my elbows so I was closer to her, and kissed her. Then I scooped her up, staying inside of her while I walked us to the shower. The cold water wasn't enough to tamp down the need we had for more.

With my cum running down her leg, my cock hardened again and I pushed her against the cold tile. As I lifted one of her legs over my hip and lined myself back up to her, I finally answered her question.

"My ribs are fine, baby."

I pushed back inside of her, testing how much she could take from me after everything she had been through. I knew Kace had already fucked her, but could she really handle us both?

"Cam," she moaned.

"That's my girl," I praised. Her pussy started squeezing me and she was already about to come again. "Let go."

The echo of her moans in the shower was like having surround sound. I was going to fuck her in that shower every chance I got.

Once again, I filled her up, thinking my orgasm would never end. I had never felt like that. It had never been like that. Even knowing Kace and I shared her, I would never be able to put my dick near another woman. For me, it would always be her.

ali

THE DAYS WENT by in a flash and the guys and I had settled into a comfortable new routine. Both of them were in full-on game mode—playing, traveling, and practicing—but still found time to be with me. They hated leaving me alone, which I rarely was, but I refused to be their babysitting obligation. I returned to my apartment on nights they were both gone because it was comfortable for me, and I enjoyed being home despite Alan still being out there.

To be honest, it had become almost easy to forget Alan even existed—again. Time had marched forward, and though I called the detective every few days, nothing ever turned up. There were also no pictures released, or even new threats made. It was almost as if they weren't bothering to look for Alan.

The pictures Alan threatened me with were something I gave an incredible amount of thought to. How would it affect me if the whole world knew about my relationship with both Kace and Cam? How would it affect them?

They didn't seem to care, or mind, but living in the spotlight was hard enough. Adding in a complicated relationship was too much, and it was too soon. Would it push them away from me?

I was getting the gist of what it meant to be with Cam, or Kace. Now that I knew them, I saw them everywhere. They had commercials, billboards, and were all over the news. Every sports channel and sports media outlet hung on their every word. They were Gods among men in their sports. It made more sense why they had seemed so dumbfounded that I didn't know who they were in the beginning.

How had I never seen them before? Or maybe I had and, I just hadn't paid enough attention.

On top of that, the media interest in them was far from just being sports related. One channel had an entire breakdown of a look Kace gave a tennis star four months prior when they both attended the same charity event. Kace told me he didn't even notice her; the angle of the shot was just right so the world over-analyzed it. Everything was under a microscope of obsession.

That was the main reason we made no attempts at public displays of affection. Unless I was at a game, we weren't even seen together. There were two pictures of me swirling on the internet, though. One of Cam consoling me at 678—the one Alan had shown me—and one of Cam kissing my hand before his game.

None were with Kace, which made any small rumors only about Cam and me. And those rumors had very little fuel since the guys shrugged the commentary off, and refocused it on their game.

After each first night alone with them, I think I fell for them—hard. After each night alone to myself since then, I missed them so incredibly much that tears sprang into my eyes.

Not one more than the other, either.

Both of them.

And still, they didn't seem fazed.

While they watched Thursday night football, I laid my head in Kace's lap and my feet in Cam's lap, stretched across my couch listening to them talk about sports. I was comfortable and felt safe, content.

It was my new normal.

When half time started, I sat up between them, suddenly brave and resolute. I climbed into Cam's lap and started kissing him, letting him know that while I appreciated their love of football, I needed them.

Cam responded instantly, grabbing my hips, and holding me tight. He pulled back just enough to ask, "You need something, Baby?"

I nodded with my forehead pressed to his then tilted my head a little to look at Kace. He was biting his lip, watching me on top of his best friend, looking like he was ready to enjoy the show. That look would have made me self-conscious before, but I felt empowered by them.

I kept my eyes on Kace as I pulled the straps of my cami off my shoulders, and exposed my breasts for Cam. He latched on, sucking and teasing me as I continued to keep my eyes on Kace. He stayed still, a small smile on his face, and his fingers resting against his cheek acting casual.

When I started grinding on top of Cam, Kace flinched a little, and I could tell he was debating on getting up and pulling me off Cam to play with me himself. He didn't, though. He watched and waited as I turned my attention back to Cam.

I leaned into his ear and kept my voice low enough that only he could hear me. "I want him to watch us."

Cam groaned, turned on by my words. He picked me up and carried me to the bed, landing on top of me and made quick work of taking the rest of my clothes off. He rose to his knees and took his shirt off before unbuckling his jeans and pulling his cock out. "Tell me again what you just asked for. Say it louder."

I blushed a little, but stayed on track. "I said I want him to watch."

Cam looked back to where Kace was still sitting on the couch, and made sure he heard what I said. Kace was still watching us, staying quiet and still, like a spectator watching a movie. He looked casual and unbothered, but I saw his chest heaving and the need in his eyes.

"If you want him to watch, let's make sure he can see." He picked me up once again and pushed me against the wall where my curtain for my bed hung. It was just even with the couch, and over Cam's shoulder, I could see Kace looking at us.

I started licking Cam's neck, teasing Kace as we held eye contact. Cam didn't bother with his jeans any more than he had. They were low enough, and when he lined himself up to my core, he drove into me hard and quickly, pinning me between himself and the wall.

"Eyes on Kace," Cam moaned. "Let him see how much fun we have together."

Kace was no longer smirking or looking relaxed; he was on the edge of the couch, barely even sitting. His forearms were resting on his knees and he was squeezing his fists together to contain the almost angry look on his face.

Maybe I was twisted, playing my own sick game and testing their friendship more than I should have. But I couldn't be coy around them anymore when we were all together.

With my eyes on Kace, and Cam driving into me, bringing me close to coming, Kace unbuckled his jeans and pulled his cock out. He leaned back and stroked as he watched, biting his lip, but with an expression I still couldn't read. We were his own personal porn.

"Cam making you feel good?" His voice was raspy and sexy.

I tried to answer, but all that came out was a deep moan of pleasure.

Kace stood and walked toward us, closing in behind Cam, who wasn't fazed at all by his close proximity. Cam just kept pumping his hips while he palmed my tits and sucked on my neck. Kace reached over Cam's shoulder and ran his thumb along my bottom lip. "You look so good when he fucks you like this."

Cam lifted his head from my neck and looked at me, tilting his head a little as he watched me. "Tell him what you want," he demanded. "You get us however you want us, remember?"

Kace nodded as Cam leaned in to kiss me again. Kace's thumb was still on my lip and stayed between our mouths as we kissed. When Cam pulled back, Kace brought his thumb to his own mouth and licked our kiss from his thumb.

"I want you next, Kace," I finally said. "I want you to take your clothes off while Cam fucks me."

Kace backed up just a little and stripped his shirt off, then his pants, becoming completely naked behind Cam. He waited like he was in line for a ride at the fair, getting more and more excited the closer he got to his turn.

I couldn't take it anymore. I was so turned on that I came hard, screaming and squeezing Cam's cock as he slid in and out of me.

"Oh fuck, you feel so good. Squeezing me so fucking tight." Cam moaned as he came with me, jerking his body and trying to stay on his feet as he slowed down.

When he pulled completely out of me, he turned me around to face the wall and placed my hands high above my head. He backed away, making it clear I shouldn't move, while Kace came up and grabbed my waist.

"You feel his cum sliding down your leg?" Kace asked in my ear. Then he took his finger up my inner thigh, through Cam's cum, and then into my mouth. "You taste him, Baby girl?"

I nodded, not believing Kace had just done that. But he was my wild one. I never knew what he would do next and that was part of the reason I climbed into Cam's lap first and made him watch. I loved making him crazy.

Taking my hips, Kace grabbed on and thrust his cock inside me from behind, just as hard as Cam had. He moved in and out of me, making it hard to keep my hands up on the wall and not fall into a puddle. Cam sidled up beside me and faced Kace while he played with my nipples.

"You should see his face," Cam whispered. "He loves fucking you as much as I do." He leaned up to kiss me as Kace brought me closer to another orgasm.

It happened so fast, too turned on by their mutual effort to keep me high. I screamed into Cam's lips as Kace reached around and stroked my clit as I came. Kace moaned his release right after me, gripping my hips impossibly hard.

When Kace pulled out, I almost fell, but Cam scooped me into his arms and carried me to the bathroom. I felt dirty, sexy, fucked, and so damn happy I could barely think straight.

Was this my new normal?

"What did I do with my bag?" I heard Kace yelling from his closet as I laid in his bed, curled up on top of Cam's chest.

At some point, all three of us started carrying bags with us so that at whoever's house we ended up, we were ready for a sleep-over. The night before, Kace and I watched Cam's game on TV at his penthouse, and Cam joined us afterward.

"The kitchen," Cam yelled back.

Kace ran from his closet to the kitchen and back.

"You'd be lost without Cam, you know that?" I giggled.

Cam was the one who always had his head on straight. Incredibly smart and intuitive. Always the sensible one. Always the responsible one. Kace would lose his left hand if it wasn't attached to his arm.

"Yeah, yeah. And he would be boring if it wasn't for me. We all have our strong suits."

"I'm gonna be plenty of fun without you once you get the hell out of here." I could feel how hard Cam was under my arm, and I knew what kind of fun he meant.

"Don't fuck up my sheets."

Cam just laughed and I hid my face. As comfortable as we had all been about being intimate with each other, I still turned pink when they talked about it.

Cam and I got a rare afternoon alone until he headed out to Kace's baseball game, and I headed to 678. The playoffs started so, naturally, Cam was going to the game. But I needed to be at work as much as possible since I had missed so much time.

Kace was exceptionally jovial for a man headed to work. The excitement he exuded was palpable. He had told me that the play-offs did that to him, but Cam told me that it was *me* that did that to him.

When Kace finally got everything together, he leaned down to kiss me goodbye and kissed Cam on the forehead. Cam pushed him away, laughing, and Kace winked at me and left.

"Bye dears," Kace teased as he shut the bedroom door.

Cam wasted no time showing me how fun he could be, and before I knew it, we had spent hours in Kace's bed. It was time for me to get to work and I dreaded having to get up. But my saving grace was that it was Monday, a slow night, and the TVs around the bar would have Kace's game on.

I was still being driven to and from work by a driver. In fact, I was getting kind of used to it. The soft leather of the back seat and quiet ride made the drive a time for me to regroup, think, and steel myself for whatever lay ahead.

That day, I wished the drive had been longer. Taken hours, maybe even days. Because I was not prepared for the twist that waited ahead.

"Hey Tony, it's getting close to game time. Can you turn on the TVs?"

He obliged but never said anything back to me, just a quick huff. He knew I was a sudden Kace Jackson fan, but I couldn't tell if he approved or not. He just seemed to get grumpy when I mentioned it.

With the bar being dead and no one in my section, I sat on a stool to watch a little of the pregame show. They were supposed to be breaking down the game and how they predicted it was going to go. Instead, they usually reported like they were TMZ and dug for any juice they could find on any of the players.

I had learned to ignore most of it. When you knew a player personally, you realized how often the news sources reported without knowing anything. I had just hoped to get a glimpse of Kace, maybe in the background.

I'm that girl now. I am borderline obsessed and just need a peek.

"This just in: Kace Jackson has been ruled out for today's game." My head jerked up, and I stared at the TV. A few other people around the bar also heard that bombshell and studied the TV with me. "Moments ago, Kace Jackson was arrested for domestic assault and led away from the stadium in handcuffs. He had no comment for reporters, but the Kings have placed Jackson on indefinite suspension pending the outcome of the charges."

Everyone around me was buzzing. Tony looked stoic. Molly just shrugged.

I was frozen. In complete shock.

My mind was swirling with questions—most of which I couldn't answer. But the one thing I did know was that Kace was innocent. He looked mean and tough, but he would never lay a hand on anyone.

The word *domestic* stuck out in my head and I ran behind the bar, grabbing my purse and my phone. I usually kept it off when I worked, so I had to wait for it to turn on and load up. I was praying I had a text or call from Kace or Cam telling me the news was gossip and it was all false. But when the phone was on, all I stared at was an empty screen. No calls from either of them.

I dialed Cam.

No answer.

I dialed Kace.

No answer.

I dialed Cam again.

Still no answer.

Tony took note of my panic and told me to take five on the roof. I nodded absently but still stared at my phone, willing it to ring.

Before I could round the bar and head for the stairs, another *Breaking News* flash came onto the screen.

"More breaking news: Cam Nichols has been arrested for domestic assault. Nichols was arrested moments after Kace Jackson was arrested for the same charge. There is no comment from either at this time, but we reached out to the Jets, who have also confirmed Nichols will be placed on indefinite suspension. The two notorious, life-long friends are said to have been in a war with one another over a woman who eventually became the target of their rage. We will have more as it becomes available."

Tears sprang in my eyes and I ran up to the roof, praying Cam would answer his phone when I called again.

But he didn't.

I paced the length of the roof several times, and my breathing became erratic. Eventually, I sat down on the same bench Kace and I were on when had our first real conversation all those weeks before, and I cried.

I didn't know what was happening, or why. I didn't know what was true, and what wasn't. I knew in my heart neither Kace nor Cam were capable of hurting anyone. How could they arrest them for hurting *me* if I had never reported them doing so? Wait, what if I wasn't the woman they were fighting over? What if there were more? What if this really was a twisted game?

I thought it, but instantly pushed it away. It didn't feel like a game anymore. It felt real.

As I mulled the situation over and over again, my phone finally rang and I answered without even looking at who it was.

"Hello?" My voice was frantic.

"Did they hurt you?" It was Mary and she sounded hysterical.

"Of course not!"

"What's going on, Ali?"

"Mary, I wish I knew! I just saw them both this morning, everything was fine!"

"Have you heard from them since?"

"No. They never called or left messages. I just saw the news on the TV at the bar. What do I do?"

"The only thing you can do is make sure the police know that you are not involved."

"This is ridiculous, Mary! If it's me they think was hurt, why was I never asked or spoken to?"

"Ali, listen to me. I love those boys, but I don't know them well enough to know if they are capable of this. Just be very careful. You haven't known them long. Are you 100% sure this is false?"

"I know they would never hurt anyone. Much less a woman. Mary, I just know! Somewhere in me. Deep. I just know..." I trailed off after stuttering along, choosing to hang up on Mary instead of trying to explain something I didn't understand.

I was with an abuser once. I was with Alan. Cam and Kace were nothing like Alan. Rationally, I knew that meant nothing. But still, I felt it, in my heart.

Cam and Kace were innocent.

kace

I STOOD AT MY LOCKER; my mind completely focused on the game. I studied the pitching stats of my opponent one more time. I put on my lucky jockstrap, said a quick prayer, and texted my mom. I thought about texting Ali, but knew she was working, so I just locked my phone in my locker. I did all my pregame rituals and turned to head to the field.

"Kace," I heard the soft solemn voice of my manager, Phil. He was in full uniform and should have already been out in the dugout, scoping things out.

"Yeah, Skip, everything okay?"

"The suits are asking to see you in the lobby outside the locker room."

What? The biggest game of the season was starting in thirty minutes and the big wigs wanted a meeting?

I nodded, because there wasn't much else I could do, and followed our skipper out of the double doors. The first thing I noted was that along with the suits were two police officers and the hairs on my neck were standing up.

"What's going on?" I hedged. I was hoping they were there to tell me they found Alan, but fear that something had happened to Ali consumed me.

"Kace Jackson?" The officers stepped forward. "You are under arrest for domestic assault. You have the right to remain silent..."

What the fuck?

I was speechless, but in my head, I was roaring. Assault? Who the fuck did they think I "assaulted?"

Without so much as a twinge, I let the cops finish their spiel and handcuff me. I was in too much shock to fight or argue.

"The league takes these allegations seriously, Kace." One of the general managers of the team spoke up. "So, despite bond that you will undoubtedly be able to post, you are not to return to the stadium until this is settled. You are suspended indefinitely."

The look on my face must have spoken volumes, as everyone in the suits backed up on instinct. My guess was, I looked how I felt—like I was ready to tear a hole into anyone close enough.

Ironic considering the charges.

When no words left my mouth, the officers started leading me toward the door and into their patrol car. As I settled into the backseat, and the officers took their place in the front, the police radio grabbed my attention.

"Cam Nichols has arrived at the stadium and will be taken into custody by Officer Samson and Officer Reese. You're free to head to the station with Mr. Jackson."

"10-4," one of the officers replied.

"Cam?" I shouted, finally finding my voice. "Cam is being arrested as well?"

"Quiet Mr. Jackson, they can fill you in at the station."

"This is bullshit!"

CHAPTER TWENTY-NINE

Cam

I BREATHED hard through my lungs. They felt raw—just like the rest of me. The past twelve hours had been pure hell.

As I arrived at the stadium for the game, I was arrested for domestic assault.

Domestic. Assault.

I always play life by the rules, but being arrested wasn't something I ever ruled out. Being arrested for domestic assault? It was unfathomable.

Once I reached the station with the police, I was given my one phone call—which I used to call my lawyer, Rick. To my surprise, he was already on his way, telling me Kace had been arrested too, and called him already.

Kace had been arrested.

We both kept Rick Bosier on retainer, and he spent hours meeting with Kace while I waited. No one had spoken to me, or offered me any explanation as to why I was in a holding room. Not until Rick finally walked in.

"Morning Cam."

Was it morning already? It was around five in the evening when I was brought in, but my phone, watch, and anything else I had on me was taken away. I had been in that colorless room, given coffee, water, and a cheese sandwich—none of which I touched. But I didn't know how much time had passed.

"What time is it?"

"Five in the morning, Buddy," Rick answered in a placating tone.

Exactly twelve hours.

I rested my head on my intertwined fingers and took another deep breath.

"So, well…" Rick began. "They are charging you with domestic assault. Before I even get started here, is there anything I need to know?"

"Like what? Did I hit my girlfriend? Is that something I really have to answer, Rick?" I yelled.

He held his hands up in surrender. "Just needed to ask, Buddy."

Buddy. Like I was a child. The little brother. Baby talk.

Rick wasn't the bad guy, but if he called me *Buddy* one more time, those charges were going to be legit, because I was going to knock him the fuck out.

"Kace is charged with the same thing," he continued/ I jerked my head up, surprised, but not really. "There were some anony-mous tips, pictures, and a damning report from a neighbor that got you two in here."

"Who do they think we assaulted?"

"Allison Hansen. Ring a bell?"

Fuck!

Two detectives walked in carrying folders of what I was sure was their *damning evidence.* I sat up straight, eager for them to sit down and fill me in. Rick took the seat beside me and whispered in my ear, reminding me I shouldn't say a word, not even react. But I had nothing to hide. Whatever was in that folder was going to be news to me, and I wasn't sure I would be able to keep my mouth shut.

I nodded, nonetheless.

The detectives introduced themselves, but I didn't register their names, or their attempt at pleasantries. I wanted them to get to the point. I wanted to know what they thought they knew.

"So, Mr. Nichols," one of them started as they took the seats across from me. "In the last month, we have received several anonymous tips regarding you, Kace Jackson, and your involvement with Allison Hansen."

I somehow stayed quiet, so he cleared his throat and continued. "Okay, so, we have here," he started, opening his folder and laying out pictures, "evidence that supports the tips."

I damn near came up out of my seat. Lying before me was "damning evidence" all right. Only, it wasn't what they thought it was. Pictures of Ali with a bruise on her face. Kace standing in front of her, looking like he wanted to kill someone—her. Me, with my fists clenched, looking like I had just hit her. More pictures from her apartment window. They were taken the night we found her, the night she told us about Alan.

That wasn't all, though. There were statements from her neighbor in 6B, claiming we had been stalking Ali. That she had seen us lurking outside her apartment on more than one occasion. That we kicked her door in the night of the assault. That she saw Ali leaving the apartment with bruises the next day.

There were statements from 678 saying that she had called in sick so many times that they began to question their authenticity. Although the people at the bar did not have any accusations, they did contribute to the overall picture that was painted—that Ali was being controlled and assaulted.

Everything they had was true, but it had been turned upside down, and painted an ugly picture. That Kace and I were the ones responsible.

"None of this was us!" I yelled. "We have been reporting her attacker for over a month now! We called the cops; we have reports showing this wasn't us!"

"Mr. Nichols, you have accused Alan Berkman of these crimes against Ms. Hansen. But as we led an investigation to find him, there were no signs someone with that name even existed. Questioning the neighbor, Ms. Hansen's father, and her co-workers all brought us to the same conclusion. You both were the only ones that could have put those bruises on her."

"Did you check any previous claims? Alan assaulted Ali two years ago and recently found her."

"There are no claims against Mr. Berkman. Ms. Hansen had a run-in with a few bar patrons back then, but not Mr. Berkman."

"You have got to be kidding me! What did Ali say? Because she knows the truth, she knows we never laid a hand on her!"

Once again, the detective cleared his throat, looking uncomfortable. "We moved forward with the investigation, and felt that we had enough for the arrests without her initial statement. You and Mr. Jackson are high-profile, and this is a public matter, not a private one."

"You targeting my clients," Rick yelled. "We demand you speak to Ali Hansen."

"We had every intention of doing so once we felt like we could bring her somewhere safe. Somewhere she would be more likely to talk."

"I had her in my arms this morning. I made love to her hours before you arrested me. She was safe, had never been safer. What the fuck? You should be looking for Alan."

"Mr. Nichols. Alan Berkman does not exist. These bruises," he pointed to the pictures taken of Ali that night in her apartment. "They were not from Alan Berkman."

"What about the pictures from outside her apartment? Why would we take those of ourselves?"

"Those were anonymously submitted. We are tracking down where they came from, but people have a right to privately report things."

"Taking pictures of people inside their apartment is a crime. Whoever took those committed a fuck crime," Rick argued.

"We aren't denying that. But what they told us about this situation remains true. And Mr. Nichols has not been honest with us. Because of that, we have no reason to think he's ever been honest with us."

"You just wanted to be the big shots," Rick seethed. "You just wanted to make the news. Arresting my clients probably gets you hard. This is all about you, not them, and certainly not Ali Hansen."

"Talk to Ali," I pleaded. "Put her wherever you think she will be safe, hook her up to a lie detector, do whatever you have to do. She will tell you the truth."

"Since your arrest, reaching Ms. Hansen has been difficult as she has not been at home, or work, when we have attempted to speak to her. Ms. Hansen will be brought in for a statement as soon as she is located."

"What?" I stood up, anxiety racing through me. "You have to find her; she could be in trouble!" My body was shaking. Ali should have been home. We were all supposed to meet at her apartment after the game. There was no doubt she heard about our arrest, and I hoped she knew to just go home and be safe.

"What about the letters that my clients received?" Rick asked. "Cam called the cops for that as well. What about those? Someone was threatening them."

Instead of answering Rick, the detective looked at me. "Mr. Nichols, can you honestly tell me that someone sent you and Mr. Jackson a letter asking for money, like this is some goddamn movie? Those letters held no traces of any evidence and led to a dead end. How do we know you didn't plant those to throw us off?"

"We were the ones that called the cops the night Ali was hurt. Why would we do that?"

"Because you knew the neighbor knew that you were there.

She told us you buzzed her apartment by mistake. She saw you outside of Ali's apartment, stalking her."

This was not happening. This was not okay.

"If you say the charges are false, let me ask you this..." I looked the detective in the eye, still taking nothing away in terms of his looks or eye color. All I saw was red. "Is there a chance you and Mr. Jackson have been duped? Could Ms. Hansen be setting you up for the money? Maybe *she* is Alan Berkman."

It was my turn to sneer, "This isn't a goddamn movie, detective."

He nodded, *touché.*

But once he left, his evidence still on the table in front of me, Rick turned to me and asked again, "You sure she isn't a part of this, Cam? Maybe Alan isn't an ex-lover. Maybe she targeted you two. Look at the facts, Cam. Have you ever met, or seen, this Alan guy? How well do you know this woman? You and Kace are always targeted, and this one escalated. You never paid up, and maybe she decided to flip the script and made those anonymous calls. Maybe she took those pictures. Cam be reasonable. Ali may just be a super fan that played a bigger game than you are used to."

I slammed my hand down on the table, shutting him up. I didn't want to hear him anymore. It may have been naive of me, because everything he said was correct.

I didn't know everything there was to know about Ali.

I didn't know if Alan was real.

We were constantly being targeted for money, or fame.

The pictures we saw never put Ali in a bad light. Just us.

We were being blackmailed to pay up, not Ali.

I could go on and on. The list of reasons it looked like a set up were legit reasons to worry. Especially for Rick, as my lawyer. His job was to prove my innocence, and being set up would do just that.

I wondered what Kace thought about that idea. I wondered if

they brought that up and he believed it? If he was ready to fight back, and put Ali in jail instead of us?

There was just one thing that kept tingling at the forefront of my mind. Something holding me back. Something that could potentially make me a stupid, stupid man.

"I love her, Rick." It was all I had to say for him to understand what may defeat me.

"Yeah, Buddy. That's what Kace said, as well."

ali

THE LIGHT WAS FILTERING into my room at an angle that made opening my eyes almost impossible—so bright and I felt the warmth from the sun on my face. My head was pounding. My body ached. I had spent the entire night crying.

Crying for Kace.

Crying for Cam.

I needed to get myself up, go to the police station and clear things up. They needed me. Yet, I found myself unable to move. I just wanted to lay there, in the quiet, away from the chaos of the outside world.

I guess that sounded selfish. They had spent the night in a jail cell, where there was no light or warmth from the sun. I figured if they had bailed out of jail, they would have come to me already.

But they hadn't.

Or, they didn't want to.

Since the day we met, our relationship had never been about us, but about my baggage. They didn't stay with me every night because they wanted it, but because they felt like they had to. I couldn't blame them for being tired of it.

I loved them regardless.

I fell in love with them, and that was why it all hurt so much. So much physical pain—in my chest, in my stomach, in my arms, in my head, in my…

I sat up with a start and pain reeled through my entire body. My head was spinning, and it was at that moment I realized I was not at home. The light didn't shine into my apartment that way. I cried all night, but that wasn't why my head hurt. And if I could move, I would run. Run straight to the police, tell them Kace and Cam were innocent. Tell them Alan was the one responsible.

I blinked, trying to adjust my eyes to my surroundings. I was in a room, but not my room. There was nothing on the walls, no furniture, no curtains, no clues as to where I was. Just a TV buzzing on the floor in the corner.

As was I—on the carpet, in the corner, buzzing. My hands were tied to each other, my feet were tied to each other and I was shaking, uncontrollably.

Then like a light, my brain turned on and I remembered.

Alan found me on the sidewalk as I ran home from the bar. I was too eager to wait on my car service. I was crying, trying to figure out what to do to help Cam and Kace.

As I had slowed down to catch my breath, I heard him behind me.

"Ali," his voice low, almost a devilish whisper.

I started to scream but was jerked down by my hair, a hand covered my mouth and Alan's hot, sour breath permeated my nose as he leaned over my shoulder from behind.

"Everyone wants to be famous; the cops are no different— easily bought with the things they want to hear. Everyone wants to be the one that brings the mighty down. Imagine getting two superstars in one shot?"

I pulled, squirmed, tugged, and swung. Anything to try and release myself from Alan's grasp and run. But that was the last thing I remembered.

My head was pounding and I had a bad taste in my mouth.

Alan either knocked me out, or used some chloroform. Either way, he was a damn coward, and I was getting sick of his shit.

Of course, that was easy to say when he was not in there with me, overpowering me, causing me pain.

Alan's words started to sink in. He had Cam and Kace arrested just to get them away from me. They had been by my side for weeks, basically since we started seeing one another. The car service ensured I wouldn't be walking alone at night, and rarely was I at my apartment without them there as well.

Staying at the penthouse with Kace—and in Cam's house—was too much for Alan. He was far from playing the lead in any savvy villain movie. Their homes were too secure for him to penetrate. They had even made sure 678 was unattainable.

And like a naive kid, I let my emotionally charged brain carry me right into his path.

There must have been a thousand other ways he could have gotten what he wanted, but he chose to feed Cam and Kace to a pack of police wolves.

I shouldn't have been surprised that they went for it. The first night we called the police on Alan, they had left with suspicions that it was Kace who attacked me, and I was "too victimized" to come forward.

The fog in my brain had all but cleared, so I sat up, assessing what I could do to escape. But even if I did get myself untied, out of that room, and away from Alan, I didn't even know where I was.

As I scooted around the floor aimlessly, the door handle turned, and Alan strolled in.

"Whoa! Look who's up. Hey, Honey bear."

"What the fuck Alan? What in the actual fuck?"

"What? You don't like the new me? Honestly, I wasn't sure I liked the new me either." He squatted in front of me, getting to my eye level. "I honest to God, Ali, only wanted some money. When you left, I just fell apart for a bit there, ya know? I spent everything I had looking for you. I lost my job. I lost my friends. Do you understand how that affected me?"

The new him? How it affected him? He was controlling before I left. He was obsessive before I ran. This wasn't the new him, he just wasn't hiding the real him anymore. But I didn't want to tell him that. I wanted him to think I saw the good in him.

Two can play this game.

"Alan, this is so far beyond anything I ever imagined you doing. This is not you." I was trying to stay calm, but my voice broke a bit on the lie.

"It wasn't me, before you. But losing you was awful, Ali. It changed my life. And having to give up the search for you because of losing my resources, as well... well, that sent me into a tailspin that only money can fix."

"I can get you money, Alan. Why didn't you just come to me, as a friend? I could have given you money!" More lies.

His backhand to my cheek came as I finished my plea.

"Bitch! I didn't know where you were! Remember?" He stood up and began pacing. "But then I saw you in that article. A small piece by a small-time reporter—his only goal being to dig up a little gossip on Cam Nichols. Ah, he made it easy. I followed you for a couple of nights, unaware of how close you had gotten with the two ballplayers." He shook his head in dismay, recounting his entire attempt to get to me. "Oh Ali, the one night I decided to have a nice, easy chat with you is the same night they showed up, went up with you, and never came down. Damn, I was pissed. I thought to myself... that bitch is living the high life and I have nothing. I just snapped." Alan shrugged like snapping was the only logical option. "But it was easy to determine that they were also the key to my high life as well, Ali. They have more money than they know what to do with. I wasn't asking for much. How come they didn't just share?"

"They probably would have, Alan, but they weren't feeling

very generous toward you after they found me bruised up from your fists."

"Oh shit," he said sarcastically, snapping his fingers. "You're probably right. Dang." He shrugged and squatted back down in front of me. "Glad I had a plan B!"

All Alan ever wanted was control and power. Neither of which he had gotten. His only form of power came when he played his damn games.

I was positive that Alan was capable of hurting me, I had the bruises to prove it. But I was not sure if he was capable of *more*. I didn't know how much danger I was really in. I did know that he wasn't hurting me, or anyone else, as long as he was talking.

"How have you not been arrested yet, Alan? The cops have been looking for you. What's your secret?" I tried to sound impressed instead of insane.

"Look at me, Honey bear. Do I look like the kinda guy that would deceive anyone? Do I look like my real name is even Alan?" he laughed, making me gasp. "You sent those cops on a wild goose chase, and all it did was piss them off. Once they were fed some anonymous tips, they gave zero shits about where I was, and who I was."

He stood up and walked to the TV, adjusting the old school antenna that sat on top of it. After a few minutes, a clear picture of the local news came on.

Tears had started coming down my face again. The monumental impact the last few months had had on my life were tugging at my heart.

And it all started with one glimpse at Kace and Cam.

The pull, the chain, the instant attraction.

Whatever it was, it made me undeniably, and unapologetically stupid, and set everything into motion. How ironic that the girl that was scared of attention fell for two of the highest profile names in the sports world—with all of the world's attention on them.

Stupid. But with no regrets.

I no longer wished to be hiding away, scared.

Falling in love with them had been profound, showing me that not only could I learn to trust a man again, but that I could trust *two* of them. I was no longer destined to be alone. I was no longer afraid of what could be with someone so right.

I still knew that there was a chance that we could never work out, but it gave me what I needed to move on, and into a healthier place in my life.

I just needed to get away from Alan, or whoever he was, and live that life.

"Okay, I am off to run errands. You can sit here and watch TV, it'll be fun to see if they release your boyfriends on bail. I bet they are pissed." His laugh was unruly, truly finding it funny. But he left, and that was all I cared about at that point. Because the joke was once again on him.

He left me.

He underestimated me.

Again.

kace

RICK HAD FINALLY GOT Cam and I released on bond before noon the day after our arrest. And, thanks to our high profiles, we were never taken to a cell—just a holding room until Rick worked his magic.

After we were free to go, Cam and I were reunited, and Rick warned us there was a swarm of reporters waiting for a comment. He advised us not to speak.

But fuck that.

The first question sent me right off the rails.

"Kace! Do you know the whereabouts of Ali Hansen, Cam's girlfriend?"

I stopped, abruptly.

"Excuse me?'"

Cam put a hand on my shoulder, guiding me further toward our waiting car. "Don't fall for it, Kace. They only want to make this worse. Don't let them."

The look on my face could have killed, and I eyed the reporter as long as I could while I walked. When I finally turned my head to get into the car, the reporter spoke up once more.

"Looks like you hit women better than you hit baseballs."

Cam grabbed me, throwing me into the car as best he could. He climbed in quickly behind me, slamming the door. Rick had arranged a car service for us to get home, so we were both in the backseat as Cam yelled, "Go!"

The driver raced off—instructed to take us both to Cam's, away from the center of the city.

Yeah, fuck that too.

Luckily, Cam was on board with me. "Straight to Bellissa's Deli," Cam told the driver.

"Sir, I have been instructed to take you straight to John's Creek. No detours."

"Yeah, that's what Rick said, but now I am saying I'm fucking hungry." Cam wasn't hungry. Bellissa's was the deli below Ali's apartment. We had to find her.

The fact that the police couldn't find her—nor could they find Alan—made me want to fight. Rick had told us she left 678 after hearing of our arrests, and hadn't been seen since. We yelled and we screamed that they had to find her.

But not one person was taking us seriously. Everyone was convinced she wasn't in danger as long as Cam and I were locked up.

We were told to stay away from her. That we would be arrested again if we were found within 1000ft of her, her work, or her home.

Yeah—fuck that too!

And despite knowing in my gut that we wouldn't find Ali at home, we were still going straight there to check, to see for ourselves.

The driver agreed to take us for "sandwiches" after Cam's speech about not being his prisoner, and that Rick was not the boss, that *we* paid Rick, and whatever else he said. I was only half listening.

We pulled up along the building and jumped out. For some

reason, I yelled, "Starving." I wasn't and didn't actually care, but it seemed like I had a role to play.

We walked toward the deli, but passed the main door, straight to the door that led to the apartments. Luckily, someone was opening the door and we caught it before it closed and locked again, entering the building in a flash.

Once we were at Ali's apartment, we knocked. I had a set of keys, but I wasn't letting myself in unless we had to. And we came close when she didn't answer after several knocks.

What if something had happened to her, like before? What if she was hurt and couldn't answer?

We didn't have to wait long before we heard the locks being opened but it wasn't Ali that opened the door.

"What the hell do you want?" An older man with graying hair was standing in the doorway. He was tall and lean with eyes so blue they sparkled. They matched Ali's exactly and I guessed it was Ali's dad right away.

"Hi, sir, we are looking for Ali," Cam mentioned.

"Do you think I would let you near her after everything I saw that you did to her? It's all over the news. It's all over the internet. It's all over the paper." He looked exasperated but kept on. "I should be asking you where Ali is. We haven't heard from her since the news broke."

He was starting to trail off, not as menacing, or mean, as he was moments before. It made me feel he didn't believe we actually hurt her.

"Philip, let those boys in here. They can help us find Ali." Mary had come running up behind him, opening the door wider as she spoke, and hugging Cam and me, as she pulled us into the apartment. Then she looked to Philip once the door was shut. "I told you, Ali told me they didn't hurt her!"

"You spoke to her?" Cam practically yelled.

Mary was nodding, "Right after the news of your arrest, I

called her and asked her point-blank if it was true. She denied it and was extremely distraught. Said she was going to fix it."

"Did she say anything else?" I demanded.

"No! And Philip hasn't heard from her either. Don't let him get sour with you, he knows you didn't hurt her. But his daughter is missing."

Philip huffed and put his hands in his pockets, a blank stare on his face. He turned to walk further into Ali's apartment.

"Philip, this is Cam Nichols and Kace Jackson. Both are friends of Ali's, by the way." Mary's attempt at an introduction was awkward considering Philip's back was to us, hands still in pockets.

"Sir, I just want to find Ali and we think we know who has her."

He turned quickly and looked our way, sizing us up. Gauging how much trust he should put into us.

"Tell me," was his only response. Ali had told us she never told him the story about Alan. He didn't know. Neither did Mary.

Cam looked at me and I nodded. It wasn't our place to spill Ali's story to her father, but we damn sure weren't going to sit by and let him think we were the bad guys.

"Does the name Alan Berkman mean anything to you?" Cam asked.

Philip's eyes got wide. "Of course, it does, Ali dated him for several months before moving to the city."

So, Cam told the story—the version Ali told us. He left nothing out, including the night we found her bruised and battered. He even told him about the letters he and I received through the fangirls. We told them the cops had been called and knew about all of it—yet seemed to do nothing.

The only parts we left out were the ones that involved us three together; naked. We both pleaded for Mary and Philip to believe how much we adored Ali without having to reveal intimate details.

After a slew of profanity and pacing by both of them, they finally stopped, understanding on their faces, and Phillip asked, "So what now?"

"I'm not sure how I know, but I feel it, with all my heart, that Alan, or whatever his real name is, is the reason Ali is missing. I don't think he would want to kill her. He's obsessed with her in some weird way, but he doesn't want her dead." I hated saying the words *Ali* and *dead* in the same sentence. It sucked it even had to be said.

Mary was shaking, bringing a hand to her mouth to hide her trembling lips. I reached out to hug her, knowing how she was feeling. But I only gave her a second of comfort before switching back to business.

"I don't know where or how—only who and why. It may help if you two call the police and report her missing, but Cam and I have had our lawyer hire a PI, and he's called everyone he has connections with to help find her."

Philip nodded, pacing the small apartment again. He didn't speak or add to the conversation. He just nodded a goodbye when we told him and Mary that we had to get to Cam's house before the police tracked us down for violating the terms of our release—or worse, the media.

Five days.

Cam and I had been holed up in his house for five fucking days.

Rick called often, but never had any news. No leads. Nothing.

Our parents had visited, and we told them the same story we told Philip. But then we asked them to leave. We didn't want the company, didn't want their comfort. Our moms weren't happy, nor were they happy to hear we had fallen for the same girl.

But whatever. That wasn't something we regretted, nor were we in a place to ease their minds about how it would all end.

Despite the temperatures getting cooler, Cam had been swimming laps in his pool every day. The cold water on his skin seemed to be the only thing that kept the fire in him at a slow simmer.

I wasn't dumb enough to get into the pool, but I did end up working out in his gym seven hours a day. Somehow, like Cam, punishing my body seemed to be the only thing I knew to do.

For the first night at Cam's, I had stayed in the extra bedroom but the second night, I went to Cam's room. Without even asking, I laid on "my side" and slept—pretending Ali was in-between us, right where she should have been.

Now, we were antsy.

And frustrated.

And downright scared.

What kind of bullshit was it that no one could find Alan Berkman, or who he really was? How have they not been able to track a single crumb from him?

I was lying on the couch in the living room, watching the highlights from the baseball playoffs that I should have been playing in. The Kings lost the series, and we were out. But the stories were more about the fact that the Kings would have won if I was in the lineup—that I let my team down.

I did let them down, in some sort of way. But I was innocent, and everything was all bullshit, so did I really "let them down"? I didn't know. I kind of didn't care, either. Losing in the playoffs felt so small. It didn't matter.

While I was in the midst of my misery, the TV shut off, and I sat up, ready to chew Cam out for not letting me finish the highlights—and my pity party. But the look on his face stopped me and instead I asked, "What's wrong?"

He was standing behind the couch near the entrance to the kitchen where he had been making us food. He licked his lips and shook his head. "I just got a call from Rick. The police are convinced Ali just ran away...with Alan, or without Alan...too scared to come forward because of us. They are sending a car to pick us up. They have more questions. Then, according to Rick, and our teams, we have to make a public statement regarding Ali and our relationship with her."

"Are they out of their goddamn minds?" I jumped up and yelled. "Who the fuck is running this investigation? This feels like some kind of fucking joke! It's no one's damn business what our relationship with her is. I don't give a fuck what the charges are, they can go fuck themselves."

I started pacing and Cam kept quiet. I ended up letting out more words, more yelling, more hysterics. I wasn't able to control myself. Cam just watched me, letting me release the warehouse of energy I had packed away.

Since the day I met Ali, my body had been ignited. I sizzled from my fingers to my toes. I was high, I was low. I was hot, I was cold. I was calm, I was rage.

It was all pent up, choosing that moment to release itself from my body.

I had been fueled with combat—the need to hit something reverberating in waves since day one. At the same time, I had finally fallen in love. Possessiveness, passion, protectiveness. I had it all. Did everyone feel that way? Was I doing it wrong?

We were being charged with assault, something I was more than capable of committing. But I would never, ever hurt a woman. I would never, ever hurt Ali. Did I have to announce to the world the details why?

And why wasn't Cam as upset as I was? We had never talked about how deep our feelings ran for Ali, but I knew he felt it as deeply as I did.

His silence and calmness confused me.

I stopped pacing, I stopped ranting. I looked to Cam, questioning.

He gave me silence, thoughts swirling behind his blank eyes.

Finally, after what felt like hours, he spoke.

"I love you."

What?

"I love you, Kace."

I tilted my head, wondering why he was telling me words I knew to be true, but never said directly.

"I'm not going to let you lose her, I promise. I love her so fucking much, but I love you, too."

"What are you saying?"

"Just that, if it comes down to it—and it will eventually—I won't let you lose her." He took a deep breath and ran a hand through his hair. He looked tired, spent. Pale. His bottom lip trembled from clenching his jaw before he loosened it again and continued. "Rick told me that you told him you were in love with Ali. We are completely, and rightfully, upset. Ali is missing, she's God knows where going through God knows what. We have bogus cops up our asses for bogus charges. The Kings losing the playoffs is being blamed on you. And if that wasn't enough, we live in a very public eye that is waiting for us to tell them the truth. This shit is not easy. It's costing us our sanity. But I just wanted you to know that despite all of that bad, I love you, and I won't let you lose her."

"Cam," I whispered, unsure of how to respond, or what prompted him to even say all that.

"There are pics of Ali and me all over the place now. That reporter calling her my girlfriend... I saw it on your face when he said it. You were pissed he opened his mouth, but I saw pain as well. You wanted to shout it to everyone that she was yours, and that you loved her, but I tossed you in the car." He shrugged. "Before we go back out there, I just wanted you to know I got your back. Shout whatever you need to shout. Be whoever you need to be."

"I love you too," I blurted. We did love one another. It wasn't a declaration of love like we felt for Ali. It was our brotherhood. Our sacrifice for one another in what was an unorthodox relationship being taken public before we were ready. We never had a plan for the future, we just knew we needed to keep the fact that we were both with the same woman on the down low. Cam was letting me know that I could stake the claim, that I could be the guy who claimed Ali when the cameras were on. He loved me that much.

I was probably scaring the fuck out of him.

I took a deep breath, calming myself down. "It's all coming to an end before we are ready. It's not fucking fair. We haven't even had a chance to talk to her about this. Fuck, it's only been a few months. We need more time. It isn't fair to Ali if we speak on her behalf, we need to be careful."

"Agreed."

"No one takes the lead," I decided. "I love you too, you fucking asshole. I'll get my shit together; I'll keep my cool. I'll survive this shit, and we will wait on Ali to move forward."

cam

KACE WAS LOSING IT.

I was losing Kace.

He had seemed inconsolable earlier. I meant what I said that I wouldn't let him lose Ali. I needed to protect him just as much as I needed to protect her.

When we made it to the station, the cops had more dumb ass questions, but we were able to answer them together, with Rick. A whole bunch of nothing that didn't mean anything, especially since we were innocent.

As we stood at a podium for our press conference—dressed in suits that were tailored to perfection, sunglasses on, hands in our pockets—I considered throwing every reasonable thing I agreed to say out the window and tell everyone to fuck off.

Instead, I listened to Rick declare our innocence. That we considered Ali a friend but were unsure of the role she played in our arrests. I scoffed under my breath as he spoke, still not willing to believe that she was off hiding with Alan, living happily ever after.

Rick thought we were insane to not even to consider the possibility, and he wanted to put that idea into the ears of everyone paying attention. He didn't understand that we didn't have a choice. I was drawn to that woman like a goddamn moth to a fucking flame. I may have been willing to stand down for Kace, but it did not mean I could change how I felt.

Kace and I agreed that we would both speak. We would each reiterate our innocence, and nothing else. No questions. At least that was what Rick thought the plan was. We owed our teams and families a few words, but we owed Ali our silence.

We owed *Alan* a little something, too.

As Rick introduced me, and I approached the podium, I scanned the crowd, taking in all the faces that showed up hoping to get a juicy story. We were on the steps outside the police station, and there must have been two-thousand reporters holding mics scattered below on the sidewalk and road. News vans had been set up along the entire block—some local, some from nearby cities, and some from national news sources.

I kept my sunglasses on, the bright sun providing the perfect excuse to hide my tired eyes. Eyes that wouldn't be as silent as my mouth.

I took my hands from my pockets and gripped the sides of the podium to keep me grounded. After a few deep breaths, I spoke.

"Five days ago, Kace and I were arrested for assaulting a woman we consider a close friend. Someone who never made these accusations herself. Someone who has not been spoken to by police at all. Which is unfortunate for Kace and me because we have no doubt that she would proclaim how false these charges are. We have not, nor would we ever, hurt her."

I looked back to Kace, silently asking if I should keep going with the plan. His nod was all I needed to continue.

"We will, however, beat the ever-loving shit out of the person we know has her." The crowd started to buzz, and Kace blocked Rick from pulling me from the mic. We agreed not to mention Alan's name since the police told us the name didn't exist, but we also wanted him to know what kind of shit he'd gotten himself into, that we weren't scared, or backing down. We also wanted Ali to know that no matter what the cops, or Rick, said, we knew she didn't run. "In the last month, we have been threatened, attempted to be blackmailed, and have done everything we could to keep Ali safe. Our arrest ensured Ali was left alone, and I have no doubt, *that* is the reason she cannot be found."

I backed away; my part was done. Kace started to approach the podium, despite Rick freaking the fuck out. Even Rick knew Kace was the wild card, and considering I was the good little soldier that just went off script, he knew Kace had no fucking script. And he didn't. We agreed to what I would say, but I kept my word to Kace, and let him be whatever he needed to be—vowing to have his back.

"You know what's crazy?" Kace started. "I don't give a shit whether, or not, you think I assaulted Ali Hansen. Your opinions are not the worst thing that has happened. Going to jail, losing my career, and everything I have, it's still not the worst that could happen. I recently learned there are worse things to lose."

And Kace was done. He said his peace, and walked away toward the blacked-out SUV that awaited us, me following behind him. We gave our teams the words they wanted, kept the secrets we owed to Ali, and let 'Alan' know he needed a head start.

ali

HE HADN'T TOLD me his real name yet, but he would always be Alan to me. The guy that had done nothing but lie to me, and everyone else, since the day we met.

It took me a few days, and Alan leaving several times, for me to figure out how I was going to get the hell out of that house. I didn't know what he was doing, but he left almost every day at the same time—usually gone for about four hours. I didn't have a clock, but I felt good with that guess. I had also discovered I was on the second floor of a house in an old school neighborhood. I still didn't know where I was exactly, but I knew I was close to Atlanta. I guessed I was in his hometown, a suburb of Atlanta, or near the college we had once attended.

Alan kept me tied up when he left, but released my hands and feet when he was there so I could eat and use the restroom.

I was not an idiot—no food meant no strength or skill, no stamina, and no sanity. So, I ate everything he brought me, praying he didn't lace it with something.

On the day I decided to run, I tried eating like normal, but excitement stirred in my stomach making it hard to want to consume anything. The TV was on the only channel it had, and

Alan was sitting next to me as we watched the same things that came on over and over. Daytime soaps, local news—which was how I guessed I was still near Atlanta—and nighttime reality TV.

Since it was only noon, we were right in the middle of seeing if John and Marlena would once again return from the dead and fall in love, again, and fight the evil Dimeras… again. I knew once that was over, Alan would leave. He would probably hit me across the cheek or chest again before he left, though. I needed to prepare myself for that. He seemed to love hurting me, and I would be lying if I said I wasn't in pain.

So. Much. Pain.

I took another bite of my spaghetti and meatballs, hoping I looked normal, as I spaced out into my happy place—inside my head thinking about Kace and Cam.

I watched them leave the police station that day Alan had first turned on the TV. Kace looked wild, rabid. Cam looked his usual calm self, but I knew underneath he was probably running just as wild as Kace. It didn't shock me that the media referred to me as Cam's girlfriend—most of the pics taken were of us. But what did shock me was the hurt in Kace's eyes.

Our whole relationship didn't seem temporary anymore. Maybe it never was, but I think I always anticipated it ending. Dating two men at the same time was not that unusual. But being *committed* to two men—who knew about it and were okay with it —was pretty "frowned-upon."

I had been so scared of being the "whore" or "slut" that slept between the two stars. I had learned just how under a microscope they lived, but it was easy to ignore when they did such a good job of avoiding, and hiding, the details of our world. I had always thought that they did that for them, to save face, but maybe it was for me, for my fear of being ostracized.

Now I feared that I would lose them. Once I got away from Alan, they may decide that I had put them through too much.

Hell, they had been arrested because of me. I knew they cared about me, but was I worth all the trouble?

My mind continued to wander down that path of uncertainty when a sudden news break interrupted the show.

"We interrupt this programming for an update on the arrests of Kace Jackson and Cam Nichols. The two have both been quiet since their release on bail five days ago. However, we have learned that they will be speaking in front of the police station momentarily…" The reporter went on, updating everyone who may have missed the original news story—which was probably no one.

I had sat up straight at the mention of Cam and Kace. Alan took notice of my change and kicked my food away, "Calm down, bitch!" He re-tied my hands and kept talking. "It's only a matter of time before their fancy lawyer gets their charges dropped, but they can't find you. So, there's no reason to get excited."

By the time he finished with the ropes on my wrists, the camera had moved to where a group of people were approaching the podium. I didn't let Alan's words bother me. I didn't feel like I needed anyone to find me. I was getting out of there my damn self. I cared more about them leaving Cam and Kace alone, dropping the charges and letting them be. I prayed that was what the news conference was about.

My heart beat out of my chest as I saw Cam and Kace approach the media area, walking behind a few police officers, and a man in his forties, with an expensive suit and dark hair. The dark-haired man spoke first, introducing himself as their lawyer. He proclaimed their innocence, and insinuated that since I—the person they were accused of assaulting—had run away, there could be no further investigation, or proof, that the guys were guilty of such uncharacteristic acts.

Ran away?

I started shaking my head no. They couldn't really believe that was what happened, could they? Surely the guys knew, after everything we had been through, that Alan was most likely responsible for me disappearing, right? Was that why Alan never seemed worried? Were the cops not looking for me because they assumed I ran away?

What about my dad and Mary? They would know I hadn't just run.

The dark haired guy kept talking, insinuating that there was a chance that I was behind the arrests, and had planned the entire thing. My heart sank even further, and my lunch made its way back up my throat, making me swallow it down over and over again.

Alan had started laughing as the lawyer droned on. "Oh, this is so perfect!" He clapped his hands, pleased with everything he was hearing. I repeated in my head that it didn't matter, that I could save myself, and would tell everyone what happened.

Then, the lawyer introduced Cam.

Sensible, sweet, sexy Cam.

He was wearing a suit that was tailored to his body—dark blue, with a white shirt and dark blue skinny tie. His hair was perfectly coifed, and his face freshly shaved. His ray bans hid his eyes, but I knew they were the same deep blue that matched his suit. He looked like he had stepped out of a magazine, posed with his hands in his pockets.

His jaw was clenched as he took his hands from his pockets and prepared himself to speak. "Five days ago, Kace and I were arrested for assaulting a woman we consider a close friend." Consider. Ice ran through my veins. I felt light-headed just by his first sentence. But I guess it made sense to believe what everyone around them was saying. His following words were lost as I had to physically work to overcome the pain coursing through me.

Right as I zoned back in, though, everything lifted. I didn't know what I missed, one or two sentences. But what I did catch was Cam glancing to Kace, who nodded at him. "We will, however, beat the ever-loving shit out of the person we know has her...."

I looked to Alan, who looked like he wanted to kill Cam. It was scarier than he had ever looked before. Cam recounted the threats we had faced, but never mentioned Alan's name. Was that on purpose? Did they know it could have been a fake name?

He finished his short speech and let Kace have a word. Their lawyer looked like he was going to have a stroke. I had no doubt that Cam's words were not part of the plan, and I knew Kace was even more of a risk with a microphone in his face.

Kace looked just as sexy as Cam. His suit was also tailored to his perfect body, only his was a dark charcoal grey. He had a white shirt on, no tie, and his shirt was slightly unbuttoned—a tattoo peeking from the top. His hair looked like it had once been put together, but I knew he had been running his hands through it. He always did when he was anxious.

He took a minute to compose himself. His sunglasses also hid his eyes, but I could tell he was eyeing everyone that stood at the base of the steps waiting for him to speak. Then finally, he scoffed and shook his head.

"You know what's crazy? I don't give a shit whether, or not, you think I assaulted Ali Hansen." *What?* "Your opinions are not the worst thing that has happened. Going to jail, losing my career, and everything I have, it's still not the worst that could happen. I recently learned there are worse things to lose."

And just like that, he was done. He walked away, Cam right behind him. The reporters were asking a million questions, shouting over each other, hoping they would answer just one. But they didn't. The cameras followed them to the SUV where they slid into the back seat, and were gone.

Holy. Fuck.

Their lawyer was red. He was pacing and typing on his phone. I could picture him texting the guys, asking them what the hell just happened. Maybe he wasn't, but I couldn't imagine any high-profile lawyer being happy with his clients not caring about their charges.

Alan had stood up when it was all over, stretching himself, and somehow acting like it was just another day. I knew he was leaving soon. I knew it was almost time for me to get my shit together and get the hell out of there.

He threw away our lunch and came back to me, crouching down in front of me. "Gotta go, babe," he pointed to the TV, "we will have to talk about that shit when I get back."

He shook his head and stood up, leaving the room. But before he got out, he turned and came back. "Oh, I almost forgot…" he got back to me in two strides and took his hand to my neck, squeezing hard enough to block the airways. I was gasping for air, watching his face transform from happy-go-lucky to deadly in an instant. "New me is tired of playing this game, Ali. I guess I need to send your fuck boys a little message."

He released my neck and closed his fist, rearing back to punch me. That was nothing new, he always hit me before he left. I just never knew where it would be aimed at.

That time, he found my face. He usually used his open hand on my face, but I got a full punch, right into the left cheek.

I fell back instantly, no sound coming from me. He stomped from the room and left me dizzy. My head was pounding, and I was rolling on the ground. I tried pulling my hands up to cover my swelling eye, but with them tied so tightly together, it was hard. I decided to just lay there for a minute, to let the pain ease before I bounded into action.

Just a minute.

That was all I could spare.

As if rising from the dead, I sat up quickly when I heard a loud bang. I looked around, trying to adjust to what was going on. I was still in the room Alan put me in, I was still at the house.

I remembered I was going to escape, but I was still there, and it was dark in the room, telling me it was dark outside.

I didn't know what time it was, but it wasn't getting dark until seven most days, so it was late.

Too late.

I looked to the corner of the room, to an area of the carpet where I had managed to hide a knife. It was only a butter knife from a lunch we had days before, but I knew I could make it work.

Alan didn't seem to be back as early as he normally was, he was usually back before dark. But I wasn't sure if I still had time to try and escape.

I heard another loud bang. That time it sounded like it was in the house—a door maybe.

Alan was back.

I resigned myself to wait until the next day. I would try again. I could do it, I would wait one more day. But when he slammed open the bedroom door with the same scary look in his eyes as he did when he left, I wasn't sure I had any more days.

He stomped toward me and grabbed me by my hair. I stood up only for him to punch me in my stomach, knocking me back down to the ground. With my hands tied, I couldn't catch my fall, and the back of my head slammed to the ground as well.

"Alan…" I groaned. Pleaded.

"I spent all day trying to figure out how to send a message to those fucking assholes. A part of me wanted to send them one of your fingers. Just cut it off and mail it to them. But that is mafia shit, and you know I get squeamish." No, I didn't know that. I didn't care. "Another part of me wanted to ignore them, let them just stew in their own shit."

He pulled out my phone from behind his back. He started

thumbing it, unlocking it. "Ultimately, I decided you're going to make a call."

My eyes opened wide with disbelief, and he shook his head. "Don't get too excited. You're not calling the cops, your dad, your friend Mary, or your boyfriends. No one that will be expecting the call and can try tracing it from their phones. But you will call someone, and you will tell them you're fine. You will beg them to tell everyone you're fine. You just can't stand the thought of calling someone close to you, you're so scared and sad. Got it?"

Who the fuck did he think I could call? I had so few numbers in my phone that it was pathetic. I wanted to roll my eyes at him. What a dumb ass plan, too risky on his part. Who's to say I won't start screaming for help?

As if reading my thoughts, Alan did something I didn't think he was capable of—he pulled a gun out and put it to my head.

I immediately panicked. All that time, all that pain, all that drama that Alan had incited, and I never once thought he'd kill me.

The panic in my eyes made Alan happy. He knew he was going to win. "The best way to punish them is to hear it straight from your mouth. I'm just not dumb enough to let you call certain people. I'm also not dumb enough to let you do anything stupid." He cocked the gun and re-aimed it at my head. "Now... let's decide who the lucky bastard is that will do our dirty work."

He started scrolling through my thirty contacts—mostly people I spoke with through my day job, people I had never met personally. A few others were from 678. One of them would make the most sense. They may hear my underlying concern and tell the police. The one thing I knew I wouldn't do was fuck up the opportunity. I would stick to Alan's plan because I had one of my own, and if I was dead, or hurt more than I already was, I wouldn't be getting out of there.

Then, as Alan scrolled through my phone, a thought occurred to me. "JJ..." I whispered.

"Who?" Alan asked.

I didn't overthink it; I just went with my gut. "There's a guy in there, his contact name is JJ. He's a work friend that lives in Atlanta, but I have never actually met him—we teleconference." The lie was rolling off easier than I could hope. Truthfully, I did teleconference with people I had never met, but their area codes were in California. Kace's was in Atlanta so I needed to be careful where I said JJ was from. "He knows me well enough to help me, but not so much he'll care."

"Okay," Alan said. "JJ it is."

He scrolled until he found the contact information. I couldn't believe it was that easy. But he knew he held the upper hand. The gun in my face ensured him I wouldn't fuck up.

The only thing I worried about was that Kace would blow my cover when he realized it was me. Or that he'd answer the phone in a manner that was a dead giveaway that he was not "JJ."

I was thankful that Kace and Cam told me their names were JJ and Nick. The night Kace gave me his number, when he came by the bar without Cam, he had tucked his number into my back pocket as he walked away. I saved it as *JJ* because that was what I thought his name was—but I never actually used the number.

By the time we were all exchanging numbers and talking, I knew their real names and saved them as new contacts, never deleting "JJ."

"We are using this phone." He held up an extra phone and I wondered if it was a burner phone. "You know what to say. Don't. Fuck. Up."

The gun was still aimed at me, and I had no doubt it was loaded. I was kind of scared of Alan accidentally pulling the trigger, he clearly didn't know what he was doing, or how to use that thing. He was bigger and stronger than I was, which was why I was there and tied up—but he wasn't in his right mind. He wasn't savvy enough to pull something like this off. I could see it clearer and clearer.

He was winging it. I just had to keep him calm.

"Okay, Alan. Let me call JJ and get it over with. I'm sure he will pass along any messages." I shrugged like it was no big deal.

Alan took the number from my phone and entered it into the other one. Once it started ringing, he put it on speakerphone and held it with the hand that was not holding the gun.

"Hello?" Kace answered. I was frozen for a minute. The sound of his gruff voice making my heart beat out of my chest. I wanted to cry. I wanted to tell him how sorry I was that I got him caught up in all of my bullshit baggage.

"Hello?" He repeated, a little more agitated. Alan's eyes got wide, fearing I was about to do something stupid. He could see the change in my demeanor. I just prayed he didn't recognize that I was longing for the voice in my ears.

I cleared my throat and tried to be as perky as possible, hoping it threw Kace off my voice long enough for him to play along. "Hi, JJ?"

Silence.

No one called Kace and referred to him as JJ. That was between him and Cam. The only other person that would call him that was me. I hoped he knew that.

After a minute, he cleared his throat. "Um, yeah?"

"Hi! This is Allison Hansen, from work." *Please play along, please play along.*

"Ali?" I could hear the desperation in his voice, the panic. I needed to cut him off.

"Yeah, from work. Can you do me a tiny favor? Please?" My *please* was desperate in my head, but I hoped it sounded sincere to Alan.

More silence.

"Okay..." he finally said.

"So, I think you may have heard my name in the news."

"Yeah..." he had no clue where I was going, but he was listening, he wasn't panicking, he was going to play along.

"I'm going off-grid for a while, I need to just get away, ya know? I wasn't sure who else to call. The cops are so needy, and my boyfriend is dangerous." I hiccupped on that word. They weren't dangerous. *Please don't believe me, Kace.*

"What is it you need?" he demanded, getting more agitated.

"Can you just tell everyone I'm okay. I ran away and do not want to be found."

"Don't you think you should tell them that yourself?"

Alan's hand started shaking, he was realizing his dumb idea was just that—dumb!

"No, no! I just, well… I was scrolling through, debating on calling them, but I remembered the last time we talked, you said if I ever needed anything, I could call."

"Yeah…"

"So just, I needed to tell *someone*." I wanted to cry again. He knew my words weren't real. He knew he wasn't "JJ from work," but I wanted to make sure he really knew. "Oh, and can you take care of my reports, I can give you my password."

Alan's eyes were menacing. He didn't want the conversation to go on any longer, but he also knew cutting it off would be suspicious. I tried to calm him with a look that I was trying to be believable.

Hurry up, he mouthed.

"Yeah, I'll get those done, Ali." I could hear the change in Kace's voice. It was calmer, more believable. *He knew. He knew. He knew.*

I steeled my jaw, the threat of tears once again creeping up on me, "The password is iLove2020."

Silence.

Lingering and ominous silence.

Alan hung up the phone and yelled, "What the fuck was that?"

"Alan, he's my coworker, he wouldn't have believed I was disappearing without turning my work over to him. I had to give him my passwords," I pleaded. All I wanted was for Kace to read between the lines and know I loved him. Him, and Cam. Both of them. Both number 20. That password wasn't real. They wouldn't be able to unlock anything with it. But it was a message I needed to send... Just in case.

Alan backhanded me with the hand no longer holding the phone. "You better hope that worked."

I wanted to roll my eyes, I didn't care if it worked or not. I wasn't spending one more night in that damn place. But pain shot through my face from his hit. Bruises on bruises.

I laid down, trying to get myself oriented and hoping he backed off for a while. I needed to get closer to where I stashed my lunch knife. I needed to make him go away.

But he didn't. Instead, he took my feet and cut the binding off himself. I was so confused, but relieved. That was one less thing I had to do.

My relief was short-lived, though. He flipped me over and dragged me to a different spot in the room. He started cutting my jeans off with a knife, nicking my skin in the process.

"Alan!" I screamed. "Alan, what are you doing?"

"Time to consummate our new lives, Honey bear. We are leaving here in the morning, we are moving on, we are going to spend our days together. And I'm so tired of waiting until we are gone to fuck that pussy, again."

On instinct, I started kicking. No way was he getting near me. That was always my worst fear, but Alan never had it in him to rape me. I could get through anything but that. I would never be able to get over it if he touched me.

He was on a power trip.

On top of kicking, I screamed. I prayed. Someone had to hear me. I saw other houses nearby when I looked out the window, so why could no one hear me?

"No Alan, please no!" I was hysterical, but I had a small moment where I was so thankful I called Kace, hoping he knew my message was real. I needed him and Cam to know I loved them in case that moment was when I died. Because I would rather die than let Alan touch me.

"Be still, bitch." He hit me again, that time in the stomach. I coughed and recoiled, pain shooting everywhere. "And when you come, I want you calling me Alvin."

Stars. I was seeing stars.

I was dizzy, and drunk on pain. It was like a night of drinking and finally laying down, the ceiling spinning and the need to vomit so pronounced. I closed my eyes, willing the dizziness to stop. My jeans had been shredded and I was almost exposed to him by the time I regained my wits. Only my panties remained.

I stilled, trying to think of what to do. Alan was unbuckling his jeans, staring down at me with lust—creepy lust. The need to purge gained momentum.

I turned onto my side, trying to hide my body. But Alan took my ankles and turned me back over. "Just relax honey bear."

Once his hands brushed my legs, I knew it was time. Time to give everything I had. I took a deep breath and pulled my feet up. As Alan started to hover over me, guiding himself between my legs, I kicked, aiming for his face.

I made contact and he instantly backed off. But he was only angrier and came back harder. "You little bitch!" he yelled again. He started to hit me again, but I knew I wouldn't be able to take another blow, so I kicked his hand. I kicked again and again. With my legs not tied, I was able to kick hard and wild.

Once he was off of me, I backed myself up to the corner where I had hidden the knife. I wasn't sure how it would help me at that point. I wouldn't have time to use it to break my restraints. But I knew I had a better chance if I could get it.

As I struggled to inch myself to the corner, I heard a gunshot and I froze. I waited for the pain to start seeping through my body. I waited for the blood to pour from me. But it never came.

I looked back at Alan, who was standing with the gun aimed at me. The gunshot buzzed by me into the wall.

Intentional. He didn't want to hit me with that bullet, he wanted to scare me. But he didn't realize I wasn't scared to die. If he thought I would let him rape me instead of dying, he was a bigger fool than I thought.

I turned back to face him but backed myself up to the loose carpet in the corner. I needed to calm him down long enough to put the gun down, to let me get the knife.

I needed to keep playing my game.

"Alan," I stated calmly. "Or can I call you Alvin? Please put the gun down. You don't want to shoot me."

"You're right, I don't. I don't have time to clean your dead ass off this floor, but I will. Don't you doubt that I will." He was yelling, his arm shaking. His words were menacing but his resolve was weakened with that gunshot. Something told me he never planned to pull that trigger, and doing so rattled him.

"We don't have time for *this* either," I said, eyeing my naked legs and his unbuttoned jeans. "Let's just get out of here."

"We have until morning. We aren't leaving until morning." He was trying to calm himself, his words getting lower.

He was weak. A small moment flashed where I felt sorry for him. He looked broken and alone. "Alvin," I said calmly. "It's okay. Just… please… come here…" The look on my face was sincere. He needed a hug. He needed to know I felt his pain. "Come here, Alvin. Just, please, let me hug you."

Alan lowered the gun and walked toward me. He knelt in front of me, eyeing me. "This wasn't how this was supposed to go, Ali. You were supposed to see me again, realize you missed me, and want to be with me forever. You were supposed to be as lonely as I was. You were supposed to love me."

"I did, Alan. I did love you. But I loved you most when you were kind, thoughtful, and cared about who I wanted to be. I didn't need you to control me. I didn't need you to scare me. But I was scared. You scared me... So, I ran." I kept my voice soft and tender, not keeping track of which name I was using. It was all a blur anyway. Everything I was saying was true, though I meant every word. Two years ago, I thought he was *the one*.

But his insecurities led him to control me. *His fear of being alone.*

Did he not see the irony in all that?

He put his hand slowly to my face, gently rubbing the side of my bruises. "Why did you make me hurt you, Ali?"

"I didn't mean to, I'm so sorry." A tear escaped my eye and ran down my cheek and he wiped it away. "Can we please wait until we are out of here to be together, Alan? I don't want to hate you for hurting me anymore."

More truth.

"I just want to be with you," he said. But he stood up and buckled his pants, giving me a moment of relief as he turned his back to me and hunched over, undoubtedly upset.

Maybe he was seeing the reality of his actions. Maybe he was regretful. Maybe this could be over.

I was hopeful.

I was sad for him.

I was heartbroken.

But…. I was *not* stupid.

I stood on my legs, still untied, and free. I quietly got closer to him, the carpet padding my steps. I could see the gun hanging from his right hand and stopped for a minute, debating if he would still be unwilling to use it on me.

I didn't care. I didn't care when I feared him forcing his body on me, why care now? Anything was better than being his prisoner.

And despite how my heart broke for the person he could have been, I knew he wasn't that person. His moment of absolution wouldn't last. I needed to fight.

As if sensing my approach, he whipped around quickly, ready to aim the gun back at me. But I never gave him that chance as I took the knife and pierced his skin, the blunt tip causing a jagged wound to his arm. The gun dropped as pain shot through his body.

I didn't want to stab him in the heart or lungs. Killing someone—no matter the circumstances—was not something I thought I would be able to live with. When I pictured escaping, I pictured him being gone while I ran. But he wasn't leaving again, and I sure the hell wasn't sticking around.

He tried picking the gun up, but I reared back and took another stab at him. This time, I got the back of his left shoulder as he cried in pain. I knew my time was up. I had to run. He was distracted by the element of surprise and the need to get his gun, but he wouldn't let me get a third chance.

As he cursed and got back up, I kicked the gun away from him, opened the door to the room, and ran—locking the door on the way out. I knew I was an idiot for not grabbing the gun, but I was panicked and frantic… my flight instincts took over.

I made my way down the stairs, not taking the time to take in my surroundings or note what else was in the house. I didn't even care. I knew he would grab the gun and chase me. That lock wouldn't hold him, just slow him down. I needed to find the front door and run to another house. But as I rounded a corner, I realized I had gone the wrong way, the front door nowhere to be seen.

I heard Alan shoot the lock on the door and start his way down the stairs. There was no more time. I couldn't run far enough ahead of him to evade the gun. I saw another door that may have led to the backyard, but again, I wouldn't be able to run. I opened it nonetheless and backed up into the house. I opened another door, a closet, and hid inside, silently closing the door just as Alan ran down the stairs toward the front.

"Ali!" he yelled. "Ali!"

Maybe I should have run out the back—by him going the other way, I would have had more time. But now I was trapped.

Stuck in a closet, praying he thought I ran out the back and was gone.

"Ali!" he yelled again, that time closer to the door I was behind. "Ali!"

I heard him retreat to the back door and then outside, still yelling for me. I thought maybe I could run while he was out there, but I didn't know how big the yard was or how long he would look.

It wasn't long before he reentered the door and slammed it shut, letting out a slew of profanity. "That bitch, that fucking bitch!" Did he think I was gone?

I could hear him breathing hard, pacing the linoleum floor below his feet. I heard the water running. He seethed as I imagined he was cleaning his wounds. I heard the water stop. I heard more cursing.

Then I heard the doorbell. *The fucking doorbell.*

In the week I had been there, I had never heard the doorbell. I was both scared and excited. It could have been the neighbors hearing the commotion, or maybe someone called the police when they heard the gunshots.

Alan shuffled to the door but didn't open it. I opened the closet door, hoping to catch a peek at what he was doing. I couldn't see the actual front door, but I saw Alan leaned against the wall next to the door, trying to peek out to see who it was.

He didn't know. That was good, right?

He held the gun in his right hand, dangling it loosely in his fingers.

Another doorbell.

Whoever it was wasn't going away.

After a few minutes of debating, Alan tucked the gun behind his back and began unlocking the door. As he opened it, it busted in and Alan fell to the ground. I couldn't see who it was, but I saw Alan reaching for the gun. I couldn't watch. I couldn't move, either. I slid down to the bottom of the closet, hiding my face in my knees. My hands were still tied, and I felt helpless.

I heard yelling.

I heard fists hitting flesh.

Then I heard another gunshot.

kace

I HADN'T RECOGNIZED the number when the phone rang, and I wasn't going to answer it. Cam told me not to bother. It was most likely more media that had somehow gotten my number.

It had been a few hours since we left the press conference. Which wasn't a press conference. It was basically Cam and I telling everyone they could kiss our asses. Upper management for the team wanted me to get up there and apologize for letting my team down, but hell no. I didn't let them down.

I didn't *do* anything.

Apologizing was admitting guilt, and I was not guilty. Maybe when I was less pissed, I would apologize for how it affected my team. But in that moment, I was only interested in finding Ali.

I was about to cancel the incoming call when I remembered one of the PI's we hired was tracing my incoming calls so on a whim, I answered it.

"Hello?"

Nothing.

I was so tired of the bullshit so I started to hang up but stopped.

"Hello?"

That time, I heard a woman clear her throat and then said words that sent my heart into rapid-fire. "Hi, JJ?"

JJ? No one fucking called me JJ. No one knew that Cam and I used nicknames. *No one except for Ali.*

But it didn't sound like Ali. Ali was a happy woman, but the woman on the phone sounded downright euphoric. And if I were to guess, Ali wasn't very happy at the moment.

But she called me JJ. That couldn't be a coincidence, could it?

"Um, yeah?" I started to wave at Cam from across the living room. He was watching me since he told me not to answer the phone, so he got up and came to listen to the conversation.

"Hi! This is Allison Hansen, from work!"

Ali? Ali?

"Ali?" Did I say that out loud?

Cam looked at me with side-eyes and a look of disgust. He shook his head, thinking someone was fucking with us.

But I couldn't let it go. I couldn't shake the feeling that the call was important.

"Yeah, from work!" She repeated, sounding more high-spirited than ever. "Can you do me a tiny favor? Please?"

The please was what did me in. It was Ali. It sounded distressed under the joyful volume she was using. Cam had gotten closer to the phone. Was Alan with her? Was he listening?

Please.

"Okay..." I finally said. *Tell me, baby, what do you need?*

"So, I think you may have heard my name in the news."

"Yeah..." I was shaking, physically shaking. Cam rested his hand on my shoulder but kept his focus on the phone.

"I'm going off-grid for a while, I need to just get away, ya know? I wasn't sure who else to call. The cops are so needy, and my boyfriend is dangerous."

We are dangerous, Angel, because we are capable of killing Alan.

"What is it you need?" My voice was getting grave. I didn't

know why she was calling me JJ; I didn't know why she was talking like that, but I knew she had a reason.

"Can you just tell everyone I'm okay. I ran away, and do not want to be found."

"Don't you think you should tell them that yourself?"

"No, no! I just, well… I was scrolling through, debating on calling them, but I remembered the last time we talked, you said if I ever needed anything, I could call."

Go with it.

"Yeah…"

"So just, I needed to tell *someone*." She sounded like she wanted to cry. Her voice was no longer joyful. She was cracking. I was not sure how I knew, but I knew she couldn't crack. Not yet. "Oh, and can you take care of my reports, I can just give you my password."

"Yeah, I will get those done, Ali." That was the moment I had been hoping she would give me. Something. Anything.

A clue.

"The password is iLove2020." My eyes shot to Cam, he looked to be in physical pain. He still had his hand on my shoulder, something he did to calm me, but it was my turn. I needed to be strong for him.

I took too long to respond, to keep her on the line. The next thing I knew, she had hung up. She was gone. And we still didn't know where she was.

iLove2020.

I knew it was her way of saying she loved us. Alan was listening, and she risked it. Cam and I sat quietly for a solid minute, me patting his back, trying my damnedest to be strong.

The sound of my phone ringing again broke the silence. Without even looking, I answered it.

"I saw the call, Kace. I traced it. We should call the cops."

I was shaking my head before he finished his sentence. The PI caught the call and traced it. He knew where Ali was. I wanted to jump for fucking joy.

But I couldn't yet. We had to go get her. "Where is she?" I demanded.

Cam had taken note of my tone and was watching me.

"We need to call the cops, Kace," he repeated.

"Fuck the cops. They don't want Ali to be safe, they want the story of Cam and me being behind bars. Tell me where she is."

Cam was now on his feet, grabbing his keys and wallet. He knew it was go-time. We were going after her ourselves.

"It's an old neighborhood outside of town. The address is a foreclosure." He rattled off the address and begged me not to go without the cops. But Cam and I were already in his car, following the GPS I programmed.

We were going to get her.

cam

I HAVE DONE some stupid shit in my days. Things that could have gotten me arrested, for sure. But nothing as bad as murder. I was never capable of taking someone's life. That wasn't me.

Until that moment.

I was ready to release all the rage I had stored away. My target was Alan's face. Not a doubt in my mind that someone would have to revive Alan to keep him alive once I was done. I even made peace with spending my life behind bars if it meant Ali was safe.

How did it get to that? How did I go from zero worries to being willing to kill?

Ali.

She captured my soul before I ever said a word to her. None of us had a damn choice in how hard we fell. And even if we did, we wouldn't have chosen any different.

There was so much we still needed to figure out, what with my best friend being in love with her too and all, but we would make it work somehow. We needed that chance.

I peeled away from my house, taking my black 760-horse-power Ford Shelby GT500 Mustang. It was a gift from Kace. A joke of sorts. We had grown up dreaming of owning a Mustang, what teenager didn't? But his first "post-contract" gift to me was that car—a reminder of how far we had come together. Yeah, I could have bought it myself, but I can buy anything myself—it was the thought that counted. He wanted to be the one that finally gifted it to me.

Bet he didn't count on it getting us down the freeway one day in a real-life game of Gran Turismo to save the girl we loved.

And it did. In record speed. Daring a cop to try stopping us.

I took the exit that the GPS told me to then a few more turns and we were in the neighborhood, parked in front of the house.

Kace and I hadn't spoken the entire drive. We both knew what needed to be done, we didn't know how, but that didn't matter—we would figure it out. That's what he and I did... we figured shit out.

We approached the house and rang the bell. Kace hid from sight of the peephole, and I did the same on the other side of the door. There were no windows we could be seen from.

We honestly didn't even know if we were in the right place. Some poor old woman could answer. It could be a hoax.

I didn't feel like it was, though. Call me crazy, but I felt Ali was close. I always felt her when she was near, and that invisible pull we had was more prominent than ever.

After a few minutes, we tried again.

The doorbell was working, we could hear it through the door. Finally, the locks started to turn and I looked to Kace, willing him to have a plan past "getting the door open." He had a one-track mind though. Rage, which I decided was an excellent plan. What the fuck did it matter, anyway?

Right as the door opened, the sense that Ali was in there was so overpowering that I kicked the door the rest of the way in. The person that was opening the door fell back from the force. I immediately recognized Alan from the pictures Ali showed us, and without any other plan, I released my rage on his face. Hitting and pounding.

I had a fleeting thought that I would never be able to throw a football again, but I didn't give a shit.

As I hit, a glint of black caught the corner of my eyes, but before I could warn Kace, Alan pulled the trigger toward him.

He missed, but he sure as fuck wasn't doing that again. I took his arm and held it straight, forcing him to drop the gun as Kace came in to take over the punches to his face.

After a few more swings, he was out cold. Maybe even dead. I kicked the gun away and called 911 as Kace ran up the stairs looking for Ali.

By the time I got off the phone, Kace was running back downstairs, a frantic look on his face and a scrap of fabric in his hand.

"It's her jeans, Cam. They're fucking shredded! She isn't up there!" Kace was losing it.

I was losing it.

"There's blood on them!" he shouted.

I looked down at Alan, a new rage igniting inside me. I turned to kick him again when I heard a hiccup. A cry, maybe?

I whipped my head toward the noise at the same time as Kace, and then we were both sprinting toward where we heard it coming from. We searched the kitchen, and started opening every door in the house.

Finally, after the longest few seconds of my life, I opened the right door—a closet near the back door. There she was, balled up in the back of the closet, her hands over her ears the best she could get them. Her wrists were bound together, and she didn't have pants on.

I reached for her as Kace made his way behind me. "Ali, you're okay, sweetheart. I got you." I think I was trying to convince myself more than I was trying to reassure her. I scooped her in my arms, and she rested her head on my chest while Kace undid her hands. I didn't want to take her near Alan, but I needed to get her the fuck out of the house.

I held her head to my chest, hoping it blocked her view as I walked past him in the living room. I heard the sirens getting closer as I stepped onto the porch. Kace was behind us but ran ahead to flag down the police as they approached. I took Ali toward my car. I knew I couldn't take her home yet, but I wanted her somewhere she felt safe.

I crouched down on the sidewalk with her still in my arms and pulled her face away from my chest so I could check her out. "Ali, baby, you're okay," I repeated.

She was staring at me; no words had left her mouth yet. She nodded as if to agree with me, but that was all the communicating she was going to do.

Kace ran up to us and crouched beside me, wiping the hair from Ali's face to get his own look, his own reassurance. "You're safe, we got you."

I know," she whispered, then laid her head back on my chest.

Chaos had ensued once the police and ambulances arrived. We were questioned while Ali was looked over by EMTs. Then she was questioned, although she wasn't very talkative. Alan was wheeled away on a stretcher, the cops assured me he would be arrested once he was stable. The blood was cleaned from mine and Kace's hands, and we found out some of the blood was not from Alan's face but had been coming from stab wounds that Ali had created.

My girl was a fighter. She was getting the fuck out of there. I knew she would have made it, but I was so fucking glad we got to her.

When it was time to take her to the hospital, they were only going to allow one of us to ride in the ambulance with her. I stayed calm, letting it be her choice. She looked to the EMT and said softly, "Neither."

My heart almost died a little. I would have rather she said

"Kace" than "neither." I hated that fucking word. But I wasn't going to argue, it wasn't the time or the place. Her safety and security were all that mattered. Before I could turn around, though, she added, "They told me I didn't have to choose."

The EMT smirked, knowing damn well what she meant, but she shrugged and said, "Come on guys, she's stable, I'll ride up front." We jumped in, one on either side of her, and took her hands. She was tired and quiet, but held our hands tightly as we made our way from the scene.

ali

AFTER ONE NIGHT in the hospital for observation, and several visitors, including my dad and Mary, I had been sent home. The cops had questioned me—both the ones that arrested Alan and the ones that arrested Kace and Cam.

Needless to say, the charges against the guys were dropped. I also threatened the cops with a lawsuit for their negligence, and defamation. Not sure how far that would go, but they put a lot of damn assumptions, and words in my mouth, all over the media without even speaking to me personally. I also threatened to sue them for being mean to my boyfriends, but again, not sure if that was a thing.

Rick, the guys' lawyer that I recognized from the press conference, assured me he would see that all justice was served. For me, and for them.

My dad insisted on being the one that drove me home from the hospital, and much to the guys' dismay, I agreed. I missed my dad, and we needed a few minutes alone to talk.

"So, two boyfriends, huh?"

"Yeah well," I shrugged. "I couldn't choose."

"Seems complicated since they both appear to be serious

about you. How does this end? Who are you thinking of choosing?"

During my five days with Alan, I had thought a lot about how it all ended, and I still didn't know. But I didn't see it ever ending if I was honest.

"Dad, I can't even think about one of them without the other."

"Well, I'm a little old school, Darlin', and I couldn't imagine being okay if I had to share your mom with anyone else. But there are two things I know for a fact." I turned his way, waiting for him to continue. I knew dad wouldn't be judgmental. He wasn't that type. We weren't as close as we had been in the past just because of how much he closed down after Mom's death. So, he never tried to be the dad he wasn't. But I respected everything he had to say, and I loved him immensely. His opinion mattered, even if it wouldn't reflect my ultimate decisions.

"I'm listening."

"Fact number one: It is possible to fall in love with two people in one lifetime. Most of the time they're at different life stages, but whatever." He waved his hand like that wasn't the point and he didn't want to steer too far off track. "Fact number two: The more love someone has in their life, the better. Now, I'm not sure how you want to take all that, but those are facts, Darlin'. Facts are facts."

That was his way of telling me he was okay with me loving two men. He was too "old school" to just say it, but he had my back. "Thanks, Dad."

The rest of the drive was silent. It wasn't until we started to pull up to my apartment building that I got the nerve to ask him a question that had been nagging at me.

"Fact one. How do you know that's a fact, Dad? Have you ever been in love other than mom?"

He shifted in his seat a little, searching for a parking spot and letting it distract him from answering me.

"Dad?"

"Well, Darlin'," he sighed, finally finding a place to park. "It's only been five days since we reconnected, and I wouldn't call it love, but I think Mary be something I've been missing in my life. Just not sure if that's okay since she was your mom's friend and all."

Mary?

My jaw was dropped open. What the hell happened while I was gone?

"Now, look. Don't start looking at me like that. I'm a lonely man, and it's been nice having her to talk to and be with. And would you close your mouth? I promise this is less shocking than your *two* boyfriends."

I busted out laughing. He had a point. I couldn't judge him if he wasn't judging me. It just seemed so fast. It'd been five days.

"Missing you was worse than losing your momma. The last few days have been the hardest of my life. I knew your momma was in a better place, but I was so scared thinking about where you were. Mary and I just connected, right away, over everything we were feeling and going through."

"I'm so sorry Dad," I started to tear up, almost feeling guilty. "I'm so glad you had her to lean on."

"And now we are going to see where it goes."

"Does she feel the same way?"

"Hell yeah, she does," he hooted.

"She has quite a mouth on her, ya know." He knew. You didn't know Mary for very long without learning about her love of *fucks*.

"She sure does," he crooned, looking so damn cute. I hoped it lasted forever. I wanted him to be happy.

Right then, my door flew open, seemingly on its own, making me jump. Then Kace leaned in, "Everything okay?"

"Of course, we were just chatting," I said with a smile. Then, because I couldn't help it, I threw a thumb in my dad's direction. "He loves Mary."

Kace's eyes got wide and he smiled. "It's that mouth, huh?"

I rolled my eyes, *seriously?*

Dad just winked at Kace and undid his seatbelt, getting out of the car. I followed and climbed out of the car. Kace wrapped an arm around me and held me close as we walked to the building.

Before we got to the door, it opened and Cam popped out, jogging to us. I jumped into his arms, kissing his face everywhere. "Welcome home, baby."

"Mmm, I'm so happy to be home."

We all four went back up to my apartment where Mary was waiting inside. She walked toward me when we came in. "For fucks sake. That fucking Alan. I swear if those boys didn't fuck him up, I would fucking do it myself." That was almost the same words she told me in the hospital, but maybe one or two additional fucks.

We sat around for about ten minutes, everyone reliving the past few days, and catching up on everything. Cam was reinstated with his team and had to head to the team hotel later. He was playing the next day, and I could see how happy he was being back with his team.

Kace's team lost out of the playoffs in three days. They didn't get over not having Kace in the lineup. Kace told me he was going to talk to his team in the next few days, but he was still refusing to apologize. He did, however, say that upper management was considering a lawsuit against the precinct for the witch hunt on him. They could argue that they cost them millions of dollars by falsely arresting Kace, and causing him to miss the games.

My coworkers at 678 had called, assuring me I could take all the time I needed. Cam and Kace suggested I quit, but I figured I would give it more time. Mary wasn't headed back, though. She turned in her resignation that morning. Between connecting with my dad, fearing for my life, and fearing for her own, she decided to retire. I was willing to bet she would be filling that spare time with my dad out in the country.

Dad and Mary stood up and began saying their goodbyes. He was staying downstairs with her, and driving home in the morning. "I will be back to check in on you in the next few weeks," he said.

"I'll be okay, Dad," I said as I looked to Kace and Cam.

He followed my eyes and sighed. "I have no doubt, Darlin', but I'm still your dad."

I collapsed onto my bed once they were gone. Kace started running me a bath and Cam started cooking. I had told them at the hospital that I was hungry and gross, and I couldn't wait to rid myself of Alan's aura that still lingered around me. I watched them move around my small apartment, working together to make sure I was taken care of. How could anyone think those two would hurt me?

I guess we had done such a good job keeping things on the down low that no one got to witness the high. But I wanted to change that. I didn't care what everyone else thought of my relationships, or how much being with them would push me into the spotlight. They were worth it.

After a few minutes, I got into the bath and scrubbed every inch of my body, then joined the guys at my small table to eat. It was the first time we had been alone since they found me, and I had a million questions. A part of me was over talking about the last week, but the other part of me wanted to clear my head once and for all.

"I know your PI traced my phone call from your phone, but how did you know to stick with my story?" My question was directed at Kace, but I didn't look up at him. I just pushed the food around my plate with my fork, hoping he didn't mind talking it out.

"You called me JJ." He cleared his throat and I looked up. He looked pained and uncomfortable, but had a question of his own. "How did you call me without him knowing it was me?"

"That night you came to 678, you slid your number in the back pocket of my shorts, when you walked away, right? I didn't realize it at the time, but I found it when I went to do laundry. I started to throw it away but ended up programming it in my phone under 'JJ.' I just couldn't bring myself to toss it. Then when Cam set us up in that group text, I saved it again under Kace, never deleting JJ from my phone. When Alan wanted me to call someone who could deliver a message, I thought about that contact, and told him JJ was a work friend."

Both guys were staring at me. I had repeated that story to the police a few times, but the guys were not always in the room when I was being questioned. They needed me to fill in the blanks just as much as I needed them to fill some in for me.

"All I knew at the time, was that I was fighting my way out of there. If he was going to let me call someone, it was going to be you two, to let you know I was okay, to hear your voice, and to try and ease whatever you were feeling. After I saw the press conference, it felt more important than ever. I didn't realize you two would come blazing into the house with no cops." I was still in disbelief that they did that.

"Yeah, we didn't have a solid plan. When we got the address, we just headed straight there, no idea what we were going to do. Probably a dumb idea in hindsight, but I'd do it just the same." Cam took my hand as he spoke and kissed my knuckles.

"So, what now?" I didn't know what I was asking. I knew they weren't leaving me. But since the day we started our relationship, Alan had always been a factor—now he wasn't. *So, what now?*

"Now," Kace started. "We get our asses in that bed and sleep until we can't sleep anymore. I don't think any of us have had a good night's sleep in a while."

I turned to Cam. "What time do you have to leave?"

"I'm not leaving. I called and said I needed to be with you

tonight. After everything, Coach didn't argue, just told me to have my ass at the stadium before the game tomorrow."

I breathed a sigh of relief to have them both there. Kace was right, I hadn't slept well, and I got my best sleep when I was in between their safe and strong bodies.

"Oh, one more thing," Kace said as he climbed in bed behind me. "Cam and I have to do another press conference. We need to give our statement to the media. You tell us what to say and we will."

I was laying on Cam's chest and looked up at him, he nodded and added, "But we can do that when you're ready, they can deal with whatever time frame you need."

I thought about that for a minute. What did I want them to say? I sat up so I could see them both, on my knees between them. Their naked chests showing as they lay in bed, arms behind their heads propping them up. The blanket was covering their lower halves and the scene was so sexy I almost forgot what they asked me.

"Earth to Ali," Cam laughed.

I glared at him and countered, "Don't mess with me, I deserve to stare as much as I want."

Kace's smile made me melt all over again. "You do. Whatever you want, we are going to make sure you get."

"I'm not the only victim in all this. You both deserve to say whatever you need to say. I didn't let Alan scare me away from you two, so I sure as hell won't fear public opinion."

Cam sat up caressing my face and kissing me softly. Kace's hands found my knee and rubbed me gently. As Cam pulled away, he looked back at Kace, and then, as they so often did, they read each other's mind.

"I love you so much, Ali," Cam whispered when he turned back to me, causing my breathing to hitch. "That's what I want to say—to you and the world. This isn't a brief fling, a weird game, or an act of depravity. It's real, and I don't want to hide."

Holding his neck, I kissed him, attacking his mouth. Trying to tell him with my kisses how much I loved him too.

When I let go of Cam, I realized Kace had sat up as well. He guided me to him and kissed me with the same energy I was just giving Cam. So many unspoken words in that one connection.

He abruptly broke free and held his forehead to mine, breathing hard from the passion we had just exchanged. "I love you, Baby. I love you so fucking much."

I felt light and free. No fear of the future, or what it all meant. Cam was right, we were real. We needed to treat it as such.

I pulled from Kace and looked back at Cam. "I love you too, Cam." And before there could be any question of my intent, I looked back to Kace, "I love you too."

Tears were streaming down my face. It felt important to single them out when I told them I loved them just as they had done for me—each taking their own moment to tell me.

Once all my tears were wiped away, I laid back down between them and fell asleep in their arms. I slept well knowing I was loved by Kace Jackson and Cam Nichols.

ali

I STOOD at the podium in between Kace and Cam, each of my hands in one of theirs. It had been a month since I had been home, and we were finally at a place where we felt comfortable speaking candidly with the media.

After his first game back, and every game since, Cam had told reporters that he was still processing everything in private. He spoke only about football, and they seemed to accept those answers. Kace's season was over, so it was easier for him to avoid reporters.

But after a lot of discussions, we all decided to face the media together, as a unit. No more hiding.

The press conference was being held at the baseball stadium just for ease of access but was outside in the commons area where I had seen the drum line playing when I was first there. It was crazy thinking back on how little time had passed, but how much things had changed.

Cam was speaking to the press first. He had prepared the most concise speech of us three of us. He was telling them the basic facts, only speaking for himself. His girlfriend was kidnapped, he was accused and arrested, and he was cleared and back with his team. He asked for continued privacy as he worked on the football season, and focusing on the team again.

Cam was my rock—always dependable and straight forward. I looked down toward our intertwined hands—he held mine possessively and tightly. I looked up to his profile, his jaw was strong and confident as he spoke. He was speaking so eloquently, with an air of dominance and control. You would not even know that underneath that tailored suit and sunglasses was the sweetest, kindest, and most sensitive man I had ever met in my life.

After Cam finished, Kace took the podium. We never let go of each other's hands, simply moved over so Kace could get to the mic. As Kace prepared himself, Cam leaned down and whispered a quick, "Love you," in my ear.

I smiled up at him, I wasn't going to give the media the chance to read my lips, but I knew my eyes spoke back to Cam better than my words could.

"I think, for the most part," Kace started, "Cam covered the basics of the last few months. All I wanted to add was a public apology to my team. This affected them, our cohesion, and ultimately our season, as I was temporarily removed from the team. For that, I am truly sorry. I think the guys know me well enough to know that this means next year will be war. I plan on getting to spring training early, and start working on rebuilding our championship franchise.

Kace was in a suit, and his stance matched Cam's—dominant and self-assured. The difference was, Kace held a hint of wild in everything he did. He was my superhero—always protective, but fun at the same time. He kept things light and unpredictable, but was just as steadfast as Cam.

After a few seconds thinking about his next words, Kace continued. "I also want to use this chance to say how thankful I am for my family, Cam's family, Ali's family, and for Cam and Ali themselves. This has been a trying time for all of us, and without their support and love, we would be lost."

Cam and Kace's families supported us. I had even become close to one of Cam's sisters, Becca. Their moms thought we were crazy, their dads didn't care, and Cam's other sisters thought anything Cam did was gross. But they all accepted us regardless.

Kace wrapped up his short speech, and then it was my turn. I was a nervous wreck. The guys were used to public speaking, but I wasn't. I had never spoken publicly, and they told me I didn't have to. I didn't owe anything to the media, or a team, or anyone. But I did want to set the tone for our future. I wanted to put myself out there, stake my claim, and not show weakness. I stabbed a man with a butter knife, for crying out loud, I could handle speaking.

The guys each took a moment to whisper to me, making sure I was okay, telling me they loved me. Then letting go of my hands, they stepped back like bodyguards, to let me have the stage.

"Hi," I started. "I just wanted to take a minute to clear up a few things. I know it has taken me almost a month to speak about this publicly, and trust me, I almost didn't. But I feel it is important to close this door, in this way."

I looked back to Kace for strength. He nodded at me, and that was all I needed. "First of all, Cam and Kace have never, ever, hurt me. Those rumors are false, and need to be dropped, once and for all. I hope that hearing it straight from my mouth is all you need. Secondly, I too, want to thank our families and friends for their support. This has not been easy on us," I motioned to Cam and Kace, "but it has been hard for our families as well. Yet, they continue to show us their unyielding love."

The next part was tricky. It was all on me. The guys didn't know what was coming because I had only decided last minute how much I was willing to say.

We knew we would send a message when we held hands on that stage, and by how we interacted with one another, but using actual words was my choice. I didn't want the guys to be asked about it every time they had an interview. I wanted it to be said and done.

But I was also a damn chicken. I didn't know if I had the guts to say, *"Hi, these two are great in bed, sorry bout ya ladies, they are MINE."* Not that I would use those exact words.

Ultimately, I decided on one more game.

Honesty without direct impact.

Passively aggressive.

And hopefully that was the last game I had to play for a while.

"Finally, I want to thank the media—all of you. Not only for being here today, but for not asking Cam and Kace about me in every sports-related interview. I know that hasn't happened yet," the crowd laughed a little, "but I am hopeful you all will give these guys a break. They're exhausted from dodging the questions. Kace even says, 'No comment' in his sleep."

I sleep next to Kace every night.

"Poor Cam cannot even remember what sport he plays anymore." Another laugh. "I have to tell him every morning that he plays football, not dodgeball."

I wake up next to Cam every morning.

"But seriously, we are all just navigating this the best we can. Our circumstances aren't conventional, and neither are we. All I ask for is a bit of privacy and understanding as we try to dust off the drama, and move forward, together. Thank you."

Together.

epilogue

1 YEAR LATER

Ali

A FEW MONTHS after our press conference, Cam, Kace, and I celebrated our first Christmas together. It may have seemed quick, but that was when Kace and I moved into Cam's house full-time. We all wanted to be together, and there was no reason to keep jumping from place to place, especially around the holidays. We even got a new bed custom-built to suit the three of us in one room. The guys had gotten so used to sleeping there that they shared the bed even when I wasn't home.

Not that I was away very often. But every once in a while, I would spend the night in my old apartment. It was primarily used as my office when I needed to get away and work. When the nights got late, the guys would tell me to stay put and get some rest, even if I hated sleeping alone.

Sleeping alone was what I did most when football season and baseball season crossed over. From August to October, both guys worked and traveled so much that we were rarely home at the same time. And I couldn't travel with them both for every game.

"That was a strike!" Becca yelled from her seat on the couch next to me.

Cam's sister and I had become very close, spending all our free time together. She joined me for Sunday Night Football and Sunday Night Baseball, featuring my guys. Cam was in Seattle, Kace was in San Francisco, and we were in the basement where the guys had set up several TVs for times exactly like the one we were in.

"If Cam gets sacked one more time, I will personally break Derreck's legs," I added to the commentary in the room, referring to the offensive lineman who couldn't block Seattle from getting to the quarterback.

Becca nodded, agreeing, before yelling, "He was out, Ump! Are you blind?"

Glancing at the baseball game, I nodded as well, agreeing with Becca that the umpire had to be blind. Then I giggled, loving having her there while we ate junk food and watched both games. Having a best friend after so many years of isolating myself was weird at first, but Becca had helped me move forward from that old life almost as much as Cam and Kace had.

"So," Becca leaned back, finally satisfied with the ongoings of both games. "When are you moving that rock from your wrist to your finger?"

Jerking my head over quickly, I smiled and furrowed my brow at her. "Excuse me?"

"All I'm saying is, its time you make this weird relationship you have with my brother and Kace a permanent one."

"It is permanent. And it's not weird," I laughed.

"My brother had a nine foot bed custom made so he could share it with you and his best friend. It's kinda weird."

Smiling softly, I knew she was teasing me. She always did. Our relationship was unique, special, and hard to comprehend for some. Still, we knew so much love that outside opinions didn't bother us much. The only thing that bothered us anymore was the attention it brought into our lives just because people were too curious to leave us alone.

After a year, though, we had also gotten used to that.

Point to my wrist, Becca cleared her throat dramatically and smiled. "Tell me when."

For our first Christmas, the guys gave me a charm bracelet that represented everything we had been through and everything we had hoped for in our relationship. We called it our playbook, like the ones the guys had for their games. A representation of the plays in our lives that made us the happiest. It was nearly full of trinkets from vacations, anniversaries, and inside jokes that only the three of us knew about.

Then there was a diamond. Something they added to the bracelet and told me they wanted to eventually move to my finger. When I was ready, they wanted to commit their lives to me-to each other- to the bond we all had and would forever be faithful to.

A marriage.

"Marrying them is impossible," I mumbled the truth.

"Eh," Becca waved off. "Marriage through the government is impossible. But through the heart, it's not. It's not like you need to change your last night, file insurance forms, and property deeds. The guys have enough money to make all that go away. All they want is their claim on you."

"I know," I smiled, listening to her repeat things I had already discussed with Cam and Kace. "I've been waiting for the right time. I thought maybe our next vacation, I would take the bracelet off and wrap it around my finger. Show them I was ready to show the world that I would love them forever."

"The next chance you three get for a vacation is February," Becca huffed. "I can't wait that long."

"You?" I laughed louder, throwing my head back. "Why are you—?"

The announcer on the TV got loud, and I scanned both

screens to figure out which one we had the volume up on. "Touchdown, Cam Nichols!" The announcer cheered as I started pumping my fist in excitement.

"That's my man! I love you, too!" I spoke to the TV as the camera got in Cam's face. He had put his thumb, pointer finger, and pinky up to say, "I love you." Something he did every time he scored. It was our little code, and I responded, not caring that Becca was the only one who could hear me.

"To answer your unfinished question," Becca sighed. "I'm only anxious to see you three complete. A forever family. Seeing my brother so happy means a lot to me. Even if the idea of him having sex with my best friend is gross."

"We are already that," I assured her, laughing at how ridiculous she was. "A forever family. But you're right, I can't wait for the perfect moment because it may never come."

What I didn't say was that before she had ever brought it up, I had already decided to take the next step with Cam and Kace. Our relationship had been about jumping hurdles one after the next, and it was time to knock the rest of them down.

Ready or not, I was taking the diamond off my wrist, and in its place, I had a new charm to add. A gift I couldn't wait to give them.

Cam

When I pulled into the garage, it was nearly three in the morning. Kace's car wasn't home, so I assumed he was still traveling back. That meant I could slide into bed with Ali and have her all to myself for a while. Fuck, I couldn't wait to slide in between her legs and lose myself in her warm...

A scream cut my thoughts off, and tiny fists started raining down on me before I could adjust my eyes to the dark room. Ducking and turning, I took the hits to my back while trying to reach back and grab her arms.

"Shhh, it's me, baby, fuck."

The pounding on my back stopped, and I turned around, reaching for the light switch. Becca's eyes were wide, her arms were still in the air, but she was frozen.

"What the hell are you doing?" I asked her, snapping her from her motionless stance.

"I was leaving!" she whispered so loud it might as well have been a scream. "What are you doing?"

"I live here!"

"You're not supposed to be here yet!" She yelled again, then faked a gag. "And you called me baby."

"Grow up," I laughed at my older sister. "I thought you were Ali."

"Well I thought you were a masked marauder."

Alan may have been in jail, but I kept this house locked up like Fort Knox. No one, especially a random masked intruder, could enter our house. Not with Ali inside. We ensured every measure was taken so that she felt safe inside her home. And every step was set as I made my way in.

But that wouldn't have crossed Becca's mind when she turned the corner and saw me.

"I didn't see your car," I nudged her.

"Chase dropped me off and he's almost here to get me. I was going to meet him outside the gate."

"He will kill you for standing out there this late. He will kill me for making you stand out there this late." Punching a few buttons on the panel, I opened the gate so my sister's boyfriend could drive to the house to pick her up. "Do you watch the game with Ali?"

"Yeah, and I knew I would drink too much. We fell asleep on the couches downstairs sometime after the last pitch of Kace's game. Ali is still down there but I woke up and missed Chase."

As if on cue, the chime of the alarm panel indicated someone was pulling in, and Becca grabbed her stuff and smiled. "Tell Ali to have fun with Kace on his day off."

Her smirk made me shake my head as I followed her to the front door. Making her cringe was my favorite pastime. "Wait till Kace gets home, and we both—"

"Blah, blah, blah," she stuck her fingers in her ears and ran toward Chase's car, who gave me a small wave.

My stomach hurt from how hard I was laughing at her. She was one of our biggest supporters regarding our relationship, but she had trouble with the idea that I had sex. After all, I was her younger brother by a year, and the concept that Kace and I shared Ali was enough to make her head explode.

I heard a soft sigh behind me as I closed the gate and turned the security back on. I saw Ali, with her hair looking wild, dressed in leggings and a tank top, walking toward me.

"There's my girl," I reached out and took her hand. "I was about to go down and get you, carry you to bed."

"I heard the alarm chime and figured Becca was leaving so I was heading to bed."

Scooping her into my arms, she laid her head on my shoulder as I did exactly what I said I would do and carried her to bed. "I missed you so much," I whispered.

She didn't immediately respond, but the slight hiccup she gave me made me feel like something was wrong. When I reached the top of the stairs, she finally whispered, "I missed you too."

"Hey," I set her on the bed. "What's wrong?"

"I miss Kace too."

"He'll be home soon. Want to call him?"

She shook her head as a few tears fell from her eyes. "I don't know what got into me, Cam. I was fine and then I saw you and I just felt so overwhelmed with emotion. I think I'm still half asleep."

"Hey," I squatted down in front of her. "Climb up in bed and close your eyes. I'm going to check on Kace and then join you."

"No," she cried again, "Stay."

"I have to grab my phone."

Fuck, something happened. Ali wasn't afraid to show her emotions, but there was always a reason for every tear she shed, and I needed to know what it was. I needed to fix whatever happened.

Pausing for a minute, I considered that Alan had somehow contacted her or that something happened to Mary or her Dad. But they were fine when I spoke to them yesterday. They were heading into town for my next game and wanted to surprise Ali. Everything seemed right.

Without changing, I slid into bed and pulled her into my arms, soothing her as she cried against my chest. In the last year, I learned that when Ali was upset, I had to wait for her to tell me why. She always told me and always made sure I understood. But she needed to get herself together first.

Right when I thought she had gone back to sleep, the chime on the alarm sounded, and her head popped up. "Kace?"

"Is that what you need, Baby? Is it Kace you need tonight?" Or I should have said this morning since it was nearly five a.m.

"I just want you both here."

We waited a few minutes, listening to Kace come in and turn the alarm back on. Then his footsteps sounded up the stairs, and Ali sat all the way up.

Walking through the door, it was as if his presence had made everything right again. Ali seemed content. His smile was bright, and seeing them both made me feel more at ease.

It wasn't the first time it had been that way. We spent a lot of time with Ali on our own, and we were always happy, but sometimes, she needed us both. We needed each other as well. It's what made our unique relationship work so well.

But just like with me, Kace immediately saw something

wrong, and his smile fell before he could even say hello. "What's wrong?"

Ali fell back into my arms, and I wrapped her up, eyeing Kace to tell him I had no idea what was happening. He pulled his shirt over his head and kicked his shoes off before climbing onto the other side of Ali.

"Come here," he pulled her. "Come see me."

She rolled over into his arms, and I stood up, taking my shirt off as well and tossing my jeans somewhere in the room. Then I climbed back in bed, and together, Kace and I held our girl as she cried.

Kace

Nothing made sense when I walked into the bedroom.

I expected to find Cam and Ali naked, wrapped in each other's arms, and two satisfied sleeping smiles on their faces. Seeing Ali in tears and Cam completely dressed through me for a loop. Panic immediately took over, and I needed to hold Ali until she was ready to tell Cam and me what she needed.

She lay between us for a while as the sun slowly rose. I was fucking tired, but sleep wouldn't come until I knew Ali was okay. Since I had come home, she and I hadn't even said a word to each other. We didn't have to. She needed me, and I was there. That was all that mattered.

I looked over her head a few times at Cam, who had wrapped his body around her from behind. His eyes were as wide as mine, waiting for Ali to tell us what was wrong.

It felt like hours, but it couldn't have been more than forty-five minutes before she finally mumbled the best five words I had ever heard. "I want to marry you."

Cam's head lifted, as did mine, making Ali turn over and sit between us, facing us both. A few more tears fell from her eyes, and I reached up to catch them before they fell down her cheeks.

"You want to marry me?" Cam asked as if he couldn't believe it.

"Yeah," she nodded. "So bad that it hurts. So much that I can't wait."

"Your tears are sad," I mused. "Don't be sad."

"I can't marry you both," she sniffed. "You said I would never have to choose but it feels like I will have to."

"Fuck," I snorted and sat up to get closer to her. "You don't have to choose, Baby. Never."

"He's right," Cam added. "Never. We've talked about this."

"Can I change my name to Ali Jackson-Nichols?"

My heart wanted to beat out of my chest just hearing her say that. My knees begged me to get on them and ask her to properly marry me like we should have. But we had done that, and she knew it was her we were waiting on. So when she moved to her knees between us on the bed and lifted up, I knew what she would do.

"I thought this would be more romantic. I thought I would wait until we were on vacation or having a romantic dinner. I certainly didn't plan on my emotions taking over and doing this in bed after you two had traveled all night. But this is how it has to be because I just can't wait a second longer. Cam," she looked over and placed her hand on his cheek, then turned to me and smiled. "Kace," her other hand went to my chest, and I grabbed it, holding it against my heart. "Will you both marry me?"

Neither of us spoke as we pulled her into our arms and kissed her. Our lips were both covering her lips, her cheeks, her nose, her neck. We tried to avoid kissing each other as we navigated every part of her skin we could find.

Finally, I looked up and smiled. "Fuck yeah."

Cam laughed and nudged me before kissing her and placing his forehead against hers. "I can't wait to marry you, Angel."

Tears started coming down her face again, but they finally looked like happy tears, so we pulled her clothes off and kept kissing her body. Cam slid between her legs and kissed her clit before running his tongue up the folds of her pussy. She shuddered, and I smiled, pinching one of her nipples and making her squeal.

"You like when he does that, *Wife?*"

"Oh God," she moaned. "I can't wait to be your wife."

"You already are, as far as I'm concerned. You're mine. You're ours. You have been since the day we laid eyes on you."

Cam hummed his agreement as he lapped at her clit harder and harder. She was squirming even more, already close to coming.

"We've been waiting for you to be ready," I continued. "We want to move that diamond off your wrist and onto your finger so bad."

"I've been ready," she cried. "So scared."

"I know," I whispered. "But you have us. Even when we are all scared, we still have each other."

Cam closed his lips over her clit as I spoke, and she started shaking as she came. The glint in Cam's eye was all satisfaction, and it turned me on even more than I already was. Watching them together like that was something I would never get used to.

Taking my place between Ali's legs, I lined my cock up to her core and teased her. Meanwhile, Cam kissed his way up her body and landed on her lips before he finally spoke.

"Marrying you has been all I've wanted since we met you. I'm so sorry you got so emotional and scared but you have to know this is the best day of my life. Knowing you're ready to wear my ring forever."

"I've wanted it for so long," she moaned, then looked at me. "Kace please. Please don't make me wait."

Smirking, I slowly slid into her core, feeling the mess Cam's mouth left behind. "I got you."

"I love you," Cam added, then lifted onto his knees. "Open your mouth. I need that tongue wrapped around me."

She finally smiled, then laughed, before opening her mouth for Cam. He gently pushed his cock between her lips as her eyes locked with mine.

"Keep those eyes on me," I teased her. "Suck his cock but watch me fuck you."

Her moan around his dick was guttural, and I pumped harder into her, nearly losing my focus.

"That's it," Cam grunted. "Let me down your throat. Fuck you're perfect."

Ali's hand reached up to cup Cam's balls, and I hissed with jealousy. "My wife," I gritted out. "Touching my best friend that way. What a bad girl."

"My wife," Cam argued. "Letting my best friend fuck her like that."

The sparkle in her eyes as we teased her was enough to make me lose my strength. Pulling from her body, I slapped my cock onto her clit a few times, teasing her and giving myself a minute. Her eyes immediately widened, and I knew she was about to come from that slight touch alone, so I pushed back inside of her, ready to feel her squeeze me.

"That's it," I grunted. "Come on my cock. Come…"

I trailed off, my words becoming moans as I lost control and spilled into her pussy. She came with me, her moans around Cam's cock making me wonder how the fuck he was still holding onto his sanity. Then he snapped, and together, we all three filled the room with the sounds of pleasure and love.

She swallowed as Cam pulled from her mouth, and I climbed over the top of her to kiss her. It had been a long time since I stopped giving a shit about tasting Cam's come on her tongue. Kissing her was all that mattered.

When we were finally able to pull away and get cleaned up, I was ready to die in her arms for a few hours. But Ali got up and went to the closet, then returned and got in bed between us again. "Just one more thing," she sighed.

Ali

I couldn't help how emotional I was.

After talking it over with Becca, all I wanted was for the guys to get home and finally tell them what I wanted and needed. Cam coming home first was a relief because he always handled my emotions with a calmer presence than Kace. Kace tended to build anxiety until he was ready to explode.

Had they both shown up at the same time, though, I may have avoided the tears altogether. But it felt like I needed to wait for Kace to speak because once I did, I knew I would tell them I wanted to marry them, and they needed to both be there for that.

Yet, when Kace showed up, more tears took over, and I lay in his arms, questioning my sanity. I had to convince myself to give myself a break. It was okay to be emotional. There were a lot of changes on the horizon, and it was a lot to deal with.

"Just one more thing," I smiled at them both, feeling relief from the orgasms they gave me.

Both of them had their backs against the headboard, the sheet covering their naked bodies, and I bounced on my knees between them. It seemed all our best and most meaningful moments happened right there in our bed, with me always tucked between them somehow.

Pulling up a small box, I handed it to Cam, then held Kace's hand. I only had one gift and knew I wanted Cam to open it.

"What's this?" Cam mused, turning the wrapped box over like it had a label.

"Kace? Can you take my bracelet off?" He smiled as he grabbed my wrist and then handed me my charm bracelet before I continued. "I only have one gift for you both. Cam you open it. Kace, you added it to my bracelet."

"Okay," Cam laughed nervously. "So it's a new charm?"

"It's the one I want to replace the diamond."

Kace watched as Cam slowly unwrapped the present. He tossed the paper to the ground and lifted the top off the sleek, black box. When he looked down, he froze, and for a minute, I thought maybe I missed the mark, that he wasn't as happy to see it as I thought he would be.

Then his eyes met mine, and I could see tears threatening to fall. Kace looked into the box, and his gasp made me turn my attention to him. He also had tears welling in his eyes, and his head shook back and forth in disbelief.

"What does this mean?" Cam asked, lifting the small charm from the box.

"It means what you think it means," I laughed nervously.

"But does it mean now, or later?"

Looking at Kace, I realized he was wondering the same thing, and I laughed again. "Of all the games we play, this isn't one I would kid around with."

Taking the charm, I smiled and held it up for the guys. A little heart that said, "Baby on Board," dangled for us all to look at. When I lowered it back down, Kace took it and added it to my bracelet like I asked him to do.

Then he reattached it to my wrist, grabbed my cheeks, and held me close. "You're pregnant?"

I nodded and smiled. "I don't know—"

"Don't," he stopped me, and I nodded again. I was going to tell him I didn't know which one of them was the father, but just like I hoped, it didn't seem to matter.

"I've been ready for marriage and a baby for so long," I sighed, looking between the both of them. "But this is all so dang scary. And I have been so emotional, which, I guess comes with stupid hormones. But once I found out I was pregnant, it was like all that fear left my body, and in its place was a realization that we have created so much love together. There isn't anything to be scared of. Like you both said, as long as we are together."

Cam was still speechless, but his eyes told me he was beyond excited. He had always been the one who wanted kids and a family. The home we lived in was one he bought, hoping for a family to share it with one day. Now, it was finally happening.

"I love you," I smiled at him.

"I'm going to be the best husband and father in this entire world," he finally whispered. "I promise."

"Me too," Kace said as he ran a hand over my stomach. "This baby of ours is going to be so fucking loved."

"I was afraid that you two would be…" I sighed, contemplating my words.

"It doesn't matter," Cam assured me. "We are a family. One with two dads and super sexy momma."

Smiling, I looked between them as our faces morphed into something goofy. Then we all fell into each other's arms and basked in what was happening. Kace reached out and wrapped his arms around Cam, squeezing me between them. Cam returned the embrace with his own. And I settled into my favorite place between them as we all finally fell asleep to dreams of the future.

THE END

To read about Cam, Kace, and Ali's first Christmas, please check out The Christmas Playbook, originally published in Our First Christmas Anthology and now available HERE.

afterword

Hope you loved this trio!

My very first book... WOW...

I thought this book would be different than it ended up being and I learned the true meaning of "letting the characters talk." So this is *their* story, not mine, and I hope you love it as much as I do.

Fun fact: Thinking no one would EVER read this, I was looking for a name for the football team when a JET flew over my head. So I said, "Ah, Ha... JETS!" never even thinking about the NY Jets. So no, this team is not "misnamed," nor did I mess up my NFL teams. I did consider changing the name, but eh... let's just pretend! hehe.

THANK YOU SO MUCH FOR READING THE GAMES WE PLAY!

about the author

Katie is a hopeless romantic, a proud mother of two, a devoted wife, and a die-hard baseball fan. She resides in Florida where she loves beach days and boat life.

There is always more to a Katie Rae book than what you think! She loves making us think while also making us swoon. You always think you know, but you have no idea, and that is what makes Katie Rae books so special.

Join the fun in Katie Rae Reader Group and sign up for Katie Rae's Newsletter!

Also, www.katieraebooks.com is now LIVE. Check out extras, events, book information, signed paperbacks, and MORE!

also by katie rae

The GAMES Series (interconnected standalones)

The Games We Play

The Lies We Tell

The Love We Make

The Way We Dance

The Way We Fight

Men of the Military (complete standalones)

Ranger

Raptor

RECON

Rogue

Miami Inferno FC Series (Interconnected Standalones)

Reckless Goals

Scoreless Nights

Twisted Assist

The Boys of Summer Novella

Pretty Boy

Man of the Month Club Novella

Love Bites

Another One Bites the Dust

Silverbell Shore Series (standalone)

Now and Then

Co-Write with Zoey Drake (standalone)

Dirty Monsters

www.ingramcontent.com/pod-product-compliance
Lightning Source LLC
Chambersburg PA
CBHW051947150726
47999CB00004B/1285